Death
in the
Rainy
Season

Mary Martin Devlin

Cuidono • Brooklyn

Death in the Rainy Season
© 2018 Mary Martin Devlin

Cover Image: Morning fog on the river Sangha, Congo
Sergey Uryadnikov/Shutterstock

ISBN: 978-1-944453-04-6
eISBN: 978-1-944453-05-3

Cuidono Press
Brooklyn NY
www.cuidono.com

To the memory of Larry

The old doctor felt my pulse, evidently thinking of something else the while. "Good, good for there," he mumbled, and then with a certain eagerness asked me whether I would let him measure my head. Rather surprised, I said Yes, when he produced a thing like calipers and got the dimensions back and front and every way, taking notes carefully. . . . "I always ask leave, in the interests of science, to measure the crania of those going out there," he said. "And when they come back, too?" I asked. "Oh, I never see them," he remarked; "and, moreover, the changes take place inside, you know."

Joseph Conrad, *Heart of Darkness*

1

At the Air Zaïre check-in counter at the airport in Brussels an African woman, her head a mound of drooping coils of spaghetti-thin braids, told the young American woman that the flight to Kinshasa had been canceled. "Until when? Tomorrow?" Sarah Laforge asked, shifting her red backpack. The woman shrugged her shoulders and, her elbows resting on the counter, curved her long, graceful hands into a broad cup as if a great question mark rested there. "*Réquisitionné*," she said. She straightened up and reached for a pencil. "*Réquisitionné*," she repeated, scratching her head thoughtfully with the pencil.

"Requisitioned," a swarthy man behind Sarah said in a loud voice. He was wearing an embroidered tropical shirt like those Sarah had seen in small ads alongside the short stories in the *New Yorker*. "Commandeered by *le Guide*. Mobutu and his barons off on a toot. To Disneyland or Monaco or wherever. Better get yourself a seat on UTA to Brazzaville. If you've got a visa," he said, eyeing her shiny black diplomatic passport. He slung his garment bag over his shoulder. "Buy you a drink?" he said.

By two o'clock Sarah had phoned the American embassy with her new travel information to be telexed to Kinshasa and had had her tickets rewritten for a flight on TWA to Nairobi where she would pick up an Air Zaïre flight to Kinshasa. She had not slept on the plane from Washington to Brussels, and now, pushing her carry-on bag forward with her foot as she waited in the line to clear passport and security checks, she felt grimy and fatigued. She tried to concentrate on the *New York Times* someone had abandoned during the night on the flight over, the news of Washington and New York already distant and curiously uninteresting.

The tall young man in front of her turned out to be African, not American as she had assumed. He passed over a green passport to the immigration officer, a pallid middle-aged woman with wisps of hair creeping down her neck, and stood speaking to her in English with an accent Sarah had never heard before. Abruptly, the woman began to yell at the tall young African in Flemish and in French, neither of which the young man appeared to understand. The line broke out in groans and complaints, until Sarah stepped forward and, using the young man's passport, filled out an embarkation card for him.

TWA had given her a lunch voucher, and she had meant to find a quiet corner in the snack bar to read or doze before boarding, but the grateful young man picked up her cumbersome bags and followed her into the crowded restaurant.

They found a table smeared with catsup and littered with plastic plates and crumpled paper napkins. While Sarah remained with her bags, the young man, who called himself Thomas—though the name she had copied from his passport was quite different—collected sandwiches from the counter.

They tried to talk, but they had such difficulty understanding each other's English that they soon subsided into mostly strenuous smiles and energetic nodding and more smiles. He had just finished six months in North Carolina, at least that was what she thought he said, where he had played basketball. Now he was on his way home to Tanzania. In Tanzania he was a student. He asked whether she was a student, too, and when she tried to explain that she was a diplomat of sorts, showing him her new diplomatic passport, he stared at it blankly as if he wondered what this might have to do with her being a student. And when she told him that she was going to Africa as a cultural attaché at the

American Embassy, he smiled and nodded so ecstatically that she knew he had no idea what she was talking about.

Sarah's head ached, and she felt dirty sitting in the cluttered, brightly lighted snack bar. Her first meeting with an African, and all she could think of was getting away to some quiet place so that she could think her own thoughts. Guilt made her irritable.

"I must go," she said, finally, gathering up her bags.

"Let me help," he said, "Thank you, for the card, for the writing. One day we meet in America, yes, in America."

In the women's lounge, overwhelmed with self-doubt, she brushed her teeth and washed her face, leaning under the faucet and letting the cold water pour over her face. Then, she dozed in a straight-backed chair near the door until the attendant came back and reclaimed it.

Sarah had just handed her boarding pass to the attendant at the gate when she heard a familiar voice calling "Mees! Mees!"

It was Thomas, all smiles and nods.

"Same plane," he said. "Same, same!" He jiggled and smiled ecstatically at this miracle.

"Wonderful," Sarah said, so sincerely that she surprised herself, feeling immediately uplifted by the thought that she had somehow been given a second chance, a chance to prove to herself that she was as patient, generous, and sympathetic to others, particularly people of the Third World, as she had always believed.

At twenty-eight she felt almost desperate to satisfy herself that she possessed the virtues and values that she prized most in others. She had already tried and failed. She had taken the fiasco of her abortive Peace Corps stint as a galling personal failure. On her way to her post in Sri Lanka, she had stopped over in India for a week of sightseeing with a friend and had come down with a case of dysentery so tenacious that she was shipped back home. She never got to Sri Lanka. The cards and letters of her friends ardently recounting their brave Peace Corps projects seemed to mock her own commitment to do something worthwhile.

Now Africa and Thomas were giving her a second chance. She was convinced that her assignment in Africa would be her personal proving ground, and she was elated.

Nonetheless, when Thomas, in the crowded plane, could not persuade the stewardess to change his seat so that they could sit together, Sarah was not disappointed. Exhausted, she fell asleep before the plane had finished its bumpy, creaking roll down the tarmac.

Hours later, she was awakened in the darkened cabin of the plane.

Thomas stood over her, pushing roughly against her shoulder. "Mees! Mees!" People around her stirred and shifted their pillows. He was not trying to keep his voice down. "Mees! Mees!"

Sarah stared uncomprehendingly up at him. She had been dreaming that she was sleeping on a train when suddenly the train hit a patch of rough track that banged her against the window.

"Come!" He pulled at her arm. Obediently, Sarah, stupefied with sleep, got to her feet and walked stiffly behind him toward the rear of the plane. The lights had been turned off, and most of the window shades had been drawn down for the movie. In a small halo of light three stewardesses in their stocking feet sat smoking and talking together.

Thomas led her to the window of an exit door. He leaned over and peered out. "Look!" he said. He watched her face intently as she stepped forward. At first she saw nothing, her eyes caught by a rim of saffron pink clouds, then she realized with surprise that it was daylight, that she had slept the hours of European darkness away.

Suddenly, she beheld, reaching up from down below, a pinnacle of pearly white snow tinged on one flank with the saffron pink of the clouds. "Mount Kilimanjaro," Thomas said happily, "Look, Mees, look!"

The plane seemed to hover in place, the majestic peak staring back at her, glinting proudly in the morning sun. Sarah reached up and held on to the rim of the window and swung her face down closer to the pane. The pinkish glow on the mountain shifted a little, and a terrible dread suddenly overwhelmed her, like a monstrous wave, rising from the depths and pulling her under. The dread had something to do with Africa, but it was all the more frightening because she did not truly know its name. She thought for a moment that she would faint, or cry the quiet, deep-welling tears of endless mourning.

"Kilimanjaro!" Thomas said behind her. "The plane circles. For hour now. Just circles."

Sarah drew back and turned away from the window. "Ahhh," she heard Thomas say sadly as she walked back to her seat.

She found her seat and pulled up the blanket that a stewardess must have draped over her during the night. She closed her eyes but knew that she could not sleep. Sorrow enveloped her like a thick, choking fog. She flicked on her light. On the bottom of the tray table in front of her someone had scratched out the word *vest* so that the sentence read "Your life is under your seat." She stared at the tray and repeated under her breath, "Your life is under your seat." It was so absurd that she began to cry. She felt the way she had the one time Michael had talked her into trying a drug that his friend in the Chemistry Department had concocted for him. She had felt insubstantial, lost, and hopeless, and she had cried and cried until Michael, distraught but sober, had driven her to the beach where they walked until dawn. Afterwards, Michael wrote a poem about it. In the beginning, in the early years, Michael wrote poems for her and stuck them with magnets on the refrigerator door the way proud parents stick up photos and the childish drawings of their sons and daughters.

A steward came down the aisle. Sarah bent over and pretended to be looking for something in her carry-on bag.

Michael Lord. Her name was Sarah Elizabeth Laforge Lord. That was her real name, but her passport read Sarah Elizabeth Laforge. No one had ever called her Sarah Lord, and no one ever would now. At Yale, after they were married, she would have been embarrassed to change her name to Michael's. Women didn't do that anymore. Even Michael, when he wrote to her during the summer weeks she spent with her parents in Maine, addressed his letters to "Sarah Laforge." Afterwards, her mother had said with the finality of her cultured New England accent, "You are too young to call yourself a widow, darling," and Sarah's father had agreed. In the New Haven papers, though, they had called her a widow. A widow baffled by her husband's suicide. Graduate student's widow finds suicide note pinned to bulletin board over husband's desk. And a final poem stuck on the refrigerator door. The police hadn't seen that. The grieving widow. *Notice to all students: the top floor and stairways leading to the top floor of Sterling Memorial Library will be closed.* No one would be allowed out on the tiny Gothic parapet terraces now. Only maintenance men. A student running past the library on his way to Wawa's for junk food had slipped and fallen in a sticky puddle on the sidewalk, had found Michael's body slumped over the fence, a bloody spike rising like a spear from his back. It was an image that came back unbidden at blank moments.

The plane creaked and bells chimed softly along the dimly lit aisles. Sarah blinked as the overhead lights were turned on. A streak of pale sunshine fell across her lap from a window across the aisle. The passengers around her still slept. As she had slept that crisp night in April when Michael plunged from the tower to the waiting black iron paling below. She had not stayed up for him that particular night. She had not looked at the note on the bulletin board or the poem on the refrigerator door. She had slept soundly until the policemen rang the doorbell at two o'clock in the morning.

"Michael was manic-depressive, darling. Everyone could see that," Mother said. But Sarah hadn't seen it at all. To her Michael was brilliant and intense, a published poet already.

Stewardesses, looking puffy and faded, were pushing breakfast carts through the aisles.

"I don't know why you persist in wearing that wedding band," Mother had said. "It gives an altogether false impression."

"A false impression of what?" Sarah had asked.

"That you're married. When people see that ring, they'll say, she's married, and that's that."

Sarah had kept the ring. It seemed such a small thing. Michael had left so few traces in her life. Had it not been for the ring and the sorrow, she could have persuaded herself that he had never existed at all.

2

"We're late," Phil Olmstead said, peevishly. "I knew we would be."

"Relax, relax, relax, already," his wife said in the heavy New York accent that she knew irritated the hell out of him. She could turn it on and off like a faucet. "So what's the hurry? A junior officer. Big Deal. You're the boss. Besides, you've been here long enough to know the plane will be late. Hours late probably, and we'll have to sit up there on that hot terrace and drink hot beer and wait and wait, so relax already."

Msumbu, the only USIA driver Phil Olmstead trusted, plowed down the highway to the airport, the horn of the white Chevrolet station wagon bleating like a beast in pain.

"Tell him to slow down, Phil."

"Tell him yourself."

"I don't speak French . . . well, not the way you do."

Patty Olmstead's French was non-existent, despite the fact that she had spent ten of the last fifteen years in French-speaking countries.

Throngs of Africans shuffled barefoot along the sandy shoulders of the road. It was close to five in the afternoon and the shops and cafés and beer joints in the shantytowns were coming back to life. A woman with a sewing machine balanced on top of her head, a baby wrapped to her back and holding by the hand a small boy barely able to walk, swayed to a stop and turned her head slowly to watch the white car pass. Her round forehead glinted in the afternoon sun like a glazed ceramic jar.

Jesus Christ! Olmstead said to himself and looked at his watch again. This was one hell of a way to impress a junior officer with the efficiency of the office, cruising into the airport an hour late. New people on his staff always made him nervous, especially women, especially this one. He didn't like her hoity-toity Ivy League background. Olmstead had graduated from the University of Oklahoma, and he would tell anyone who asked that he was proud of it. His own daughter Shelley was at Brown, but that was different. She had to compete. It was a hard world. You couldn't do it all with a University of Oklahoma diploma in your back pocket. This Sarah Laforge . . . He wondered briefly what she looked like. Probably too fat, too enthusiastic, too intellectual, a radical. Oh, God, Olmstead thought, probably a radical feminist. It made sense, there were so many of them coming out of Washington these days.

Olmstead himself felt younger every day, he was only fifty-two, almost fifty-three really, but the young women of today were beyond his comprehension, absolutely beyond. His wife, now, Patty, she was a woman he could understand, a woman who had her hair done once a week and who spent most of her time planning bridge parties. Olmstead believed that you could always trust a woman who had her hair done once a week. But these young women today, who could figure them out? They had to have their own MBAs, their own PhDs, and what the hell, their own BMWs, and they thought cooking and fucking were cities in China. Especially these feminists, these radical feminists. Out to save the world. Olmstead's problem was that he didn't think he had the energy to deal with this Sarah Laforge. Not in this heat, not in this climate. He wanted peace and quiet, the routines of the office, pushing the papers back and forth to Washington, now and then arranging a concert at the American Cultural Center for a jazz group or a lecture by an economist, the usual stuff that didn't seem to do much good but, then again, didn't do much harm either. Olmstead had accepted the Kinshasa post for two reasons; first, it was a hardship post with a twenty-five percent salary differential, and with his daughter at Brown and a hefty mortgage on their Washington house, that fourth again came in handy; second, via the grapevine in the State Department he had picked up the gossip that Zaïre was a sleeper, a post with a terrible reputation but in reality a beauty: terrific housing and cheap servants, great French restaurants, so many embassy personnel that Washington kept losing count, which meant that he and Patty could play bridge every night of the week if they wanted to and never get bored with the same old crowd. It was a sleeper all right, and Patty had walked in and taken one look at the house and garden and swimming pool and thought that she had died and gone to heaven. Everything was perfect. Peace and quiet and the fattest paycheck he had seen in years. And the climate wasn't even half bad, though few would admit it. A little smothery in the rainy season, but was Washington any better in July and August? A nice, docile number two at the Cultural Center, no fuss, no ripples, that was all he asked.

As they approached the airport, scraggy bush replaced the tin-roofed shacks along the roadway, and, behind the linked wire fence of the airport, the rusted and burnt-out carcasses of crashed aircraft lay scattered in the high grasses alongside the runway.

Olmstead looked out at the field and panicked. In the distance, he could see the Air Zaïre DC-10 sitting near the terminal. Sarah Laforge was on the ground and in the airport. What the hell would she do when the goons in black reflecting sunglasses started in on her?

"She's going to panic if she hits immigration without me there," he said.

"Did you tell him to slow down? He's going to kill somebody, I swear to God he's going to . . ."

"He's not going that fast . . ."

"Not going that fast! I swear to God. How much faster can he go, I ask you?" She leaned her head carefully against the seat and closed her eyes. "Why should she panic? She has a diplomatic passport."

It wasn't hard to find Sarah Laforge at the airport. She was the only passenger left at the immigration window, and Olmstead thought she was going to jump into his arms when he came up and said, "*Merci, capitaine*," to one of the soldiers behind the partition. The guy was probably a sergeant, but Olmstead always called them capitaine anyway, or sometimes colonel. It made them feel better.

"So . . . what was the hang-up with immigration?" Phil Olmstead asked, as Msumbu started the car. He sat in the front seat next to the driver and turned around to face his wife and Sarah Laforge in the back seat, his locked hands draped casually over the back of his seat.

"They said my cholera immunization was not in order. They—"

Phil and Patty Olmstead burst out laughing. Olmstead slapped the back of the seat with his hand.

"The old rusty needle routine? Did they pull out the rusty needle?"

"Yes, they said I . . ."

"Yep. That you had to have your shot to clear. Now that, honey, was your *last*, and I do mean your last clue, that you were supposed to fish a few dollar bills out of your bag, slip them into your passport, and hand it back over the counter. It's routine. They do it all over Africa. *C'est l'Afrique*," he said with a bored wave of the hand as if he had lived in Africa all his life. This was his first African post, but he knew that Patty wouldn't contradict him. Olmstead laughed again and shook his head.

Sarah tried to force a smile. It still seemed to her miraculous that the awful moments in front of the window were finally over. Not a window really, an opening in a partition, waist high, and behind that partition she could see black arms and hands, no faces, and the dark green of uniforms with guns in belt holsters. There were three soldiers, and they kept pushing her passport back, not accepting it, and finally the hypodermic needle appeared. Once she had lowered her head to peer up behind the partition to see their faces but could not.

"It was frightening," Sarah said.

"Oh, well, it's just one of the games they play down here," Olmstead said, yawning. "You'll soon get used to them."

Sarah was too weary to attempt an answer. She stared at the man who would be her superior for the next two years. She had never before seen people with such strange-looking hair. Phil Olmstead's hair was pitch black, plastered down in meticulous stripes over his pink scalp, and his wife's hair looked hard and plastic as if turned out of a Barbie doll mold.

"You must be tired," Patty Olmstead said. At the airport she had stayed behind in the air-conditioned car, lazily extending her hand when Sarah got into the back seat.

"Yes, I don't know . . . The plane circled forever over Nairobi," she said, shivering at the memory of the white flanks of Mount Kilimanjaro. "I think I'm well into my third day of travel, and boarding in Nairobi . . ."

"The Great Stampede! Oh, the Great Stampede, Patty! She got the Great Stampede treatment, remember? They open the door of the airport waiting room and it's off to the races, right? You have to make a mad dash across the field for the plane and all these African mamas with their baskets and babies are beating you around the head getting up those stairs, right? And once you get inside, there aren't enough seats for everybody, so some of them go, and some of them that have the right kind of cash in their *pagnes* to slip to the stewardesses get a seat or get to squat down in the aisles when the plane takes off. Right? Is that what happened? Remember, Patty? Did you get a seat, Sarah?"

"Yes. I guess I was lucky. I had assumed seats were assigned," Sarah said. She had fallen into a seat just opposite the rear door, and when the plane took off, a young woman with a baby squatted in the aisle next to her seat. When Sarah remonstrated with the stewardess that the woman had no seat, the stewardess had looked at her blankly for a moment, then, asked, "*Alors, quoi?* So? Do you want to give her your seat?" To her shame Sarah had looked away without answering. Another failure. Though she had held the baby all the way to Kinshasa, even after he wet her skirt.

"You can't assume anything here," Olmstead said, slowly shaking his head. "*C'est l'Afrique.*" So far, so good. Olmstead liked her. She didn't look like a radical feminist . . . and most of all, she didn't look enthusiastic, not enthusiastic at all. Sarah Laforge looked whipped. Absolutely whipped.

Peace and quiet, that was the name of the game he intended to teach his new cultural attaché to play.

3

The embassy assigned Sarah a large, light-filled eighth-floor apartment swept by cooling breezes from the river which lay just beyond a garden across the street. At the rear of the building, as part of the compound, sprawled the American Club, where Americans and other expatriates congregated from the early hours after dawn until well into the night. The club had tennis courts with a pro, a swimming pool, a snack bar serving American-style fast foods, with meat and supplies flown in regularly from South Africa and a large hangar-like space with a cement floor and a tin roof where garage sales were held on Saturdays twice a year, where teenagers skateboarded or watched videos on a large screen, and where their parents square danced on weekends.

At night Sarah fell asleep to the soothing pock-pock-pock on the tennis courts below. She woke to the squeals and cries of children arriving with their mothers or nannies for an early morning swim. A sweet hum of excitement carried her swiftly through each day, and she slept heavily through the night, awaking however with the sense that the night had been filled with momentous activity. Nursing a hot cup of coffee, she would gaze out into a world of glaring color: blues, greens, reds, oranges, pinks, a white so white that it bruised the eye. A week or so later, when her sleep became lighter, she learned what happened during the night. That was when the storms came: scrabbling and thundering, heaving down thick shafts of water, scrubbing, scouring everything so that the whole world was fresh and clean when she pushed aside her curtains in the morning. As the day slipped away, the crisp, clear lines of morning would begin to blur and smudge; the dust crept back, gray white smoke veiled the palm groves and flame trees and jacarandas.

She passed long days in her office at the American Cultural Center, getting to know the staff, the office routine, discussing her work with Phil Olmstead. She declined Olmstead's invitations to his bridge club and after two months had met few people at the embassy outside the American Cultural Center.

So, she hesitated a moment and let the doorbell ring a second, long imperious peal before opening her door to a rather short, buxom woman dressed in riding clothes.

"Hey!" the woman said in a Deep South accent. "I'm Augusta Pearce. Gussie. The Consul General. And I've come to make your acquaintance." She stepped past Sarah into the room. "Well, to check out the competition, if you really want to know the truth. Someone, I won't say who, told me that I should." She flipped back her black hair, parted in the middle and hanging in straight, limp sixties fashion to her shoulders and stood studying Sarah.

Sarah laughed, feeling her spirits rise. "I'm glad you did. I'm lazy about getting to know people." She lied matter-of-factly. The truth was that she had become more and more reclusive. Sometimes she felt as if a part of herself had withdrawn to a distant place, like a wounded animal holed up inside a cave, licking its sores.

"Oh, don't feel you have to apologize." Gussie Pearce walked around the room, nonchalantly poking her head around corners and picking up magazines and books.

"Not a bad place, is it?" Gussie said. "Last assigned to the former ambassador's secretary. So it has a few little goodies that wouldn't be parceled out to your ordinary embassy employee. The ambassador thought she was the hottest little piece on two feet, and that goes a long way in the goodies department, dudn't it?"

"Would you like some coffee? Or I could make a pot of tea," Sarah said. Gussie followed her into the narrow kitchen.

"You wouldn't happen to have a real, honest-to-goodness drink, would you, hon? Something like a nice little ol' B & B? The sun has gone down," Gussie said.

"As a matter of fact, I do. Phil Olmstead showed me the commissary today, and I picked up some things. No glasses, though, except these plastic things that were left here. My things haven't arrived yet. Now . . . what was it you said you'd like?"

Sarah had the eerie feeling that she had started to drawl, that Gussie's accent had invaded her system like some intrusive odor.

"A B & B. Bourbon and branch water, that's what we call it down in Mobile."

They took their drinks back out onto the shadowed terrace off the living room and talked. The lights of the last ferry from Brazzaville, a dark listing hulk with bare bulbs strewn around the top, bobbed slowly across the river to Kinshasa. They had another couple of drinks, and Sarah decided that she liked this Consul General. She liked her very much. She judged her to be near forty and rather more candid than was absolutely necessary. Gussie seemed a woman who never had a thought cross her head that she would not immediately, happily, put into words and share.

"You're goin' to love it here, hon. You really will. Take my word for it," Gussie said again. She rested the heel of one boot across her knee. "This is my second tour here."

"You fell in love with the country. So you came back. I can understand that. I don't think I've ever been in a place where the beauty and the squalor won't let you alone for a minute. And the people, all those high spirits, that gaiety, where does it come from? In all this misery. I'm still confused by what I see, but I'm not surprised that you love it here."

"I fell in love with a guy, hon," Gussie said flatly. "I fell head over heels in love with a guy. Listen, Sarah, not all of us females have your looks. So, when we do meet a guy and something clicks, we don't just wander off into the blue. After I finished my tour here and was posted back to Washington, I watched and waited, and sure enough, one day Consul General came available, and I grabbed it. Believe me, there aren't many people in the State Department lying awake at night wondering when a suitable post to Zaïre is going to free up. Good God! Look at the time! I left the Riding Club hours ago!"

Reluctantly, Sarah put down her glass and accompanied Gussie to the door.

Gussie laughed and leaned forward quickly and pecked Sarah on the cheek. "Listen, you call me, you hear, and I'll show you around. There's not much about this town that I don't know. I'll show you the ivory market, the parrot market, the malachite market—whatever. I know this place inside out and backward. The only place I don't know is the *cité*, that's the native quarter. But Carter Everett will be only too happy to take you out every night of the week to the *cité*. He's our CIA man, chief of station. Hey, come to think of it, he's a Yale man. Like you, Sarah. Skull and Bones and all that. Dishy, hon, and I do mean dishy. And that crazy wife of his leaves him on his own down here while she's back in the States studying to be a minister. A preacher! Can you imagine! Well, maybe someday the good Lord will give her enough sense to hang onto Carter. Listen, I'll bring Carter by your office tomorrow and introduce you to him."

"Oh, no, Gussie, honestly."

"Carter is one of the most charming men in the world. And one of the nicest. Nothing to fear. Sure, he's married. So is my man, Josh Hamilton. Josh's wife is one of the biggest lushheads in Kinshasa. You'll meet her. Starts drinking in the morning. And Jacques Delpech! Wait until you lay your eyes on him, hon! Handsome isn't even the word for him. Beyond handsome. Tall, rich, and gorgeous. Owns a string of breweries all over West Africa. And a terrific person. You'll see, this place is like any other, Sarah. All the fantastic men are married." She turned toward the door. "Whatever that means down here."

4

The Swiss Air 747 en route to Kinshasa began to nose down, lowering over the Stanley Pool on its way into Njili airport. It was the usual crowd in first class. White businessmen returning from meetings in Europe or the States. Sleek Africans, their broad smiles filled with the confidence of wealth and power, in expensively tailored *abascos*, the vaguely Chinese-looking suit that Mobutu had decreed must replace the European business suit and called the *abascos*, short for *à bas costume*.

"And who do you think is riding in the back of the bus, sitting back there big as life, putting the make on this skinny, little Peace Corps gal? Flat-chested, long, stringy hair. I kid you not . . . I saw him. I was coming out of the john, and I looked way back, and there he was . . . It's Boketsu. Sure as hell. Fat and shiny as a hog." Sam Wofford's bullhorn voice thundered above the soft clatter of the flight attendants suddenly full of energy as they prepared the cabin for landing in Kinshasa.

"Bull," Joe Snead said. "If Boketsu Bika *is* on this plane, and if he *is* heading back to Zaïre, you know for sure he'd be sitting up here with us, swilling champagne and spooning the caviar. All forgiven. That ol' I.V. full of greenbacks strung back up, drip, drip, dripping into the ol' Swiss bank account."

Across the aisle Jacques Delpech kept his eyes closed and pretended to sleep. At the mention of Boketsu, memories swirled around his consciousness, tugging like a floating tree branch that sweeps down the river, hits a snag, then pulls at it, until the branch breaks free and flows along swiftly with the current again. The familiar gossip. And Sam was always on top of it. Who's in. Who's out. Very important to the foreign businessman. More important than who's sleeping with whom. Unless it's your own wife, of course. And maybe not even then.

Jacques sat upright and disentangled himself from the clutter of blanket and newspapers. The plane bumped its way down through the clouds, losing altitude very fast. The lights in the cabin flickered, and fat drops of condensation fell from the ceiling.

"*Oh, merde, la douche!*" someone groaned.

"Hey, hold on, fellas, don't take us down so fast," Sam Wofford said, ducking his head and reaching for a newspaper.

He and Joe Snead held newspapers over their balding heads. In the silence the water made loud, pinging sounds as it hit the paper.

"It must be hot as hell down there tonight," Joe Snead said.

Below, Jacques could see a few scattered patches of light in the thick darkness. His mouth and throat felt dry.

Jacques continued to stare at the darkened world below, ignoring the carroty blond stewardess who had been flirting with him since the plane left Zurich. She probably assumes my wife will be standing there at the airport, he thought, waiting to collect her husband, and that I'm making damned sure that I come through the gates clean and innocent. But wives don't meet husbands at airports in Africa; drivers do that. They arrive hours early, they wait and wait. Before they go to the airport to collect *patron*, they wash the car, sweep it out, dust and polish, polish and shine. Then after the long, dusty drive to the airport, they clean and polish again. And then they climb the steps to the terrace of the terminal and wait for the lights of the huge plane to pierce through the darkness, ever so slowly at first, then they watch enthralled as, all of a sudden, the giant roars to the ground, speeds past the terrace, and disappears into the night before rolling back slowly, triumphantly, into the light.

No, there would be no wives waiting in the V.I.P. lounge tonight, only drivers and expediters from the companies of the European businessmen, household flunkies for the wealthy Zaïrians, or embassy staff detailed to meet incoming officers and visitors. Wives would already be asleep in the cool bedrooms of villas along the river or in Djelo Binza high on the hill overlooking the city.

Or there would be no wives at all. It had been almost a year since Janine had left Kinshasa, taking Suzanne home to Brussels, for their usual vacation, she said, but the vacation had never ended, she had never returned. She had sent long lists of things to be packed up to Dieudonné, their cook and the only houseboy who could read. Dieudonné had anxiously packed every single item himself, even at such a distance courting Madame's approval, never allowing himself to wonder about Madame's absence.

Sam's husky monologue could be heard over the clickety-clack of seat belts being released as the 747 pulled to a stop obliquely facing the airport. Canned music, an old-fashioned popular song in French, stuttered over the public address. In the pale overhead lights of the cabin the passengers looked tired and disappointed, as if they had been promised that their jolly, boozy afternoon in the skies would never end. Jacques stood leaning against his seat, waiting for the bump of the stairs against the plane.

There was an angry shout outside as the stairs thwacked hard, and a beefy stewardess released the locks and whipped the door open.

Unhurried, Jacques waited his turn to leave the plane, and finally fell in step behind the Pakistani, who had handcuffed his briefcase to his wrist. Without much success, he kept adjusting his coat sleeve and his grasp of the briefcase so that the handcuffs wouldn't show.

As Jacques stepped outside the plane, the warm, moist air clogged his nostrils with the peculiar smells of dust and smoke, the smells of Africa, and he felt happy. Home. Home again, home at last. He started across the dark tarmac toward the lights of the V.I.P. lounge.

"*Patron! Patron!*" came a high-pitched African voice. Jacques looked up toward the terrace. His driver Louis stood below a rusty light fixture hanging loosely from the dirty wall.

"*Patron! Patron!*" Jacques waved at the tall, lanky black man, scrawny as a child, who stood flailing both arms, jangling from side to side, and smiling as if he could not contain his jubilation. Jacques lifted his head, and as always, grinned in return. The rituals of the airport.

Inside the V.I.P. lounge Jacques dropped his briefcase and sat down beside Sam Wofford on one of the dingy white overstuffed divans that were spread in clusters about the room. They had turned over their tickets and baggage stubs to their expediters who had gone off to collect their bags in the chaotic baggage room, where boys ran down the broken conveyer belt to fetch bags from the Swiss Air trolley for the expediters who would then take them to waiting drivers and cars.

Tall women in dark print tops and long, ankle-length skirts called *pagnes* twisted about the waist in what President Mobutu had decreed as "authentic" dress circulated among the rumpled-looking passengers taking orders for beer and whisky. The women swayed as they passed by on their high-heeled shoes with pointed toes, their massive rumps rising and falling beneath their tightly wrapped *pagnes*.

"Did you really see Boketsu on the plane, Sam, or were you just trying to get a rise out of the boys?" Jacques asked.

Sam had subsided into a half-doze, abandoning for the moment the strenuous gregariousness he assumed with his cronies. He was a bulky man, tall—over six feet three—and barrel chested from incipient emphysema as a result of smoking three packs a day since he was sixteen. In the Vietnam War his right leg had been badly mangled, but his slight limp did not dispel a sense of his tremendous athletic power. He ate hugely, drank everything in sight, and screwed just about anything that moved, black or white. He was the only man Jacques knew who had come down with the clap seven times in one year. The threat of AIDS in Africa had done nothing to slow him down.

From lowered lids Sam, like a somnolent crocodile, watched the room. "Yeah. It was definitely Boketsu," he said, turning his large head slowly to face Jacques.

"Then, why wouldn't he be in here with us?" Jacques said.

"It's not likely that he would queue up with the riffraff to clear immigration."

"He's not here because he got into a black Mercedes parked next to that C-130 over by the fence."

"Then he and the Old Man must have kissed and made up," Jacques said.

"Yeah. You know the Old Man. He'd rather have the camel inside the tent pissing out than outside the tent pissing in."

Sam sighed and lowered his eyelids again and settled back to watch the movements of one of the *serveuses.*

In 1982, Boketsu had been one of the youngest, brightest and most trusted members of Mobutu's regime, until the bright young man had started a rumble to overthrow the president and take over the country. When Boketsu lost control of his men and his plot unraveled, he had been lucky to get away to the safety of exile in Switzerland, and, later, Brussels. There, he had become one of the most vociferous critics of the president and his regime. American congressmen courted him and quoted him. Capitol Hill found in him the kind of wisdom and insight that Americans always attribute to foreigners who speak fluent English with an American accent. Boketsu became a favorite with the press, particularly with the Belgians, and they crowded around him at his beck and call as he lamented the waste and corruption in his native land under the disastrous leadership of Mobutu.

Jacques had not seen Boketsu Bika in two, perhaps three years. It seemed longer than that, after that furtive meeting in New York on the Staten Island Ferry. Bika had been furious with him, spitting out his venom in a wild mixture of Lingala, Mongo, and French, the crazy language that they had used as lonely boys at boarding school in Belgium, shut away from their families, from their country, from Zaire.

"He's a good guy, Boketsu," said Jacques. "Really smart."

"Good-looking girlfriends, too," Sam said, putting down his beer and heaving himself up from the low divan. "Is your car here, Jacques?" Sam's protocol man, stood bowing and smiling before them. Sam handed over to him his magazines and briefcase.

"How long will you be in town this time? Or are you just passing through on your way to Johannesburg?"

"Three weeks, maybe four. How about some tennis on Saturday before lunch? American Club."

"Fine. I'll meet you there at noon," Jacques said, though he dreaded the battering Sam would put him through. He could not recall ever playing a game with Sam at a decent hour when the sun was not biting through the sweat and blurring his vision. Like some madman, Sam preferred to play in the blazing heat, claiming that this kind of sweating kept his weight under control.

There were only a few stray diplomats from the Turkish embassy still waiting in the lounge when Louis appeared at the door with Jacques' luggage.

It was past midnight as they walked through the dimly lit and deserted rotunda of the airport. There would be little activity until dawn when passengers would begin arriving for the Swiss Air turnaround departure at six. The dingy little boutiques of African handicrafts, masks, ivory and dusty malachite were closed. The lights in the sign over one shop still burned; the glass of the sign had been broken and the bare bulbs showed through the cracks. The sign was written in bad French and worse English: "*Souvenirs d'Africain/Vente d'objets d'art.* African Rememberings/We sell things of art." A couple of vendors selling cigarettes with names like "Good Look" and "Pink" had settled down for the night with their cardboard and rags; they sprawled near the entrance steps and played a game of cards.

Across the parking lot Jacques saw the blond stewardess bend down and slip into the back seat of Sam's Mercedes.

Louis kept silent, steering the big black car out onto the broad road leading to town, waiting for Jacques to ask how things were at the house and what had happened during his absence. Louis could remember—that was before Madame married *patron* and changed the big black lettering on the gate to Villa Beau Rêve— when the immense house on the river had been called Villa Bondeko, which meant friendship and brotherhood in Lingala. Some of the fishermen on the river still called it the Bondeko.

People, mostly men, still swarmed along the sides of the road, lit by the dusty orange light of street lamps. Laughing and shouting at each other, they strolled along in the debris-littered sandy shoulder of the road. Their skinny, spindly arms gesticulated toward the dark trees. The roiling rhythms of Kinshasa music, monotonous and sensuous, spilled from roadside beer gardens and cafés.

It was a long way to the big house on the river, almost an hour, and it seemed longer to Louis because *patron* was in one of his quiet moods.

Along the roadway women crouched in the warm sand behind makeshift tables of crates and wooden boxes on which they displayed their wares: a half-dozen packs of cigarettes intricately arranged in a pyramid, boxes of matches, small stacks of canned tomato paste, a dented, misshapen tin bowl of palm nuts, mangoes. Short white candles stuck into a splash of wax spread small circles of light in the darkness where the light of street lamps did not reach. Some women nodded in sleep in the candlelight. They were always there, these women, silent, patient, watchful, along the streets and roadways of Africa, arranging their pitifully small supply of items into elaborate patterns of shape and color.

Once they had passed through the noisy, turbulent *cité* and approached the center of Kinshasa, the raucous nightlife disappeared. The streets were quiet and deserted, except for a few chauffeur-driven Mercedes slipping along the wide avenues lined with trees and the high white walls of villas.

Louis turned into the Avenue de la Justice, where prostitutes in bright spangled hot pants and boots and garish wigs leaned against mango trees. As the car came into view, they sprang forward dangling condoms, grayish white, like underwater creatures, and shouted their invitations. Jacques looked up as they passed on the left the walled villa where Boketsu Bika used to live, just before he left the country. It was a monster of a house around which the former owner, a *colon,* had built a high stucco fence, a rarity before Independence. Now all the great houses crouched behind their walls. On the corner the *colon* had proudly had his initials, G.O.D., worked in fancy Portuguese tile inlaid in the wall. When they were still boys, after peace came to their country, and they could leave their gray stone boarding school under the leaden skies of Bruges, Bika had said that he would one day live in the house of G.O.D. And he had. Bika had been so proud to be a member of the government, working until all hours of the night, pushing and scheming to get his reforms approved by Mobutu.

Jacques lit a cigarette. The International Monetary Fund representative lived in the house now.

As soon as Jacques stepped into the foyer, he could smell the sweet odor of Dieudonné's hemp. Every room was open and lighted. The polished marble floors glowed. Music played softly in the lamplight, and the night breeze fanned the gauzy draperies back and forth through the rows of open French windows along the terraces. A Simon and Garfunkel tape, Dieudonné's favorite, played on the stereo. The rituals of homecoming. Light fell from windows around the swimming pool. All was peaceful and quiet. Expectant. As if the rooms had just emptied a moment before. As if little girls with shining, mischievous faces and broad snaggle-toothed grins would burst in at any moment, crying "Surprise! Surprise! Welcome home, papa!"

"*Bienvenue, patron,*" Dieudonné said, his grizzled head bobbing from left to right, his eyes yellow and glazed from an evening of smoking. "*Bienvenue.*"

He straightened the decanters along the bar and watched Jacques warily as he dropped his jacket and tie on a chair before going to close the windows to the terrace, shutting out the swimming pool, the swimming pool out there in the darkness beyond the lights.

"It is going to rain. For sure it will rain tonight, *patron.*"

As if in answer, a jagged flash of heat lightning cut across the moody black skies.

"Fix me a whisky before you go to bed, Dieudonné."

"Oui, *patron.*"

Behind him, Jacques could hear Dieudonné's bare feet slapping against the floors as he moved unsteadily about the house, closing the doors to the terrace and turning out lights. Paul Simon sang

"Same Old Tears" to the empty room. Jacques could hear his two Rhodesian ridgebacks snuffling in their sleep alongside the pool. They always slept there during the rainy season.

In the bedroom Dieudonné had set out a decanter of scotch and a pitcher of ice water. Jacques looked at his watch. Twenty past one. He picked up the telephone and dialed, staring at the blank white walls as the telephone faraway rang and rang.

"*Allô? Oui?*" Nicole croaked, her voice choked with sleep.

Jacques stared at the walls. "I wonder if you could come over and be of service tonight?"

"What kind of service?"

He waited. "I thought you might have the answer to that." There was a long pause, and Jacques could imagine the flash of hot anger storming across her high, broad forehead. He wished that, for once, she would be angry enough to refuse. But Nicole was too ambitious for that.

"Okay . . . Give me some time."

"Sure," he said, placing the telephone in the cradle, and stretching out on the bed.

5

By the end of the week Jacques had stopped expecting Boketsu to call. Even supposing that he had gone directly from Njili to the president's palace in Gbadolite, which was likely, he would have called by now. Perhaps Bika had decided not to forgive him.

In Jacques' two-month absence from Africa a serious problem had cropped up in every brewery. The new machinery for the plant in Kinshasa had arrived in Matadi on schedule, or almost, but two trucks had already broken axles on the potholed roadway that was gradually going back to bush between the port and the capital. His plant foreman in Lubumbashi, a young man not yet out of his twenties, had been carried off by cerebral malaria in less than twenty-four hours. A vicious fight had broken out in the plant over the foreman's job, leaving one man with a broken leg and the bottling hangar a mess of broken glass and burned plastic. Jacques had little time to think of Boketsu and broken friendships. But he did. He could not help himself. He could not think of anyone, except his father, who had been more important in his life than Bika.

The head office of Delpech breweries was a two-story nondescript cream stucco building on the outskirts of the city near Ndolo airport, which until the late fifties had been the capital's main airport. Since then, Ndolo was used mainly by the dozens of bush pilots, darting in and out in their mud splattered, frail aircraft, who flew passengers, mail, and cargo for businesses and missionaries. For two days Jacques' plane had been waiting there, ready to take him to Lubumbashi. It was a long flight out, over eight hours, and there was enough work there to keep him in Lubumbashi for at least three days.

In the years since Albert Delpech, Jacques' father, had dredged up all his savings and thrown them into the suitcase of a departing third-generation Flemish *colon* who had founded the most modern brewery in Zaire, the business had prospered even beyond old Albert's expectations. In the wake of their long colonization, the Belgians had bequeathed to their former subjects their love of beer. Delpech beer became the champagne of the *cité*. Only once did the fortune of Delpech breweries falter. In the late seventies, rumor spread in Shaba and Equateur provinces that Delpech beer caused impotence. Sales dropped to near zero over the next few weeks. Albert Delpech, a slight man with the temperament of an eccentric schoolmaster, watched with disbelief as his thriving business circled the drain. Eccentric, perhaps, but shrewd, Albert Delpech sat up late one night and worked out his strategy: he changed the name of the beer to Simba, Swahili for *lion,* bottled the beer in a new brown bottle, and paid scores of men to sit around in cafés and beer gardens boasting of their sexual prowess after drinking Simba. When six men in Shaba claimed to have fathered a male child after drinking only one bottle of Simba, "*la brune*" was launched on its prosperous journey.

Jacques stood at his desk, stuffing into a briefcase the papers his secretary handed to him. In a low singsong, the secretary identified each file as she passed it along to him. It took them a moment to realize that they were not alone, that Josh Hamilton had come into the room and closed the door behind him. He stood watching them, his eyes wide.

The secretary clicked shut the briefcase, turned the combination lock, and set the briefcase upright on the desk. Ducking her dark head discreetly, she slipped past Josh Hamilton.

"Josh? Aren't you supposed to be working? Want to come along with me to Lubumbashi? Good beer out there."

Josh lowered his head like a rebellious child and shook it vigorously back and forth. "No," he said finally. He walked stiffly over to a chair in front of Jacques' desk and sat down.

"Jacques. Listen, do something for me, will you?" His voice was tight and hoarse.

"Sure. If it can wait until I get back." He pushed back his sleeve and glanced at his watch.

"No. It can't wait, Jacques. Really can't wait." Josh Hamilton sat up very straight and reached out and put his hands on Jacques' desk. He was a tall, thin Englishman, good-looking in a frail, feminine way, so blond and fair that he was obliged to wear a hat, even in the shade. Even so his narrow forehead was pocked with scars where small cancers had been removed. He was boyish and fun-loving and there was something weak and inconclusive about the slope of his chin. For over ten years he had managed the largest diamond-buying office in Kinshasa. Josh had all the right contacts and lived in grand style in a hilltop house overlooking the city with his wife Fiona, two children, three parrots, a green monkey, and two enormous Dalmatians, which no one bothered to house train. At their cocktail parties a guest always ended up with a wet leg, with no apologies from the host or hostess. Still, invitations to Josh and Fiona Hamilton's parties were much sought after. They were British, they were dashing, they had money and a certain rather seedy style. They did exactly as they pleased and didn't give a damn what anyone thought. Jacques found them the most frivolous people he had ever met, but, then again, they did not seem to have anything in their lives to be serious about.

Jacques stared at the small pocket of saliva in the corner of Josh's lips.

"What is it?"

"Just now . . . coming through Binza village . . . on my way back downtown after lunch. I . . . I had . . . It was an accident. I . . . It was crowded, you know how it is in that patch with all the dinky shops and stalls and damned Africans all over the road, coming at you from every direction, not looking where they're going, they never do, and I . . . I was going along and out of nowhere, I mean, Jesus H. Christ, I couldn't possibly have seen this kid, out of nowhere comes this kid . . ."

Someone cranked up a heavy truck in the courtyard below, and it backfired with a deafening blast. Josh jumped and stared at the window.

"So what happened?" Jacques could feel his hands going cold.

"I . . . I . . . I . . . hit this kid. She ran out from . . ."

"A little girl?" Jacques said, his voice barely a whisper. He tried to raise his hand to loosen his tie, but it lay there next to his briefcase, useless, trembling.

Josh said nothing.

"Was she hurt?" He waited. Josh stared out the window. "You don't want to answer? Think you don't have to answer for anything, is that it, Josh? Is that it?"

Jacques wiped his forehead and lowered his voice. "Answer me, Josh. Was she badly hurt?"

Josh gave a slight nod.

"Dead?"

The word echoed around the still room. Josh Hamilton still gazed out the window.

"Must be . . . I must have . . ."

"Jesus Christ! You don't know for sure?"

"What the fuck, Jacques! No need to shout! It wasn't my fault. She came out of nowhere . . . Boom! Right into the car!" He smashed his fist against the palm of his hand. "It wasn't my fault."

Jacques swung his briefcase off the desk.

"Nothing's ever your fault, Josh. Think about it." He headed for the door.

"Jacques, for God's sake! I need your help. You're the only one who can help."

"Why me? Go to your embassy, to your ambassador what's-his-name. They will know what to do. I can't do anything."

"Yes, you can, Jacques." Josh Hamilton stood up and rubbed his palms against his thighs. "It's simple. I'm not asking much. And I'll pay. Whatever. That's no problem."

"Pay me for what?" Jacques watched him with disgust. The small pouch beneath Josh's sloping chin was shaking.

"Look, you've got garages here. All this equipment. Trucks. Cars. You've got it all here. Everything I need. I want you to have your men paint my car."

"Paint your car?"

"Right. New color. I can't . . . I have to have a new color."

He followed Jacques down the steps. "I drive through that fucking village three, four, hell, I don't know how many times a day. How many ways are there to get downtown? They'll recognize me or Fiona. They'll remember the car. They'll drag me out of the car and stone me to death. You know how they . . ."

"Buy a new car."

"I can't . . . I mean, I don't want to. Jesus, it took me nine fucking months to get that Jag down here . . ."

"You can get a new Mercedes within a week. Stop whining."

"Bloody hell, Jacques, everybody in Kinshasa drives a fucking Mercedes. I want my Jag."

In the sunlight of the courtyard, as if mesmerized, Jacques walked over to the metallic blue Jaguar XJ6 parked in the shade of the building.

"Fiona's car," Josh said. "She wanted my car and driver to go to lunch at the InterContinental."

Jacques stared at the car, clean and gleaming and innocently blue. He walked around the car to the passenger side. Then he saw it. The sideview mirror jammed back against the door, the streaks of mahogany red starting at the mirror and disappearing over the top of the car. Jacques stepped closer. There was something caught in the mirror hinge . . . something small and mostly pink, splattered with red. He reached out his hand to touch the familiar thing. He pulled at the still slippery thing, twisting it from the grip of the hinge . . . a little girl's barrette, a cheap, plastic barrette with a dark clot of hair stuck in the wires. *The barrettes on her wet pigtails had made a loud click-click against the concrete when he turned her over, finally, onto her back, his hands numb. Célestin, the second gardener, little more than a child himself, kneeling on the manicured grass, wailing, his hands clasped as in prayer, "Oh, s'il te plaît, patron! Oh, s'il te plaît, patron!" Over and over, beside the glimmering swimming pool. And from her mouth, a kind of yellow string tinged with green, like the yolk that seeps from a cracked egg being boiled too quickly.*

He could feel his knees weaken and the heavy briefcase dragging him to the ground.

"Jacques?" Josh said. "Jacques?" Reluctantly, he took a few steps forward. "Jacques? I say, you look as if you're about to do a toss up."

Jacques turned away and seemed to be looking at the front bumper.

"It's only blood," Josh said. "No dents. I checked myself."

"Brown," Jacques said after a moment, his back still turned. "Brown is the only color we can do."

"Brown will do nicely," Josh said.

6

Mobutu telephoned at six in the morning, his gruff, gravelly voice rumbling over the flimsily patched telephone lines, and invited him to breakfast. Mobutu sounded jovial and full of energy. Mornings were his good times; he rose long before daybreak and liked to receive over breakfast around the long table on the front terrace of the presidential residence above the rapids.

Jacques dragged himself out of bed and started his shower. The house was built so far out onto the river bank that he could hear all the familiar sounds of the morning fishermen down at water's edge singing and shouting as they prepared their nets for the day. Along the marshy banks the reeds swished and crackled as the fishermen poled their pirogues through the shallows.

Jacques stared glumly at his reflection in the mirror as he shaved. Lubumbashi had not been a reassuring experience. He would have to return in another week or two. Perhaps he ought to think of taking on a partner, someone to share the grind.

Jacques drove himself out to Mont Ngaliema since Louis lived far out in the *cité* and would not appear for work for another hour. At the crossroads in Kitambo, with its jumble of tin shanties and drink and cigarette stands and gasoline stations, already thick with cars and trucks and pedestrians on their way to work in the textile factories and in the villas of the wealthy, he turned a sharp right up the road to Mont Ngaliema and Camp Tshatshi. He passed the little park where, as a boy, he and his sister Isabelle had raced around the tidy footpaths on Sunday afternoons in search of their friends. In his memory it was still a place of green mystery and enchantment, even though now most of the animals had died and the exotic plants and shrubs had disappeared into a tangle of undergrowth. Only a few antelope, a scrawny, mangy okapi, and a male lion with faded and patchy tufts of fur stared forlornly at passersby.

At the gates of Camp Tshatshi, soldiers of the Presidential Guard, as colorful as tropical birds in their green uniforms with épaulettes and cuffs of red and yellow and fez-like leopard-skin hats with plumes of red, yellow and green feathers, leaned against the gatehouse smoking cigarettes. The sergeant recognized Jacques and, grinning expansively, bobbed and waved him through, while a young soldier at his side bent down and peered curiously as Jacques drove through the gates. He followed the road past the barrack houses, more and more dilapidated with every passing day, doors dangling from broken hinges, ragged curtains knotted at windows, rusted tin roofs, debris strewn about the bare yards. Here and there a woman sat listlessly pounding manioc in a wooden bowl. For a while Jacques drove toward the river then turned left past the front of the president's compound to the parking lot.

There were only a few Mercedes, five or six, parked in the lot. A small group at table, then. In the old days, with his father, when Mobutu had been in power for only a few years, there was no formality, no protocol. They sat around the huge table and ate cold cuts, cheeses, omelets and fresh jam, homemade jams of mangoes and watermelon and figs. It was like a big family gathering every morning with the disorderly table and children scrambling to give all the adults good-bye kisses before climbing into the minibus that would take them off to school. And Jacques' father and Maman Mobutu, Marie-Antoinette, the first Maman Mobutu, grumbling and scolding her husband for eating too much and gaining too much weight. Both of them gone now, Maman Mobutu, dead in her thirties of heart disease and Albert Delpech swallowed up in the rain forest.

Jacques heard laughter in the antechamber. "You're expected," one of the president's guards said, nodding toward the long hallway. In the antechamber off the entrance foyer three guards were watching a Bugs Bunny cartoon. A cardinal sat in a highback Louis XVI chair squinting at *Paris Match*, his glasses dangling from his mouth, the magazine held up close to his pink face.

The small rooms to the left and right of the long hallway were empty. Jacques walked through the enormous room where the president officially received and out onto the terrace.

"Don't get up, please, don't get up, *citoyen Président*," Jacques said, as he always did, but, also as usual, Mobutu rose and took his hand. Mobutu smiled mysteriously and cocked his head to one side.

"*Mon frère*," Jacques heard someone say behind him. Boketsu Bika stepped out onto the terrace, and Jacques wondered why he had not anticipated the president's little surprise.

Mobutu laughed as Boketsu and Jacques embraced, then clapped his hands and ordered pink champagne. "Just a little," he said, "to celebrate. It is good to celebrate, *n'est-ce pas*, when a brother comes home again?"

They drank to the brother who had come home again, and talked in generalities, as Mobutu preferred to do now, about the country. Two days before, a copper barge in tow had broken loose and had smashed up on the rapids just below the residence. "We will go and have a look later, if you like. The carcass is still there. A nesting place for crocodiles. With all our problems we have to lose a load of copper! Nasty luck."

They listened for a moment to the rumble of the rapids, for Jacques a curiously exhilarating sound that he remembered from so many such mornings long ago with his father.

"Bika, now it is your problem. You are my new Minister of Mines. Give Gecamines a lesson in river currents. It's your problem now."

They all laughed. Jacques noticed that Mobutu used the familiar "*tu*" with Bika, and that Bika was smiling a great deal and doing a lot of anticipatory nodding. Watching the two of them, Jacques felt weary and sick of heart. Who could ever have predicted this?

Bika, the perfect courtier. Jacques began to wonder when he could take his leave without giving offense. He wanted to weep with anger and sorrow at seeing his once proud and noble Bika bow and scrape.

Behind his tinted glasses Mobutu was observing them. He wore a gabardine *abascos* of dark iridescent mauve gray and a silk ascot of purple and white polka dots. He looked relaxed but wary. Jacques tried not to look at Bika, sitting forward on his chair, a fixed, fatuous grin on his face. He felt a flood of intense, vicious hatred of Mobutu. What kind of deal had he struck with Bika to get him back behaving like a puppet on a string? Behind the French windows Jacques could see a dozen or more flunkies—spear carriers as his father had called them—peering out, following every gesture of the Man, waiting for their turn to petition, to wheedle, to beg. The champagne glasses, only half emptied, made wet circles on the glass table.

Mobutu shifted in his chair.

"I mustn't keep you from your work," Jacques said, rising from his chair. "Excellent champagne, *citoyen Président.*"

Mobutu and Boketsu got to their feet. Boketsu took Jacques' arm and murmured his good-bye to the president.

"Ah, Jacques, you are a good boy," Mobutu said, slapping him on the shoulder. "Keep an eye on this brother of yours. Make sure that he is a good boy, too. Will you do that, hein? Will you do that for me, Jacques?"

Boketsu squealed with laughter as if he had never heard anything wittier in his life.

They stood next to their cars in the naked sun. Boketsu wanted to ride with Jacques, his driver following them into town, but neither made the first move to get into the car.

"I'm sorry about your little girl," Boketsu said after a long silence. "Suzanne was . . ."

"It was Sabine. You never knew her. She was only three."

"I'm sorry."

A white Peugeot pulled into a parking space. A chauffeur in a navy blue *abacos* held the door for a short, wiry white man in a tennis outfit who headed up the walk to the entrance.

"And Janine?"

"In Brussels."

"Ah," Boketsu said. "I'm sorry."

Jacques burst out laughing. "Oh, for God's sake, Bika! Don't be so pious! You hated the bitch."

"Of course I did. Disgusting *flamande!*" Bika spat to one side, then slapped his thighs and bent over laughing. "I hope she rots in Brussels! I'm giving a party on Saturday. I'll send my driver with a *pour mémoire*. Come, *mon frère,* it will be like old times."

"Will it?" Jacques asked, feeling weary with memories and loss.

"Of course. Why not?"

7

Despite a torrential downpour during the night the heavy vines of purple bougainvillea on the walls of the American Club were already covered with gray, gritty dust by the time Jacques pulled into the parking lot a little before noon on Saturday. The American Club was set well back from the Avenue de Shaba. Behind the high walls there was a gravelly parking lot where Jeep Cherokees and Ford Broncos, orange with mud, baked in the sun alongside the chauffeur-driven cars of the embassy crowd or the businessmen from local establishments of General Motors and Goodyear and British American Tobacco and Gulf Oil or any of the other international corporations with headquarters in Kinshasa. Like other well-placed "Europeans," Jacques Delpech belonged to the American Club, which, along with other European clubs and "cercles" around town, gave the large expatriate community a social center.

The late morning sun stung at Jacques' neck like angry bees as he hurried past the long, airy dining area where a handful of American teenagers sat at picnic tables and watched a video of Indiana Jones and drank Gatorade.

Inside the club's small restaurant he found Sam Wofford sitting at a corner table, drinking beer with Carter Everett and Joe Snead and a sunburnt younger man whom Jacques had never seen before. They were all eating hamburgers and french fries, except Sam, who sat with three open bottles of Simba in front of him.

"Jacques! Hey Ho! Pull up a chair," rasped Sam, his breathing shallow and labored.

"I thought you wanted to play tennis." Jacques shook hands with Carter Everett and Joe Snead and held out his hand to the pink-faced younger man.

"Jacques, Bill Donovan. Bill, Jacques Delpech. President and Directeur Général of Delpech Breweries," Carter Everett said.

"Among other things," Joe Snead muttered under his breath, and they all turned to look at him.

"What's that supposed to mean?" Jacques asked. He spoke English with the slightly dainty, lilting accent of the Indian nanny who had cared for him as a child.

"Only that Jacques Delpech, well, you'll find this out for yourself, Bill. Jacques Delpech is a very big man in Kinshasa. Ain't that so, Jacques ol' boy? In tight with the Man." Snead reached out and pushed Jacques' shoulder with a pudgy hand. "And now big buddy Boketsu is back. Minister of mines. Somebody's going to make some serious money, eh, Jack-O. What do you say?"

Jacques raised his hand and signaled for a beer. He ignored Snead, who tilted back his chair and grinned around the table. Snead was a man close to fifty with the chronic greasy look of the overweight. He dressed in polyester and wore white socks, even when taking his winter vacations in Europe. He draped his thinning blond hair across his scalp from a point just above his left ear and fancied himself a ladies' man but could never get beyond the odd fanny pinch and sly feel for fear that his wife Doris with her mean terrier eyes might turn on him. Snead had been in Zaïre for over five years and somewhere in Africa for the last fifteen. He headed the Zaïrian operation of Americo International Construction and Development Corporation, and some said that he had it written into his contract that he would not have to serve in the United States. Not until his bundle was made. Everyone in the European circle knew that Snead took big-time bribes and made big-time deals. More than one wife had at one time or another taunted her husband with Doris Snead's jewelry and clothes. Most wives didn't understand how diamonds and Chanel suits and Johannesburg plastic surgeons could materialize out of tractor deals and road and bridge contracts, but Doris Snead did.

A grimy fan barely stirred the air in the close corner of the clubhouse. Outside the dirty window children splashed in the pool and tried to get the attention of their mothers who sat clustered in groups, gossiping and rubbing themselves with suntan lotion. On the far side of the pool Jacques saw Nicole, her black hair twisted Indian style into one thick braid, her head held stiffly out of the water, gliding about in that awkward dog paddle Frenchwomen do to keep their hair dry.

Sam Wofford absentmindedly pulled on his beer and watched Nicole make her way slowly around the pool toward a young diamond dealer sunning himself on a lounge chair.

"Looks like a water moccasin, that Nicole," Sam said. The other men turned to look.

"With the embassy, Bill? USAID?" Jacques asked the young man, who had turned back to his hamburger and french fries.

"No. Bill's a second secretary. Political section," Carter Everett said. Bill Donovan chewed and nodded in agreement.

"Upstairs," Joe Snead said, rolling his eyes as he brought his chair forward. "Upstairs," he whispered melodramatically, "Bill works upstairs with the big boys at the embassy."

"Christ!" Carter Everett said. "Cut out the shit, Joe."

Sam snorted and swung his bleary eyes from Carter to Joe and back again. He looked pleased as a kid, and Jacques realized that he was drunk.

"I thought we were going to play tennis, Sam," Jacques said, as Carter Everett and Bill Donovan stared at Joe Snead.

"Not today, m' friend," Sam spoke slowly, slurring his words. "Today I'm self-destructing. Sittin' right here self-destructing all morning long. Goddamn tropics. Makes you self-destruct . . ." His voice trailed off. He frowned at Carter as if Jacques' interruption had made him miss something important but he could not seem to remember what.

Carter had leaned forward, his elbows on the table, his hands steepled over his empty plate. His lean, patrician face was unsmiling and severe as he stared at Joe Snead. Bill Donovan, sensing the tension, had pushed away his half-eaten hamburger.

So, Bill Donovan is CIA, Jacques thought, big deal. And it was just like Joe Snead and his nasty fat boy routine to needle Carter Everett and at the same time let everyone know that there was nothing in Kinshasa, Zaïre, that could get by Joe Snead. Not even the secrets of the second floor of the American embassy were safe from him.

Carter Everett was not a man to make any effort to disguise his dislike of Joe Snead. Carter had served almost thirty years with the CIA, most of them in posts in Africa. It was said that Mobutu himself had requested his return as Chief of Station in Kinshasa, where he had spent three years in the late seventies. Washington had obliged, believing that Everett was exactly the right man to "handle" Mobutu.

The rickety screen door slammed shut, and Nicole Scott, followed by the young diamond dealer padded over to the table in bare feet. A damp towel cinched in a sarong around her waist, Nicole leaned against Jacques' chair and placed a proprietary hand on his shoulder. A silly grin spread over Sam Wofford's broad face.

"Hullo, gang," the young man said. He winked at Sam and picked up one of his beers and drank. "Coming down to ski on the river tomorrow? The company boat's been overhauled good as new. Guaranteed not to stall and dump you in the middle of the river."

Carter Everett yawned and stretched. "Not tomorrow. Poker night tonight. I don't know yet whether there will be a tomorrow."

"I'm in," Sam said, shifting his hefty frame drunkenly. "Don't forget now, Carter, I'm in. If I'm not there at eight, send your driver 'round for me. Just send for me. I'm in, hear me, Carter?"

"Aw, come on, guys. The more the merrier. Josh Hamilton's got three new parasails. And the crocodiles won't be biting. Bring out the embassy boat, Carter. Nobody uses it anymore."

"Next Sunday maybe," Carter Everett said.

Nicole swayed into Jacques' shoulder but smiled at Carter. Nicole Scott had been married for over ten years to a German freelance agronomist, who worked mainly for the Lever plantations in the bush. When he returned to Kinshasa, he and Nicole took up whatever kind of marriage they had together until he drifted off again. During his apparently unregretted absences Nicole taught French at a vaguely respectable institute and sought out clients for private lessons among the expatriate executives. She was a tall, rather mannish-looking woman made ardent by vanity and her desire to raise her status in the expatriate community. In the summer when a CEO's wife left early for vacation, Nicole discreetly took up with the husband, always with the hope that one day she could move into the wife's place for good. She was one of those women marooned in the tropics, grown soft in the life of privilege granted even those Europeans, like her, who were shunted to the periphery of that life. She had become a well-known local convenience.

Jacques shrugged off Nicole and pocketed his cigarettes. "I'm off," he said, starting for the door. "Let me know when you want to play tennis, Sam."

"Hey, m' friend," Sam said drunkenly, "Hey, Jacques! Don't you want to watch me self-destruct? I'm goin' to sit here all afternoon and self-destruct."

Carter pushed back his chair and stood up.

"Wait up a minute, Jacques. I'll be right with you."

They walked in silence toward a circle of shade under a flame tree.

"I hear you've been cleaning up after Josh Hamilton again," Carter said.

"Somebody has to. He's not big enough to do it himself." He turned to look at Carter, cool and clean in the torrid heat. "How did you hear about that?"

"I spend just about every night in the *cité*. Remember? People tell me things. Anyway . . . the little girl's family is very grateful for all you've done."

"Josh and Fiona have been white people in Africa too long. They've forgotten that there are some things you don't just walk away from, have a servant draw you a nice cool bath, pour you a strong drink, and then dismiss it all. They've been in that big house up on the hill too long," Jacques said.

A Jeep-load of young Peace Corps workers pulled to a stop in a swirl of dust and grit. They kicked off their sandals and, whooping noisily, ran toward the pool.

A moment later, a tall, remarkably pale young blonde wearing a short white beach wrap strolled into the gates from the Avenue de Shaba. She paused a moment, set down her straw bag, and with a graceful gesture, gathered up her thick, unruly hair into a pony tail.

Jacques and Carter fell silent as they watched her walk toward the pool.

"Probably somebody on temporary duty at the embassy," Carter said.

"What makes you say that?"

"She was carrying *The Bongo Banner,* the embassy newsletter, in her beach bag."

Jacques turned his head, staring after the girl.

"And she's wearing a wedding band," Carter said.

Jacques laughed. "Hell, Carter, sometimes I think you see too much."

"Don't forget my poker game tonight," Carter said.

"Okay. If I'm not running too late. I'm going to put in an appearance at a party in Djelo Binza."

"Boketsu?"

"Yes."

"Feel good to have your best buddy back in town? And in good odor with the Man?"

Jacques hesitated a moment. "Yes and no."

"Think he'll behave himself this time?"

"As far as I can tell. Looks to me as if he's pretty much teacher's pet now."

"I hear Mobutu may have shelled out as much as twenty million to get Boketsu back into the game."

Jacques felt as if a stone fist had hit him in the stomach. "That much?" he whispered.

8

Jacques left Bika's party in Djelo Binza early. Somehow he had been reassured by the looks of Bika's house with its bug-splattered fluorescent lights overhead, its plastic furniture and ugly, tasteless lamps with their plastic shades awry, its untidy ashtrays. There were few if any signs of twenty-million-dollar affluence there, and he began to take heart that Carter Everett's information might be unreliable. But the atmosphere at the party threw him off. Something seemed wrong. For one thing, he was the only European. There were too many men and only a sprinkling of women, not one of whom he recognized, and so young that Jacques suspected that they were prostitutes brought in especially for the night. He was struck by the fact that all the men, most of whom he had known since he was a small boy, were Mongos, Bika's tribe. It was odd, for at most gatherings in the years since Mobutu came to power, tribes mixed together quite casually. The men, including Bika, did not seem focused on the gathering as a party. They drank, smoked, laughed, flirted with the girls, but somehow Jacques had the impression that the real business of the evening was elsewhere: in the privacy of the kitchen, out on the terrace.

He circulated perfunctorily among the guests, vaguely ill at ease, and made arrangements with Bika, who listened enthusiastically but distractedly, to meet privately during the coming week.

Called away to a last-minute appointment, Carter Everett left Bill Donovan and George Kowalski to set up the food and drinks for the poker party. Kowalski was a young paramilitary man on a temporary duty assignment with a dozen or so other CIA men sent out to train a cadre of anti-terrorists for Zaïre. Rumors of Libyans making their way from eastern Zaïre to the capital had flared up again. The paramilitary mission was Washington's way of stroking Mobutu.

The Chief of Station's residence was located on a dimly lit, potholed street within a stone's throw of the Playboy Club. It was a rather peculiar house, for sections of the ground floor were mirror images: there were two entrance doors, two foyers, two sitting rooms, and two smaller alcoves for more intimate conversations. In this way, Carter Everett, as that night, could have guests come and go on the West side, while other, more public guests were being received and entertained in the other set of rooms on the East side.

A houseboy brought in a steaming dish of chicken *mwambe* and placed it on a heating tray on the buffet. Donovan and Kowalski finished setting out cards and ashtrays on a table in a circular screened porch at the back of the house. The evening was humid but pleasant; a large fan whirred overhead and gently ruffled a stack of paper napkins on the sideboard.

It was close to midnight when Jacques Delpech decided to join the poker game. He lowered the windows of his car and drove along the river in the soothing damp of the night. A convivial quiet had settled over the mango-arbored streets; the large villas behind white walls looked a ghostly blue in the glare of fluorescent guard lights. At the American ambassador's residence, two men played tennis under floodlights. The fronds of palm trees made dry, rustling sighs as a fresh breeze swept in from the river.

He passed under a grove of overarching mango trees where two small boys, street kids, were trying to shake loose fruit that they would sell along the roadside the next day. One boy had climbed onto the shoulders of the other and with a long bamboo cane whacked at the thick foliage of a tree.

Up ahead, he saw the Playboy Club with its burnt-out bulbs nervously blinking "layboy lu" into the darkness, and turned into Carter Everett's street. Several cars were still parked along the wall, and he was glad, knowing that he could delay for another few hours the emptiness of the house on the river.

That evening most of the players were regulars who turned up at Carter Everett's gates on Saturday nights whether a poker game was going on or not, a part of the ebb and flow of temporarily unattached men in any African city. They came to talk and to drink under the mimosas by the pool, and then around one or two in the morning they went with Carter to the *cité* to drink and dance and listen to Papa Wembé's music in dusty beer gardens.

Sam Wofford was in his usual place, and Jacques could see that his pendulum had for the moment swung to sobriety. He studied his cards with his sleepy crocodile eyes and grinned. He was winning a little tonight. The young CIA men called Carter "chief" and kept the refreshments flowing. Remnants of the chicken *mwambe* bubbled on the hot tray.

"Jesus!" Donovan said. "Listen to those frogs! Don't they ever quit?"

The wheezing, rasping, croaking, chirping cacophony of creatures in the garden pelted the house like stones.

"The other night out in the bush, coming back from Kikwit, in the middle of nowhere, you'd have to have ear plugs to get to sleep. Gimme good ol' Times Square any day of the week," Kowalski said.

"It's the rainy season. When the rains stops, they ease up," Jacques said.

"It's sex," Sam Wofford said. "It's all sex. I read it somewhere. Even the mosquitoes, that high-pitched whine of those mosquitoes coming at you, it's all those mosquitoes out to score. Especially the females, they shut up when they've got what they were looking for."

Jacques dealt another hand.

"Speaking of females," Donovan said, his pink face eager in the lamplight. "I've got some intelligence here." He did a drum roll with his fingers. "New girl in town, fellas, heads up! A luscious new babe!"

"Yeah, who's that?"

"USIA has a new lady. Cultural attaché."

"Oh, USIA," Sam Wofford said, disappointed. "Not my type."

"A widow," Donovan said.

"A widow?" Sam said.

"Yeah. A young widow. What's wrong with that?"

Jacques laughed and yawned.

"Gussie Pearce brought her around early this evening," Carter said after a moment, without looking up. "She's lovely. Really quite lovely."

9

Guy Marceau sat at a table in a quiet corner of the Brasserie Georges VI and watched the lunch-hour crowd of passersby hurrying along the rue Royale in the cold, biting March rain. *Sale temps! Quel sale temps!* he muttered to himself and picked up another Marlboro, carefully tearing off the filtered end before putting the cigarette into his mouth. Filtered cigarettes were his concession to his wife Margot's nagging; when she was not there to see, he tore the filter off and threw it away. For the hundredth time, he made a mental note to keep the Marlboros for evenings at home and good, healthy, strong Gauloises for the office. *Les jaunes.* The strongest and best.

He checked his watch and leaned forward to look out the window down to the corner of the street. The pavement, the sidewalks, the buildings were a wet, slick, gunmetal gray. Even the people hunching behind their umbrellas. Gray. Nasty, filthy Paris weather. And the rain wouldn't even wash the dog shit off the sidewalks.

Inside the Brasserie George VI the pitch of noise and bustle of lunch had begun to subside. Marceau looked at his watch again and cursed. Guichard never minded wasting any one else's time. That was his style. Showing that he was the boss and that he could make his subordinates cool their heels for close to an hour after fighting their way through the umbrella-clogged sidewalk crowds and ending up with soaked feet and damp trouser legs. That was Guichard's style. Making people uncomfortable. This brasserie, that was Guichard's style, too. Old style France, gleaming copper and brass and leather and chic women and men from chic offices on the rue Royale and the Place Vendôme, coming in and throwing off their expensive Burberry raincoats and scarves, carelessly, just like that, as if they were cheap old things picked up for a few francs at Monoprix. The women showing a lot of leg as they slid into the leather booths. A slim young woman with a briefcase caught his eye and scowled, and Marceau swiftly looked away.

"Guy! *Salut!*" Bernard Guichard bellowed good-naturedly over the noise of the room. He unbuckled his raincoat and threw it over the back of his chair, carelessly. A Burberry.

Bastard, he sneaked up on me, Marceau said to himself, holding out his hand but not rising from his seat. Bernard Guichard sat down and rubbed his hands briskly together. He was a tall, round man with sleek, lustrous surfaces. Glossy eyelids stretched tightly over rather large, protuberant eyes, and he had a nervous habit of raising both hands and smoothing back the graying hair at his temples with the heel of his palms. "*Sale temps, hein?* Let's see, what shall we have? Have you ordered?"

Marceau snapped out his order of a *steak frites* while Guichard went into a long discussion of his health problems with the waiter who stood tapping his pencil against his pad and nodding sympathetically. Finally, with a sigh, as if he were laying his head on a chopping block, Guichard ordered a *steak frites*, "to simplify things," he said.

They ate efficiently, ordering a second carafe of red wine, and talked mainly of the dismal end-of-winter weather, the daily rains, the floods in Auch, dampness in their fuel lines, but it seemed to Marceau that Guichard had a gleam in his eye as they worked over the subject. They finished their coffee, and Marceau lit another cigarette.

"*Alors . . . ,*" Guichard said, grunting a little as he leaned over and fished through his briefcase. He pulled out a gray plastic Swiss Air ticket folder and a French passport and tossed them down in front of Marceau.

"Those are for you," Guichard said.

"These are for me?" Marceau responded, picking up the airline tickets. Inside were three or four Swiss Air baggage identification tags and a packet of tickets. "What's this? My secretary usually gets my tickets from the office upstairs. Is this something special?" He did not trust Guichard. It would be just his style to play some mean, nasty joke so that he could have a good dinner-party story. "Is this a joke?"

"No joke at all," Guichard said solemnly, putting on that self-important, I'm-a-dignified-boss look that made Marceau's skin creep.

Marceau dragged on his cigarette and picked up the passport. It was his passport with the same old photograph—his secretary always kept it in her desk—and about midway, on two pages toward the back, a visa with the flaming torch seal of Zaïre. The visa gave him the right to *nombreuses entrées et sorties* and the *carte de séjour* of a permanent resident. Back to Africa. Back to the good life, fancy cars, fancy houses, servants falling all over each other. Good-bye stinking hellhole Métro, gray skies and dog shit. Marceau clamped his jaws together. He was afraid that at any moment he would start to squeal with joy. And that bastard Guichard sitting there watching him. What if it was all a big joke anyway?

"And you want me to head up the office down there?"

"Something like that. But not really. We have people on the production side to supervise the operation. They're in place. Or almost in place. By the end of June, that's our target. No," Guichard dragged out the word and glanced quickly about the room, where only a middle-aged man and a young blond dawdled over their coffee and spoke in whispers. All of the waiters had disappeared below. "No," Guichard said again. "You won't be heading up the office. But . . . this is more important. Much more important, in our opinion, and believe me, we have gone over and over your assets for this particular situation. "

Marceau despised the way he threw around the "we" and the "our," always trying to make it clear that Guichard was on the inside, where the big decisions were made, and that Marceau was not. He had to wait until someone came along and threw his passport and some airline tickets in his face.

"This particular situation may be a little tricky," Guichard went on. "But knowing the way business goes in Africa—I learned a lot in Gabon, you can be sure of that—I think you can handle it and get the results we want. Basically, Petro-France wants you to *represent* us in Kinshasa."

Guichard drew a folder of papers from his briefcase and began to go through them while Marceau sat smoking. "Let's begin with Boketsu Bika—Boketsu is his family name—and you may have followed . . ."

"I have. *Petit salaud*, isn't he? A regular bastard. Turncoat. Ratted on the whole gang down there, Mobutu in particular, and now he's back lapping up the cream. Right? *Petite crapule, hein?*" Marceau tore off the filter of another cigarette. One thing he was good at was getting the number of these guys who supposedly "ruled the world."

Guichard ordered another coffee, and Marceau a brandy and a pack of Gauloises. The middle-aged man and his blond companion had disappeared, and their waiter stood leaning against the bar reading a newspaper.

"*Alors, quoi?*" Marceau said, when Guichard had finished his dossier. "The usual payoffs, hein?" What was all this melodrama? "The same old African cha-cha-cha, hein?"

Guichard smoothed his glossy hair back from his temples and fixed Marceau with an icy glare. "No, *mon cher ami,* it is not the same old African cha-cha-cha. We're talking here about an 800-million-dollar-a-year oil strike. One of the richest, potentially *the* richest oil strike Petro-France has ever made in Africa. And Boketsu Bika, according to our sources, is going back down there to be named Minister of Mines."

"So . . . okay, okay. I'm reading you loud and clear. Do we rent this Boketsu, or is he a lease-purchase?"

"A rental. Hopefully, a long-term rental. And the situation is potentially promising enough for us to go back to one of our old policies. The company is tired of getting these guys on the payroll and then have them start to dick us around. We've got to have more control. Have someone who speaks our language. Someone who knows how to keep Africans in line, keep them from getting too greedy for their own good. This time we're going after the black man's white man, too. It's been a good arrangement in the past. It's up to you to make it work in Zaïre. Boketsu's white man is his childhood friend, a Belgian businessman named Jacques Delpech. We want you to hit him first, soften him up, then go after Boketsu." Guichard shot his wrist forward and glanced at his watch. "I'm late," he said, getting to his feet. "New secretary. I have to go over some dictation with her." It had stopped raining, and a hard wind buffeted scraps of paper along the gutter. "We have to talk again. And you want to check in with Robert. Time is of the essence. *Essentiel.* The company would like you in place within ten days."

"Ten days! God Almighty, what will Margot say to that?"

"That's another thing, Marceau. The company feels that you could negotiate this tricky situation better if not . . . encumbered, as it were . . . by your wife. If you could come and go as you please, get yourself into the swing of things in the expatriate community."

Marceau cringed with embarrassment. The company didn't think Margot was . . . very chic. Poor Margot. She was an earnest, hardworking Alsatian who liked nothing better than scrubbing the kitchen floor on a Saturday morning, peeling potatoes straight from the garden. Her hands were always a mess. Guichard was telling him that the company was sending him off to the tropics alone. Marceau lowered his eyes, afraid that Guichard would read the joy in them.

Marceau lit a cigarette and visualized a huge, airy house in a grove of palm trees, curvaceous girls in bikinis around a pool, canisters of Gauloise cigarettes, *les jaunes*, in every room of the house, day and night, especially the bedroom. And not a single, puny, puking filtered Marlboro anywhere.

10

Even before Guy Marceau stepped out of the car, he looked up at the Villa San Diego and said, "I'll take it." Biding his time, waiting to find a house that would suit his new status, Marceau had spent two months in one of the best suites at the Hotel InterContinental, playing tennis and sunning by the pool, hanging out at night in L'Atmosphère, Kinshasa's trendiest nocturnal playpen on one of the top floors of the hotel, a slick, high-tech disco with psychedelic lights.

Marceau quickly fell in with the fast-talking, fast-dealing Lebanese crowd who drifted in from the casino around two each morning. The "Lebs" were Marceau's kind of people: out for the high stakes, mostly in diamonds, and not afraid to get their hands dirty. They changed Marceau's money at the best rate in town and awed him with their casual brutality.

Toward dawn one morning a fight broke out over a mulatto prostitute that ended with one man being hauled out into the foyer and tossed over the balcony onto a marble table two flights below. "His head is smashed," someone called up from below. "*C'est o.k.*," Chehab, the ringleader, a burly man with a thin, feathery mustache, said, peering over the railing, "I was afraid you were going to say that the table was smashed." "The table *is* smashed," the other man said. "*Enfin*," Chehab shrugged, turning away. "Money will take care of it. *Ça se paye*." Marceau liked that. It had style.

It was Chehab who got him the lease on the Villa San Diego, which belonged to one of the black bwanas of the government. For Marceau, who despised Americans, the name nonetheless gave a touch of the complications of modern power to the splendid villa, which was located at the top of Djelo Binza with a panoramic view of two capital cities, Kinshasa below, and Brazzaville across the river in the Congo, as well as a sweeping curve of the great Congo River. It was the kind of house that could make a short man like Marceau feel tall, the kind of house that would impress even a snob like Guichard.

"*Alors,*" Bernard Guichard said, "Let's hear how things are going." He sat down opposite Marceau on the terrace with his back turned, deliberately it seemed to Marceau, to the magnificent view of the city, hazy in the afternoon heat. "Bring us up to date. You suddenly dropped us."

"The telephone lines are cut half the time. The bastards hack them in two when they run short of money. Look out there at that goddamn spaghetti." Marceau gestured toward the street where telephone wires sagged and looped in tangled black knots.

"Pay them off, *cher ami*. Do I have to come all the way down here from Paris to tell you that? Do I? If so, Petro-France has selected the wrong man for the job we have to do here."

"I *have* paid them off," and don't *cher ami* me, you asshole, Marceau thought. "I've got two of the *salauds* on a regular monthly payroll, for God's sake."

Guichard frowned as Marceau's voice rose. In the *boyerie* he could hear the soft chatter of the servants stop abruptly. Guichard looked at his watch and waited.

"I haven't found the guy responsible for this *secteur* yet," Marceau said in a subdued voice. "It's like trying to kill a damn snake: you pay one guy off, and two or three others step into his shoes." Goddamn! Marceau thought, only a few months on my own and already they've got the bloodhounds from Paris snooping around. Goddamn! He could feel his ears burning, turning a telltale red.

"*Enfin, passons,*" Guichard said. "Tell me something about your contacts. That's what we need to know. Any key people in the government?"

"I'm working my way to them through my contacts. Starting at the top. How's that for a shocker, hein? What do you think of that, hein? Any day now I may be called to the residence. The President's in town, you know." Marceau crossed his legs and lit another cigarette. He shifted nervously from cheek to cheek.

Guichard sat watching him. Marceau dragged deeply on his cigarette and unleashed a fit of coughing.

After a moment, when Marceau had lapsed into breathless wheezing, Guichard said, "Ah yes, your contacts. *Parlons-en.* One of the reasons we thought I should come down. I'll be frank with you, Guy. You're associating with the wrong element . . ." He held up his hand for silence. "Don't worry, we know who they are, we do our research, after all. The Lebanese are shady characters, almost to a man. In and out of favor with the government. Untrustworthy. Too involved with smuggling and money laundering. These are not, and I can't stress this too heavily, these are not the contacts Petro-France has in mind. We want you to move with the very top society: diplomats—have you called on the French ambassador, by the way? Courtesy call? No?—all the top executives naturally, and especially the businessmen who have been here a lifetime, not just those who come and go with the big corporations. The permanent ones, those with friends among the ministers. I don't think you'll find a single Lebanese on that list."

"Wait a minute, just wait a minute. Who do you think got me this house? A Lebanese, that's who. A Leb with influence. Look at this spread! Right next door to the Minister of Transportation and on the other side the Minister of Plan. Why do you think the street hasn't a pothole in it, hein? Minister of Transportation. The whole street is crawling with black bwanas. I'll be playing tennis with the Minister of Plan every morning before the month is out. They all play tennis, these black bwanas. Look at that tennis court next door. Lights and everything."

"Petro-France is expecting you to do more than play tennis in Zaïre, *cher ami*." He paused. "Have you started to work on Jacques Delpech yet?"

At the mention of Delpech, black, roiling rage surged through Marceau. A stampede of images of late nights and early mornings in L'Atmosphère pounded through Marceau's brain raising a cloud of grimacing faces, blue arms, orange ears, twisting, undulating, under the spiraling lights, so many faces, named and unnamed. And then one night three weeks ago, everything rational, practical, and sane had gone out of his head: Marceau had fallen in love, not gradually, not cautiously, but like an overloaded river barge going smash on a sandbar in the middle of the night. His body ached with the torment of it. And at the center of that torment: Jacques Delpech.

"In three months you don't meet everybody, for God's sake. I've been working with my contacts at the top. The President's in—"

"You said that. At any rate, when you are circulating in the right crowd down here," Guichard cleared his throat expressively, "you will meet Jacques Delpech. You know about Boketsu, but perhaps, my dear fellow, you haven't quite figured out what Delpech means to us. Delpech grew up in Zaïre, boyhood friend of Boketsu, tribal brothers as a matter of fact. Delpech was initiated into the Mongo tribe with Boketsu in one of those puberty things. Very, very Zaïrian, if you know what I mean." Marceau did not, but he said nothing. "You're going to pitch both of them. You can't do one without the other. Delpech's father supported Mobutu before he became the *Président fondateur*. Jacques Delpech grew up around Mobutu and his set. He is one of the few Belgians Mobutu trusts. Boketsu has just come back, he always set himself up as an idealist, against government corruption, et cetera, et cetera. He's going to try to keep his hands clean. For a while. Delpech is his friend, his tribal brother. He's family. Besides, you know these Africans. They have to have their white men around to tell them what to do. Look at the Ivory Coast. Who's running that show now? We are. France has more people down there now than when it belonged to us. *Enfin*, if Delpech says jump, Boketsu will ask 'how high?' Especially if his fall from great moral heights is cushioned by a great deal of cash."

"Okay, okay, Bernard, I know that you guys in the corner suite have this all figured out, I know I just *live* down here, that's all, I'm not in some fancy office on the Place Vendôme like you guys, but it doesn't take a genius to see that you've got this thing ass backwards. Come on now, let's be serious . . . in the past, and you guys aren't the only ones to know this . . . outside the corner suite we hear some things, too . . . the deal got the okay from the big man at the top. Hein? Why not target Mobutu and let *him* tell his minister what he wants to do?"

"Too expensive, that's why. Mobutu would cost too much. The top man always costs too much. And is not nearly as reliable. Look at the Congo."

"And this Belgian," Marceau asked. He could not bring himself to pronounce the detested name. "Is he a rotten apple ready to fall from the tree, or will I have trouble shaking him loose?"

"Hard to say. He's a businessman in Africa. The species is not well known for its moral rectitude. He's rich . . ."

"Rich? So he's supposed to get himself mixed up in a bribery scheme to get richer?"

"Precisely," Guichard said, throwing his head back. "As someone said, One can never be too rich or too fashionable . . . uh, or one can never be too rich or too . . . uh, chic . . . One can never be . . . something of the sort. I forget who said it . . ."

"Well, I think we can be pretty sure it wasn't De Gaulle," Marceau said.

"The point is, everyone always wants more, hein? And Delpech may not be as rich as he thinks. All of his money, so far as we have been able to find out, is invested in Africa. Our sources tell us that Guinea may nationalize his brewery in Conakry within the next few months. If so . . ." Guichard snapped his fingers. "Poof! And he has recently separated from his wife. His wife has always been expensive and will become more so. Divorces are expensive, *un point, c'est tout.* He has a child. Or two. I forget. At any rate, one can never be too . . ."

"Rich. I think I get it," Marceau said.

A scowl flitted over Guichard's smooth forehead. "I must go. I want to be on the Swiss Air flight when it comes up from Johannesburg in the morning."

"First class? Not a chance. First class is always sold out weeks and months in advance, even on Sabena."

"Not in Africa, *cher ami,* first class seats are, happily, *always* available." Guichard pushed himself up from his chair and smoothed back the hair at his temples. "I'm sure that one of your Lebanese friends can manage that detail."

Before the gates of the Villa San Diego had closed behind Guichard's car, Marceau was at the telephone.

"*Allô? Madame est là? Allô? Allô?*" Marceau leaned his head against the wall and waited. He was perspiring and breathing heavily. Suddenly, he whirled around like a madman and threw the telephone against the wall. "*Ah, les salauds!* The bastards! They've cut the wires again!" he whimpered.

11

Sarah's office was located near the rear of the American Cultural Center and looked out onto the ivory market where row upon row of ivory artifacts glistened in the sun. Beyond the tables heaped with carved elephants and necklaces and bracelets, vendors displayed dusty tribal masks and soapstone or wooden totems that had been buried for months in the moist earth to give them an antique look. Close to the curb, boys dozed in the shade of oil paintings propped against piles of rocks, paintings of local scenes on Matadi flour sacking stretched over crude frames: garish depictions of fishermen on the river, full moon over a thatched mud hut, glossy African women, their faces bemused as if discovering with astonishment their magnificently full and shapely naked breasts. Further down the street, near the exit of the Cultural Center parking lot, sickly African gray parrots and bewildered monkeys in bamboo cages slumped in the heat.

There was a sudden commotion of thin squeals and laughter, and Sarah looked up from her desk. A gaggle of small boys was pushing and shoving at each other, trying to shinny up a palm tree to recapture a scruffy-looking monkey that had escaped from one of the bamboo cages. The monkey clung to the tree trunk, looking back over its shoulder, wary, ready to spring into action.

"Phil. I didn't hear you come in. There's a loose monkey up a tree. He's having a great time up there. Just look at him!"

"Ah, c'est l'Afrique, Sarah, c'est l'Afrique." Phil Olmstead carefully patted the strips of hair covering the top of his head and laid a thick folder on Sarah's crowded desk. "Monkeys in a palm tree. Happens all the time. You're not in California anymore, Sarah. Or is it Maine?"

"Maine," Sarah said, opening the folder. "So, what do you think of this linkage proposal?"

Phil Olmstead slid into a chair next to the window. "I don't know, Sarah. We'll have to think about it. Mull it over. You know what I mean? Give it some thought." He settled a leg across his knee and stroked his ankle thoughtfully. "We don't want to get in over our heads. Not in this heat."

Sarah idly turned over several pages, giving herself time so that she could ask, in a voice that would not sound baldly stubborn, why USIA could not go ahead with plans to set up a linkage between the University of Kinshasa and an American university or college. She had discovered the proposal in the files abandoned by the previous cultural attaché and had almost shouted *Eureka!* this makes sense, this could make a difference. She set to work on the project, figuring out details down to specific universities and departments in the United States that might be interested in sending a professor each year to Zaïre and accepting a Zaïrian professor on their campus. She had already called on several professors at the disintegrating university campus in Djelo Binza, where students wandered aimlessly around gutted buildings with broken windows, sagging, unhinged doors, and rusty, foul-smelling liquid from toilets oozing down the outside walls. Earnest, neatly dressed teachers clustered around her, their eyes timid with embarrassment, seeing for the moment what she saw and feeling ashamed. They were desperate for books, intellectual stimulation, anything that would bring them out of their impoverished stupor.

"What exactly do we need to think over, Phil?"

"Well, just about everything. I mean, it's not ever good to rush into these things. That's been my experience and, believe me, Sarah, I've had plenty of experience when it comes to these Third World projects. Plenty of experience and not all of it rosy, you can bet your bottom dollar on that." He tugged at his sock and sighed.

"I mean, just for instance, who the hell, if you'll pardon my French, in his right mind is going to want to come down here and spend a year in Zaïre, for God's sake?"

"You did, Phil. And I did. And besides it would be only nine months. An academic year."

"Nine months can seem like a year. Ten years even. Take it from me, Sarah, I've been there. And besides academics are picky. Fussy people prone to complaints. Never satisfied. We don't want that. I can't stand that, all those problems, holding somebody's hand, trying to find him a hamburger that tastes just like McDonald's."

"The hamburgers at the American Club taste just like McDonald's."

"No, they don't."

"Close."

"How should I know? I never go near the place. Patty won't let me go there. Swear to God and hope to die. Patty thinks I'd spend my time ogling the babes around the swimming pool. Or the cute young things in their tennis outfits. She's jealous, my Patty, swear to God."

Phil Olmstead's brow flushed as pink as his scalp.

Sarah quickly picked up the folder and began shuffling the papers again. "I can think of at least two art history professors, specialists in African art, who would snatch up a chance to come here to do some research and teach. English and American Studies. Just the basics. It doesn't have to be anything fancy."

"What would they do for books? You gotta have books, Sarah. They've got nothing here. Zilch. Zero. Nada."

"*We've* got books here at the Center. And every college and university library in the States tosses out duplicates by the boxful every year. I can write and request those. I know where to start with that."

"And housing? Where do we put them?"

"I talked with the General Services Officer at the embassy, and she assured me that there will be no problem. There is plenty of housing for A.I.D., and some places are vacant."

"I don't know, Sarah," Phil Olmstead groaned. "I look into my crystal ball, and I see problems. Problems, problems, and more problems. And work, my God, the work! All those papers to Washington flying back and forth, makes me dizzy just to think about it."

"I'll do the work, Phil," Sarah said. "With pleasure."

Olmstead straightened his leg and put his foot on the floor.

"You know, Sarah, I honestly believe you will. I'm beginning to figure you out. You really want to do this, don't you?"

"Yes. And I'll make it work. Trust me, I will."

A little boy on a bicycle raced through the aisles of the ivory market, spinning clouds of pumpkin-colored dust in his wake.

"If that's your idea of fun, Sarah, then, I say do it. Write up the project, start to finish, and I'll sign off on it. Get it to those bozos in Washington before they've had their second cup of coffee before lunch. Time I shook headquarters up a little. Show them what it's really like to work your butt off, if you'll pardon my French, to get a good thing going."

He stood up and shook out his pants' leg. "You wouldn't want to come over to the house tonight to start your bridge lessons? It's a small group, just two tables. I could get you started."

"How nice of you, Phil, but I promised Gussie Pearce that I'd go with her to the Italian ambassador's garden party. Now I'm sorry I accepted. My shipment hasn't arrived, so I'll have to wear whatever I can find."

"It's probably sitting out at the airport somewhere. *C'est l'Afrique.* I'll send an expediter out to the airport tomorrow, I promise. Gotta be out there somewhere." He shambled toward the door. "And don't you worry, Cinderella, about that party. Even in rags you'd be the most gorgeous dame there."

Sarah laughed and said, "Tsch! Tsch! Mr. Olmstead, better watch those sexist remarks."

Grinning and leering like a tongue-tied kid, Olmstead ducked his pink head and shuffled out the door.

Sarah whirled her chair around and switched on her computer. Outside her window, the palm trees had begun to pitch and shudder in a sudden squall of rain. The fugitive monkey and the small boys had disappeared. She glanced at her watch. She had just enough time to draft a couple of letters before Gussie dropped by to pick her up. Nothing like good, honest work, and plenty of it, to ease the heart and soul. Damned if I don't sound exactly like Mother, she thought. It had been a long time since she had summoned up Michael's suicide note, going over and over it like a conscientious archeologist sifting and sorting through ancient debris, looking for the one piece that would provide the clue to her private mystery. She thought she understood more of Michael's particular misery now, but she still had not figured out what role she had played in it. She only knew that she felt healthy and strong, not crippled and bent as she had when she left Yale. And she was not at all unhappy that Gussie had promised to introduce her to the most fantastic men in Kinshasa at this fancy garden party.

She gazed contentedly at the screen, her fingers working over the keys. I'm off and running, and I'm going to see this project through. Even if I have to work like hell, if you'll pardon my French, every day of the week.

12

Jacques Delpech came directly from his office to the Italian ambassador's garden party. That morning he had returned, relieved, from another trip to Lubumbashi where the plant appeared to be returning to normal production after a series of fights, strikes, and the usual transportation problems. A Sabena stewardess, one of his wife's friends, had stopped by his office and left off a long, abusive letter detailing Janine's plans for a separation and a financial settlement. The letter read like the whining of an old, miserly, distant relative, secretly aware that her claims on your life and money are bogus.

Though Jacques, like other businessmen in Africa, made it a point to keep up his social obligations—parties were never simply parties but ways of getting information and making necessary contacts—he had come to the Italian ambassador's residence primarily in search of his accountant, a young bachelor who played mahjong on Thursday afternoons with the ambassador's wife and was a regular guest at official receptions.

The long drive leading up to the residence was lined with drivers, chatting and smoking, standing alongside Mercedes and Peugeots. Flame trees glowed orange, and plump scarlet blossoms fallen from tulip trees stained the gravel drive in ragged blood-red circles. Grey guinea fowl, which the ambassador believed would kill any snakes in the garden, noisily roamed the lawn, glistening acid green in the late afternoon sun.

Barefoot houseboys in starched white uniforms with rows of gold buttons moved silently through the crowd offering trays of drinks and hors-d'oeuvres. Women glittered in heavy gold jewelry and diamonds and wore cool, brightly colored dresses that bared their shoulders and arms. They swayed back and forth trying to balance their drinks and keep their thin high heels from plunging into the soft, moist lawn.

Jacques was standing under an arbor of bougainvillea talking with his accountant, slightly apart from the general flow of guests in the garden, when Nicole Scott, in black Thai silk pants and a blouse like a man's tuxedo shirt, interrupted them.

"I've brought someone to meet you," she said, looking at Jacques and ignoring the young accountant, who turned and strolled away. She was deeply tanned and held by the arm a short, dark-haired man with a mustache. "This is Guy Marceau."

Jacques turned and looked down at the man at Nicole's side. As they shook hands, Jacques was startled by the man's expression and wondered what stories Nicole could have told him.

"Guy is with Petro-France," Nicole said, and Jacques smiled, remembering her almost mystical faith in the power of oil company executives. In one of her more recent liaisons with a Mobil oilman, Nicole had almost snatched the gold ring, but the man's wife had refused to give him a divorce, and the affair had limped along and died after the Mobil man failed to appear at a rendez-vous at the Hotel Meurice in Paris.

"I've got a terrific party house." The short Frenchman's face appeared to be struggling to find a pleasant expression. He had a tidy little body and long, expressive hands with fingertips stained amber brown. "Nicole can tell you what great parties we have."

Amused, Jacques raised an eyebrow at the proprietary "we" and glanced at Nicole. "I'm sure."

"Don't we, Nicole?"

"*Formidable*, really terrific," she said.

"Yes, *formidable*," Marceau said, his angry hawk stare never leaving Jacques' face.

"So, Petro-France has set up an office in Kinshasa, has it? I knew that the drilling in Equateur has been successful," Jacques said.

"Splendid offices. In the C.C.I.Z. building, opposite the InterCon. You should drop in sometime. Sixteenth floor. Beautiful view of the river. The city, too, and Brazzaville." He seemed barely able to get his words out, so absorbed was he in scrutinizing Jacques' face.

Jacques lit a cigarette. The small man seemed awfully keen on local real estate. "Do the elevators work?"

"Sometimes," Marceau said, a quick flash of anger darkening his eyes. "I mean, sometimes they don't work."

The Centre Commercial International du Zaïre building sat like a dead and decaying glassy monster of modern architecture amid the profuse tropical growth along the river. Twenty stories tall, it had been built by the French at an extravagant cost to Zaïre in the late seventies with so many payoffs that there was apparently little left over to construct a functioning building. The electricity rarely worked, shutting down the elevators, the air-conditioning, lights, and office machines. Since the windows were sealed and the stairwells pitch black holes in the middle of the building, corporations steered clear of it and most of its offices were vacant. The ground floor had become a hangout for beggars and salesmen of trinkets and ashtrays in the ubiquitous copper and malachite and ivory.

"My card," the Frenchman said. "We must meet for lunch."

"Oh, yes, mine, too," Jacques ran his hands through his pockets. "Ah, sorry. I don't seem to have any. Happy to have met you."

With that, he grabbed a glass of pink champagne from a passing tray, lifted it briefly in salute, turned, and was gone.

"The usual cocktail party vanishing act," Nicole said dryly as they watched Jacques walk away toward the ambassador's wife.

"He didn't like me," Marceau said.

"He's jealous, that's all."

She looked so lost, standing there on the terrace in her simple outfit among the chattering crowd of perfumed and smoothly coifed women, self-conscious, preening themselves in their latest indulgences from the elegant boutiques of Paris, Brussels, and

Geneva, that Jacques stopped on his way to thank his hostess to introduce himself and ask if he could get her a drink.

"It's so hot, thank you," Sarah Laforge said, fanning herself with the stiff invitation she had received for the party.

She wanted a scotch and soda, and Jacques was surprised, having expected her to ask for a simple tonic or a Coke. Perhaps she was not a missionary, after all, but then, what would a missionary be doing at a diplomatic party? Peace Corps, probably. She was dressed in a dark blue batik print peasant skirt and a simple white, gauzy blouse with dark circles of perspiration under the arms. She looked damp, hot, uncomfortable. She wore thick-soled leather sandals, and Jacques noticed that she had delicate, surprisingly slender feet for a woman so tall. Her thick, springy hair, a sun-streaked strawberry blond, masses of it, kinky, tightly curled, was pulled back in an elastic band at the nape of the neck. She was definitely an unusual presence at the Italian ambassador's garden party.

"You look familiar," Jacques said, when he returned with her drink. "Haven't we met before? It seems to me we have."

"I don't think so," Sarah said, her wide set blue eyes full of amusement.

"You've heard that before?"

"Yes," she said gently. "A few times." She drank thirstily. "Are you French? Your name sounds French."

"No, Belgian."

"Then let's speak French, shall we? I never speak the language, except with my assistant, and my servant," she said in fluent French. "I'm always with Americans. I think I ought to speak the language of the country I work in."

She had the manner of a schoolteacher, and he thought with painful longing of his father and his self-discipline, his humorous obsession with self-improvement.

Sarah fanned herself. "It's so hot. I'm not used to the heat. The air-conditioner doesn't work in my apartment, and my shipment hasn't arrived."

"Ah, *c'est l'Afrique*," Jacques said.

"What does that mean?" she asked sharply.

Jacques looked at her. "I don't understand," he said, "you speak perfect French."

"I know," she said impatiently. "I know, but everybody goes around saying that. Every time I say something, they come back with that. I don't understand what it means."

"Why, I suppose it means that you can't expect everything to go smoothly here. Things aren't necessarily logical or efficient or dependable. As they are in your country, I'm sure." He was rather rattled by her abruptness, but her accent made him smile. She sounded like a peasant from a potato field. "Are you French-Canadian?"

"My father is. Was. My mother, though, is very New England, a descendant of Jonathan Edwards. The Puritan minister. The last gasp of Puritanism really." She felt like a backward teenager babbling away with this man who looked as much like a movie star as any she had ever seen. Yet he seemed totally unaware of how attractive he was. To her great surprise, and irritation, she found herself wanting to impress him. "I'm sorry, Puritanism probably doesn't mean much to you, does it?"

"No, not really. But no need to apologize." Up close, he could see a splash of golden freckles covering her slim nose and her cheeks. Her skin was very pale and moist and her eyes round and childlike.

Over her shoulder he saw Augusta Pearce, the American consul, step out of the shade of a papaya tree and start across the lawn toward the terrace, her bright party smile firmly in place, closing her eyes as she lifted her face to the afternoon sun.

"I should know more about your country," Jacques said, disappointed at seeing Gussie Pearce bearing down on them. "You are American, aren't you?"

"Oh, yes. Yes, I am," Sarah said, jumping nervously as Gussie put her hands on her shoulders.

"Yes, what, dahlin'?" Gussie asked, looking flirtatiously at Jacques. Her high heels screeched disagreeably against the flagstones; the toe of one shiny black patent pump was smeared with guinea fowl turd like a dollop of white and green whipped cream.

"Mr. Delpech asked me whether I was American, Gussie."

"Of course, she is. She's our new cultural attaché. Dudn't she look just as American as can be?" crooned Gussie Pearce, wrapping her fragrant arms around him. *"Trois fois . . . à la belge,"* she said, kissing him three times on the cheek, darting her pointed chin back and forth. She then leaned back a little, still pressing against him, and rubbed her lipstick from his cheeks with her fingers. Jacques suddenly remembered Carter Everett's surprising comment about Sarah Laforge at the poker table, Donovan's young widow, the new girl in town. She's lovely, really lovely, Carter had said, keeping his eyes lowered.

Finally, satisfied, Gussie released him and turned to Sarah. "Look at you. Aren't you sumpin'? I leave you alone two minutes, and you end up with the handsomest man in Kinshasa. Now, aren't you a hoot?"

13

From the terrace of her eighth floor apartment Sarah spent hours watching the busy life of the immense khaki brown river: the battered and rusted ferries wallowing and thrusting their way over to Brazzaville and back, bicycles and people and animals hanging off the sides and lying or standing on the roof; the smart vedettes, small and powerful, speeding across with one or two passengers rich enough to pay for a comfortable crossing in deep-cushioned privacy; the fishermen standing tall in their crudely carved pirogues, silhouetted against the setting sun, casting their nets onto the swiftly flowing waters. From where she sat, the fishermen looked as if they were miraculously standing on top of the water. On some days, the river was so thick, all the way across to Brazzaville, with floating clusters of water hyacinths that the Congo looked like a great green and violet meadow where she might look out and see a long line of tall African women, bulging baskets swaying back and forth on their heads, strolling across in their measured steps, coming to town to hunker down in the dust of the sidewalks to sell their wares.

Down below, on the other side of the street, stretched the gardens of the late General Boboso, Mobotu's tribal brother, his "godfather", a key figure in his rise to power. The General's gardens were a wild growth of palm trees, flame trees, jacaranda spilling blue and violet into wayward patches of banana trees, and white and pink frangipani whose sweet, cloying odor she could smell on her balcony in the night, after the riotous thunderstorms, when the winds calmed. In the evenings, in the few minutes before the sun plunged over the rapids, sugar bats swarmed down from indigo skies into the fruit trees of the garden, their thin screeching chatter sounding like a schoolyard of small children at play.

During the day she worked hard at the Cultural Center, making great strides with the university linkage program, which, as it took form and obstacles were eased aside, seemed to Phil Olmstead one of his more brilliant undertakings. Satisfied that she had stumbled upon a rewarding project, Sarah was content to let him boast and plump up his feathers. She could make Olmstead look good in Washington, and Olmstead knew it. He was like a young kid in the throes of his first puppy love. He made sure that Sarah got plenty of invitations appropriate to her status, and urged her to take up his offer to teach her bridge.

In the mornings now she woke up to the sound of Malu grinding coffee beans in the kitchen. Unaccustomed to servants, she had at first nervously wondered whether there would be enough for him to do, but Malu had worked for Europeans for years and, smiling a little, had without a word taken a mop and bucket from the kitchen closet and started his daily routine. Sarah bought him tennis shoes at one of the trading stores because it distressed her to see him working in his bare feet. The shoes immediately disappeared, and Malu with his shy smile, was as barefoot as before. When Sarah asked him where the shoes were and explained, once more, that he must wear them at work, he lost his smile and was unable to look at her face. The next morning, when he called her to breakfast, she found the shoes, neat and white, sitting reproachfully in front of her tray on the little table on the terrace. Sarah put the shoes on the floor, and she and Malu never mentioned them again. She referred to Malu as "my servant," never as "my boy," although she knew that the embassy crowd, behind her back, made fun of her for doing so. She realized that this was a detail, but sometimes small details could matter a great deal. Besides, Malu already had white hairs sprinkled over his close-cropped head. He is my servant, she said to herself, not my boy.

"Quite frankly, your letters sound awfully happy, my dear," her mother wrote. And Sarah was happy. Sometimes almost light-headed with happiness. Still, she worried that she might be heading toward some kind of trouble. Since shortly after her arrival in Zaïre a slightly fetid odor hung over her and never totally left her. She showered morning and evening, and sometimes again when she returned from a dinner party at night. She shampooed her hair every day, experimenting futilely with one shampoo after another. During the weeks when the air-conditioning broke down, she would soak a bath towel, wrap herself in it, and go to sleep naked on the lounge chair on her balcony. In the mornings, even before the sun hit her eyelids, the smell would awaken her. It was oppressive, a nagging worry that would not go away.

"I've tried everything," Sarah said to the Pakistani woman who ran the American Club beauty salon near the embassy. "I don't know what else to do."

The woman lifted strands of Sarah's thick, long hair and smelled it.

"Asma. Come here, would you?" she called to a birdlike young woman dressed in an orange silk tunic and pants who was folding towels at a table on the other side of the room.

"Smell that," she said, digging her long fingers into Sarah's hair. "Smell."

"I smell it, yes."

"What is it?"

The birdlike young woman bent down again to Sarah's hair. "Mildew. Your hair has mildewed," she said in a loud voice to Sarah as if she were somewhat deaf.

"Mildew?"

"Yes, it's mildew. Your hair is too thick. It won't stay dry. Not in the rainy season."

She leaned over and brought another section of thick hair to her nose. "Your hair smells like death," she said. "You must cut it."

"Cut my hair? Short?"

"Yes. Cut it off, the shorter, the better. You don't want to go around smelling like death, do you?"

14

Bika's car was parked in the drive next to the entrance steps, and two bodyguards with M-16s standing just inside the gates gave Jacques a short salute as his car pulled in. Jacques paused and turned before going into his house, to make sure that the gates were closed.

He found Bika sitting as usual on the back terrace overlooking the river.

"What are the guns for?" Jacques asked, loosening his tie. "Something new?"

"Not really. Just a precaution. I feel better with them these days, that's all."

"Problems?"

"No more than the usual. I wanted to talk. Away from people." He sounded dispirited.

"Then I'll change. Be right with you."

"No hurry. Take your time. Your boy fixed me a drink," he said, lifting his glass.

When Jacques returned to the terrace in a tee shirt and faded jeans and loafers, they moved with their drinks to chairs away from the house, at the very edge of the terrace. It was habit. A reflex. Though most of Jacques' servants had been with the house for years, he assumed that at least one and perhaps two were in the pay of the *sureté*.

"Has the terrace sunk, or has it always been this low?" Bika asked, peering over the low wall.

"It's the same as always. The reeds are high at this time of year."

"God, I feel as if I'm sitting in the river. Do you get any crocodiles in the garden?" He stood up and for a moment gazed down the river toward the rapids.

"Once. A long time ago. The boys killed it, a big old granddad, we ate crocodile steak for a month. I've never wanted to touch the stuff since."

"Ah, your father, up on the plantation, getting the boys to make him crocodile stew. With caterpillars! Fried caterpillars! I never saw a thin man eat so much!" Bika finished in a high-pitched squeal. He was talking himself, or trying to talk himself, into a better mood, Jacques thought, remembering the old times.

"And the grub worms. I know the grub worms in Iyondo are better than anywhere else in the world," Jacques said. He could see himself sitting with his father in the dark shade of a mango tree, eating a bowl of chicken with grub worms from a calabash bowl. Sometimes, in Europe, dining in the luxury of crisp white tablecloths and napkins, polished silver, flowers, golden crusted breads, fine wines, and beautiful women, he would suddenly be overwhelmed with hunger for the faintly metallic smell of the cool dust under an African shade tree and the hot, spiced-nut taste of grub worms.

They were silent for a moment, watching the fishermen pole their way out of shallow waters.

"Those were the good old days," Bika said, lighting a cigarette. He tossed his lighter on the low table between them. It was a slim, gold Dupont, monogrammed. A gift from a woman? From Mobutu? It lay there like a tempting letter marked *confidential* that would reveal the mysteries of the new Bika. From his youth Bika had been dapper and *soigné* in the French sense, but never elegant. He was not a swank like his Zaïrian contemporaries who sank hundreds of thousands of dollars into ankle-length sable coats, stored in Geneva, silk pyjamas, gold bracelets, Rolex oyster watches, Mont Blanc fountain pens. In the old days, Bika looked down on those who fed their vanity so foolishly. The Dupont lighter, however, was swank.

"Were they?"

"Yes," Bika said after a moment. "Those were days when you woke up every morning, and hope was as bright and real as the day before. Those were good days. Those days are gone." He raised his hands over his head and clapped for another drink.

Alphonse, the second houseboy, shuffled out to the edge of the terrace. Jacques noticed that he had a ragged tear in the bottom of his none-too-clean uniform pants. They were getting sloppy. He would have to take them in hand. One of these days.

"I'll have another whisky, what about you, Jacques?"

"A beer. I have to go out tonight."

"Look at your boys," Bika said as Alphonse pulled the French door closed behind him. "What hope do they have? They have barely enough money left over each week to buy manioc for their families. What hope does anybody have? If it weren't for petty bribes and thievery how would the civil servants scrounge enough to get by? Everywhere it's like VAT. If you're a market mama, do you know how many palms you have to grease to get on the boat to Kisangani? Six, if you're lucky. The rail system is disappearing, more and more roads are being washed out with every rainy season, the hospitals have been plucked clean except for a few rusty iron beds. And not being replaced. The telephone system, even if you make your payoffs, is virtually useless. Oh, what the hell," he mumbled, as Alphonse came out onto the terrace. "It's all pretty useless."

"*Et la famille,* Alphonse?" Bika asked, taking his whisky off the tray.

"*Ah, un peu bien, patron*, pretty fair, boss," Alphonse replied, with the kind of humble smile that invited Bika to slip a few zaïres into his hand when he left the house.

"It's not good," Jacques said. "In fact, it's never been so bad. Last week I had to sink $10,000 in a cell phone. I was forced to. There was no alternative."

"I know. They're all over town. A status symbol the way the old Motorola radio used to be. You came into a restaurant, put your briefcase on the floor and your Motorola on the table and the girls' eyes lit up. And now it's the cell phone."

"Those two Americans are making millions on the cell. And all of Africa is ripe, ready for them."

"Yeah. The old whore is dead, but the undertakers can still make a fortune off her gold fillings. How's your business?"

"Worse than I could ever have imagined."

"That bad?"

"It's hard to keep going without decent railroads and roads. I thought for a while that I was going to have to close down in Lubumbashi."

"Do you ever talk to the Man?"

"As often as I get a chance."

"And?"

"He doesn't listen. He doesn't hear anybody except those toadies who wall him in from day to night."

"Isn't this what I told you would happen? Five years ago, didn't I tell you what it would be like if nobody put a stop to it? You didn't want to listen to me then . . ." He leaned forward, his round black eyes bulging, his two hands holding his drink down between his knees.

"Sure . . . sure." And I don't want to listen to you now, Jacques thought, because you've been bought off. Because even if you try, you won't be able to pull it off this time either. Bika had fallen into the habit of dropping by the house a couple of times a week, sometimes more, but they had not slipped back into the easy intimacy of the old days. Bika had become evasive, secretive. He was up to something, Jacques was sure of it.

The marble of the terrace shimmered with the purplish-red flush of the setting sun. In only a few minutes, darkness would descend, like a blank lead curtain dropping precipitously from the red-gold skies. In Europe he found it disconcerting the way light lingered and waned before giving way to darkness; and in the mornings, the same hesitation of night to let go of the darkness, to yield to the sun. He could never get used to it.

Jacques asked, "Do you talk like this to your *confrères* in the government?"

Bika laughed, a low, scoffing snort, and studied him for a moment. "Don't worry. I'm not starting over again. I'll smoke another cigarette, then I have to be off." He pulled from his pocket book matches from a chic French restaurant in town and lit a cigarette. "Tell me. I'm not going to, but suppose I did decide to go up against the Man, what would you say this time? What would you say now?"

"You just said you weren't going to oppose him," Jacques said, and Bika took note of the impatience in his voice.

"I know. I said, 'let's suppose.'"

"Then, I would probably say the same thing I did before. For exactly the same reasons."

"Then, it would be 'no.'"

"It would be 'no.' Until you or someone else has enough support throughout the country to oppose Mobutu and put him down, I will say 'no.' I don't want to see another Liberia situation here. Because that's what we would have. Tribal warfare like South Africa and Liberia and Ethiopia and Mozambique and Somalia . . . goddammit, all over this continent! You know it. A handful of people can't grab guns and take over the television station and overthrow Mobutu without the two hundred or so tribes in this country sharpening their machetes and hacking each other up. Whatever we may think about what the country has come to, you have to give him credit for giving the people a sense of national identity. For putting a lid on all that bloody tribal conflict. You, of all people, Bika, ought to recognize that what he has done is not a small thing."

"I do. Of course, I do. But it's not enough anymore. It shouldn't be enough for anybody who cares about this country. It shouldn't be enough for you."

"Ah, Bika, *je t'en prie*, be logical."

"Oh, I am logical. That's why I came back. I thought that I could make some difference. I didn't care how small or insignificant it was. Just a difference. I wasn't expecting much."

"Well, you must have worked out some conditions, some ground rules with the Man before you agreed to come back. What kind of deal did you make with him?" Goading Bika now, pressing him, admit it, admit you sold out for cold cash.

"Oh, you know Mobutu. He likes to play it by ear. Let us just say that I'm back. Nobody has thrown me in jail or shot me. Not yet."

Bika drained his glass and gazed across the river to Brazzaville where lights had begun to appear in the taller buildings.

Jacques said, "It looks to me as if you landed pretty well on your feet. Minister of Mines in Zaïre is at the top of the heap. You could do something to get copper production raised. And Petro-France will be pumping millions of dollars into foreign exchange."

"So it would appear. The best estimates are that they will be grossing seven hundred fifty million dollars a year. Big money for them. Big money for us. Right?"

"That's stupendous. A rich strike. Seven hundred fifty million. Hell, Bika, you ought to be able to make a difference with that kind of money."

"Oh, yeah, sure, if any of it hangs around in the central bank long enough. Or if I'm Minister of Mines long enough." He heaved himself out of his chair and leaned against the low wall with his back to the river. "I have to go. Maybe dinner with my niece tonight."

"Do you mean that you might be dismissed?"

"Dismissed, no. Moved along, maybe. Sent off to Washington as ambassador, something harmless like that. Out of the way, but muzzled. It looks like a turnover in government every six months. That seems to be the Man's latest strategy. It keeps everybody happy and makes them more efficient and eager at the feeding trough to get all they can before the next hog comes along and nudges them away from the golden swill. If you're out, you keep nodding and dancing his tune thinking that your turn is going to come one day soon. And if you've just been turned out, well, you've got a full belly. You're contented for a while. At least, that's the theory. It seems to be working."

"I guess so. I don't hear many complaints."

"Neither do I."

The terrace suddenly flooded with light as Alphonse turned on the outside guard lights, throwing the river into darkness.

"Well, *mon frère*, I think Alphonse is trying to get rid of me," Bika said, leaning a little on Jacques as he lifted his briefcase from beside his chair. "I must go. I see you've changed the name of your house back to Villa Bondeko."

"Yes. What the hell does *Beau Rêve* mean anyway? Another one of Janine's ladies' magazine ideas."

"But we both know what brotherhood means, don't we, Jacques?" Bika said, shaking Jacques' hand and looking at him solemnly.

"Yes." It felt to Jacques as if years of peaceful closeness with his best friend came back to him at that moment. "Yes, we do. And I hope it still means trust, Bika. I want you to trust me. You're still holding back. I know it. And I don't like it."

Bika said nothing. Jacques leaned over and crushed out his cigarette. "Wait. Your lighter. Here, you're forgetting it."

Bika tossed the lighter into the air before slipping it into his pocket. "Guy Marceau. Have you run into him yet?"

"Yes. Once. He represents Petro-France here. I don't think he likes me."

15

Outside the newspaper shop a flock of beggars and hawkers had cornered a young woman as she stepped out of her car. In a contraption made of rough boards mounted on wheels a man with no legs scooted across the street to join the fray, pushing himself along by slashing at the pavement with hands bound in strips of old tires. Cripples with deformed legs and twisted bodies dragged themselves around in the sand, a child in rags jabbed his withered stumps toward her face, and street hawkers who regularly congregated in front of the shop because Europeans stopped there to buy foreign newspapers shoved at her hand-carved boxes of wengay wood, toy helicopters and bicycles and boats hand-crafted of wire coat hangers and discarded bits and pieces of tin, and malachite necklaces and ivory bracelets. A man with a hole where his nose should have been and a grotesque, gaping mouth with no lips shook his callused hand at her and bleated, *"Donne, mamy! Donne!"* The other beggars took up his cry, and soon the little street echoed with their clamor, *"Donne, mamy! Donne!"*

Jacques Delpech, coming out of the shop with a handful of magazines and newspapers, which were delivered regularly to his box there, looked up briefly at the noise. It was a common sight, nothing out of the ordinary. He started for his car, where Louis sat with the motor running.

"The Belgian businessman!" the woman called in English, and when he caught her eye, she tried to smile.

"Ah, the cultural attaché!" he laughed. The beggars began to scatter as he walked toward her, except for the man with no nose who lowered his voice and murmured plaintively, "*Donne! Donne!*"

"Should I give him something? I can't give them all something, can I?" Sarah asked.

"No," Jacques said, and slipped a ten zaïre note cautiously into the beggar's hand.

"Jacques Delpech, I remember your name now," Sarah said, as he escorted her into the shop. "The handsomest man in Kinshasa, Gussie would never forgive me if I had forgotten your name."

As they turned into the shop, Jacques heard a scuffle and thud. The other beggars had thrown the man with no nose into the sand and were beating and kicking him.

"You don't have to stay. I'm all right now." She gazed distractedly around the shop. "It was like being shoved into the middle of a Hieronymus Bosch painting. I wasn't afraid. I don't like Hieronymus Bosch," she said, after a pause.

Jacques could not stop looking at her and was afraid that at any moment she would notice his rudeness. Sarah Laforge was transformed. Her thick mass of tight curly hair had been clipped into a rosy blond halo that somehow made her look taller and slimmer. She was elegantly dressed in a linen skirt and an electric blue silk shirt. She smelled of expensive French perfume.

"You don't have to stay," she said again.

"I don't mind. I'll see you back to your car. You might end up in another Bosch painting."

She gave him the shy smile of a bright and cunning child. "I want to buy a card. A baby card. For a new baby. Gussie told me to look here."

La Détente, run by an obese Belgian woman, was a jumble of a shop frequented by Europeans and moneyed Zaïrians with European tastes. To one side there were stacks of magazines like the *Economist*, *Jours de France*, *Time*, *Paris Match* and fashion magazines several months and seasons out of date, and the major newspapers of Europe three days to two weeks late. Everything from novelty fountain pens and key rings, jigsaw puzzles, costume jewelry, L'Oreal cosmetics, cookbooks in various languages and Astérix comic books were scattered around on tables and in display cases.

Sarah located the greeting cards. "They're all too humorous," she said, shuffling rapidly through them. "I want something nicer, more serious. I want something really, really nice."

"A boy or a girl?"

"A girl," Sarah said, her face lighting up. "It's a girl. My servant Malu, his wife has had a baby, and they named her Sarah. For me. I was touched. On Sunday they brought the baby to show me."

She frowned, reading each one of the cards intently before setting it back on the display. "Here, I think this one will do," she said finally.

"Does the mother read?"

Sarah's round blue eyes clouded with confusion. She glanced down at the card and turned it over in her hand. He had never seen such honest eyes, eyes that without a moment's hesitation, seemed to fling open the doors of her mind and heart. Come in and look around, they said, look as much as you like, I have no secrets here.

"I want to pick up the *Herald Tribune*," he said, and left her still looking at the card. He had spoiled her happy mood, and he was annoyed with himself. She had been so delighted with the idea of her houseboy naming his daughter after her. He picked up the newspaper. He hoped the daughter was real and not just a baby her houseboy had borrowed to bring to show her in order to get money, and presents to sell.

As he paid for the newspaper, he saw her slowly putting the card back on the shelf.

Outside, a stillness had fallen over the street. The beggars had disappeared, and the few remaining street hawkers sprawled listlessly on the sidewalk and showed no interest in Sarah and Jacques. The street was deserted. Louis dozed behind the wheel, the motor of the car still running.

"Would you like to see my presents for Sarah?" she asked, brightening again.

She took two tiny dresses, one pink and one white, from a package in the car and held them up for him to see.

In the cloudless sky behind her blond head, black streams of sugar bats swirled noisily around the mango trees lining the avenue.

"They're hand-smocked," she said. "I found them at one of the tradings. In a heap on the floor, like everything else. Made in China. Look at the detail."

Around her pale neck she wore a thin gold chain, almost invisible, with a small diamond that nestled in the hollow of her breastbone and that moved and sparkled in the fading sunlight. She fingered the pink and coral threads of the smocking, smiling thoughtfully. She had forgotten the card and was happy again.

"Very nice," Jacques said. The next day he would be leaving for two weeks in Guinea, then two more weeks in Brussels doing battle with Janine and her father and her lawyers, awkwardly taking little Suzanne to the park and then to lunch at the Villa Lorraine. He was about to join the ranks of those men who see their children occasionally for stilted lunches in expensive restaurants with obsequious waiters in black fussing, interrupting, intruding. He would not see Sarah again for a month, possibly longer. "I wonder . . . would you like to come by the house for a drink? Watch the sunset on the river?"

Her look at first was puzzled, then vague, and he realized with dismay that she was going to say no.

"I'm afraid I can't. The new ambassador is having a big dinner party, and he's asked me to, kind of, hostess for him. Command performance, my boss says, and I have to be there early." Her great blue eyes stared up at him merrily. "The new ambassador, his name is Virgil Peacock," she said, wrinkling her nose mischievously. "That's his real name."

Jacques laughed obligingly.

That night, lying awake in bed, listening to the night sounds in the garden, Jacques ran his meeting with Sarah Laforge through his mind over and over and tried to understand why he had such tender longing for this woman he hardly knew. He saw her proudly holding up her gifts, the tiny pink and white dresses. The sparkle of a diamond at her throat. Her lovely mouth sagging with disappointment over the card. The animated play of her eyebrows as she talked. Just the idea of a little girl wearing the dresses she had found for her made her face glow.

In his imagination he reached out to caress the curve of her lovely, pale face. Sarah Laforge did not look like a woman who would let a three-year-old child wander off and drown while she gossiped with friends and had a pedicure in the bedroom.

16

"Come along with me on Guy Marceau's boat," Bika said. "We may have a chance to talk. Things have happened."

"I promised to ski with Josh Hamilton's crowd," Jacques said. That crowd on Sunday, Gussie Pearce had said, would include Sarah Laforge. "Why Marceau?"

"Because he has a boat that befits my status as a minister," Bika said with a girlish giggle. "God almighty, wait until you see it. Besides, I can't hang out publicly with the diamond fellows."

"You mean, oil men are different?"

There was a pause. "So, *mon frère*, see you at the islands. Bringing a girl?"

An image of Sarah Laforge, the soft afternoon light shining on her golden halo of hair, drifted through his mind. She suddenly seemed as distant, as unattainable as a lonely boarding-schoolboy's crush.

"No. You?"

"Sure. One of my nieces."

Jacques laughed. "See you at the islands."

He was driving too fast along the Route des Poids-lourds, hit a pothole, and almost lost control of his car. He slowed down and concentrated on the road. There was no hurry. Josh and Fiona were always the last to pull out of the docks. He looked forward to being out on the water and getting tired enough to sleep deeply. For over a month his own thoughts and problems had smothered him.

"You never should have married her," his mother, her blue grey head trembling with palsy, had said in the gloomy half-light of her stuffy apartment. "She's a low and cunning girl. The cheap, common sort that always costs a fortune in the long run. She married you when you were most vulnerable, when you were grieving for that father of yours. She knew what she was doing."

Germaine Delpech spoke as sternly as her quavering voice would allow.

"Janine is not a loving mother," Jacques said.

"That's beside the point," his mother retorted. "Utterly beside the point. What happened to little Sabine is typical of that dreadful place. How many times have you heard me say, and the good Lord above knows that I said it often enough to that father of yours: in Africa the white man lives like a king and dies like a dog. Your sister died like a dog because your father loved that wretched place so much that he refused to make a life for his family anywhere else." She was not going to let go: her bitterness against Albert Delpech had sustained her for years.

Mother and son retreated behind their old, familiar barricades. After his sister Isabelle's death, his mother had left Zaïre and never returned. Not even for her personal effects. Just like Janine. Jacques had stayed in Zaïre with his father. Jacques remembered the quarrel in the night, his mother's screams, her hysterical weeping, his father's stern accusations. It was in 1971 during the week of celebrating the Trois Zeds—Mobutu's official renaming of the country, the river, and the country's money—that Madame Delpech and her friends at the Cercle Hippique had flown in a cargo plane painted in the colors of Zaïre's new flag—red, yellow, and green—with Isabelle and Haut Boy, the young stallion Isabelle planned to ride in the jumping competition in Elizabethville, renamed Lubumbashi by the president. Stubborn, foolish about Haut Boy, Isabelle had insisted on staying with him and the other horses to keep him calm during the flight. Germaine Delpech, her spirits high on champagne and the party mood in the front of the plane, objected perfunctorily, and Isabelle had her way. Only to be crushed by Haut Boy when the C-130 hit heavy turbulence just outside of Lubumbashi. Even in those days, only a decade or so after the Belgians had pulled out of the country, the hospital was inadequate to save Isabelle's life.

"*Le bateau de Monsieur Hamilton,*" Jacques said.

The two waiters from the Cercle Nautique lifted the cases of beer from the trunk of the car and, stooping forward, the muscles of their necks bulging, shifted them to their backs and started for the docks.

Out on the covered verandah of the club he found Josh and Fiona Hamilton drinking mimosas with Gussie Pearce and a red-headed young journalist from the *New York Times*. And no Sarah Laforge. Jacques smiled grimly to himself and ordered a beer.

The journalist's name was Rick Riveira. He did not look a day over twenty-five.

"Rick doesn't speak French, Jacques. Carter Everett had to fish him out of the airport at three o'clock this morning. Carter is the only person alive in Kinshasa at three in the morning." She examined the glossy red finish of her fingernails closely. "This is going to be an English-speaking day. For those of us who speak it." She turned to the red-headed young man. "You do speak English, don't you, hon?"

Josh Hamilton threw back his head and laughed. He always laughed excessively at Gussie's drolleries, especially when his wife was present.

Peevishly, Fiona Hamilton pulled an Earl Grey tin from her beach bag and sat dribbling dark brown shreds of hashish onto cigarette paper.

"You're an animal, you know that, Fiona?" Josh said, ruffling her wispy blond hair with his hand. The deep pockmarks along his hairline gleamed in the sunlight.

"Whatever works," Fiona said. "Does anyone have the *slightest* idea what we are waiting for?" A quiet, diminutive woman with languid mannerisms, Fiona spoke with a husky Midlands accent. Traces of youthful prettiness lingered about her slender, tanned face and uncertain green eyes. She had come to Zaïre with her family as a child and could not stand the idea of living in England. So she and Josh stayed on, year after year, and grew richer and richer, even though company promotions passed over Josh. Like the rest of the Hamiltons' life, it was assumed that the source of their wealth did not bear looking into.

"I told you," Gussie said. "Carter is dropping Sarah Laforge off. She had some trouble with her car."

Rick Riveira sat drinking champagne very fast.

"Carter? And Sarah?" Fiona said, inhaling deeply. "Interesting."

Jacques stubbed out his cigarette irritably and finished off his bottle of beer.

"I'm full of interesting tidbits, hon. Remember that." She brushed back the sides of her long hair. "Donovan and Kowalski, you know what I caught them calling Carter the other day in the APO room at the embassy? I was in there picking up my mail in that little bitty room off to the side. Anyhoo, I heard them call Carter and his deputy 'rusty zippers.'" She clapped her hands, her broad mouth gleeful. "Idn't that a hoot? Of course, those kids worship the ground he walks on. But, Carter a 'rusty zipper'! I walk up to them and I say, 'I wouldn't be too sure about that if I were you, Kowalski.'"

Rick Riveira lowered his glass. "I don't get it," he said.

They all looked at him. Josh was the first to laugh.

"You will some day, hon. Trust me, you will."

"Well, I think we should g. o.," Josh said, standing up and pushing back his chair. "Everyone else is already out there, and I want to ski before lunch."

The *New York Times* man gulped down another glass and grabbed his camera. Gussie protested without conviction that they should wait a little longer, but Josh and Fiona gathered up their things and headed for the boat. Suddenly tired and spiritless, Jacques trailed along behind them with Gussie and the journalist and debated whether or not he should spring some excuse and head back to the house. The tender, warm glow clustering for so many weeks around Sarah's name vanished. At the mention of Sarah and Carter the day had tilted askew.

As Josh and Jacques were finishing loading up the boat, the rickety wooden pier began to shake, and Sarah Laforge, in white shorts and a black polo shirt, ran toward them, a small, apologetic smile on her face.

Jacques watched Carter turn his car around in the drive, and head back into town.

Down the river from the Cercle Nautique, scattered around the upper end of Stanley Pool, beyond the decaying piers where sunken or half-sunken barges and riverboats rusted in the garbage-laden brown water, lay a cluster of small islands, some of them no more than bare sandbars. For swimming and water-skiing there was less danger of crocodiles in the middle of the river around the islands where the current ran swiftly, though mishaps did occur from time to time, the most notable being a German ambassador whose signet ring showed up in the belly of slaughtered crocodile some years after his disappearance one balmy Sunday afternoon.

From a distance Josh Hamilton recognized the tents and umbrellas of their usual crowd and steered the boat slowly in and out of the narrow channels among the islands toward Joe Snead, who stood next to an enormous beach umbrella on top of which perched a framed *Life* magazine photograph of Queen Elizabeth II. It was a long, thin strip of land with clumps of scrub bushes along the rise in the middle. The sand was white and as soft to the touch as finely ground flour.

They dropped anchor and began to wade ashore. Jacques looked away quickly as Rick Riveira helped Sarah down from the boat into the water. Jacques had scarcely spoken to her as the boat sped down the river.

"Jacques? Ready with the skis?" Josh asked.

"Ready." He quickly shucked off his jeans and shirt and heaved himself into the boat.

The stretch of river off the islands was already thick with boats and water skiers. From time to time obscene shouts went up as a group of parasailers from the German embassy dropped into the path of the skiing boats and narrowly missed being run over. For over an hour the two men spelled each other with the boat and skis until Jacques' back and arms ached.

"Quittin' time, boss, as Gussie would say. I'm ready for the booze," Josh said as Jacques climbed back into the boat.

Back on the island Sam Wofford, his great hairy belly hanging over a sliver of orange swimsuit, sprawled under an umbrella with Joe and Doris Snead. The women sat topless, sunning themselves, though it was gray, overcast, a typical dry season day, and drinking champagne. A little to one side Sarah Laforge lay stretched out on a beach towel, talking earnestly with the young reporter. Sarah was not topless. But Jacques noticed that whenever the men's eyes strayed, they wandered slowly over Sarah's routine bikini.

"Uh oh, just what we've all been waiting for. The little Frenchman and his big boat. My, my, just look at that," Gussie said, taking off her sunglasses.

Guy Marceau's enormous boat pulled up, cut engines, and anchored in the deep water directly in front of them. On each side of the prow *Nicole* was painted in tall, gold letters.

"Looks like Nicole has a live one this time," Doris said.

"At last," Fiona said.

Under a red-and-white striped awning on the deck, Guy Marceau, Boketsu Bika, Nicole Scott, and a very young and attractive black woman in European dress sat having lunch at a round table with a starched white cloth. Three Zaïrians in bright wax print *abascos* jackets and dark pants stood with their backs against a wall.

"She can have him. That little guy gives me the creeps," Doris said. A swarthy woman with hair dyed deep black and raccoon eyes outlined in black, Doris Snead, thanks to her Johannesburg plastic surgeon, had a middle-aged face drawn back into a permanent expression of self-satisfaction.

"Oh, I dunno," Gussie said, rubbing her thighs with suntan lotion. "He has nice buns."

"Now there's maybe a story for you, Mr. *New York Times* man," Joe Snead said, gazing pensively at the lunch party.

"What? The little Frenchman's nice buns?" Rick Riveira asked with a smirk, watching Sarah out of the corner of his eye. When he left Sarah's side to get another beer, Sam Wofford had quickly taken his place. Riveira now slumped next to Sam Wofford and had begun to match him, beer for beer.

"Cute. Cute." Joe Snead stood up and brushed the sand from his legs. "That African sitting there having lunch with Marceau is the Minister of Mines, Boketsu Bika. Ever heard of him? There might be a story in that, right, Jack-O?" He pulled his chair next to Jacques.

"Riveira doesn't speak French," Jacques said.

"Ain't that a shame?" Snead lit a cigarette and flicked the match toward the water. "A couple of weeks ago I offered to have my men put in a new road to your buddy's plantation in Equateur." Snead dragged on the cigarette and waited, but Jacques said nothing. "Boketsu said thanks but no thanks. Can you figure that one out? No skin off my teeth. We had our equipment up there anyway. No big deal."

"Didn't anybody else except me hear the boy say that lunch is served?" Gussie asked.

"What do you make of that, Jack-O?" Snead asked again.

"Not much," Jacques said, as he got to his feet and walked off toward Sarah.

He picked up a large Mexican sombrero from a pile of hats that the Hamiltons always carried to the beach.

"Here. You'd better wear this. You're going to be burned."

"Today?" Sarah asked, sitting up straight. "There's no sun. It's going to rain."

"It isn't going to rain. It's the dry season. The sun is up there, and you'll get a terrible burn."

"The others aren't wearing hats."

"The others are already tanned. And they aren't as fair as you."

"I hate hats," she said, her childish round eyes blank and glassy.

"Suit yourself," he said, feeling foolish standing before her with the ridiculous hat in his hand.

The Sneads' houseboy had set up a long folding table covered in a white cloth on a flat stretch of the beach, and had spread out platters of smoked salmon, cheese, cold chicken, deviled eggs, salade niçoise, tomato aspic, and cold cuts. Josh stood at the head of the table and uncorked champagne bottles. Gussie assumed her place next to him and handed out plates and silver wrapped in white napkins. Gussie Pearce's affair with Josh Hamilton had begun in the horsy colonial decor of the Cercle Hippique shortly before the end of her first tour in Kinshasa, and had mellowed into a humdrum gossip item which interested almost no one, including Fiona, until very recently when she had apparently decided that she had every right to be an aggrieved wife.

Fiona Hamilton was a woman fond of poses: at a younger age she had fancied herself the Brigitte Bardot of Africa, an eternally tanned sex kitten with a pout and a mane of blond hair, until the devastating African sun had faded the eyes, the hair, the pout. Fiona now saw herself as the wronged wife whose red-rimmed eyes lent a note of tragedy to an already poignant face.

Fiona sat under her umbrella, smoking and reading *Paris Match*. "Do you really think that Princess Di is having it off with her bodyguard?" she asked dreamily. No one answered.

The roar of a jet taking off from Njili rolled over the water. Everyone looked up and watched the plane curve over the river and head north.

"Sabena," Sam Wofford said.

"Four hours late," Joe Snead said.

"Late or not, there goes my payload. 683 kilos of brand new z's headed to the good Sisters of misguided Charity in Minneapolis, Minnesota. Or to their PR firm in New York, I guess," Sam said. He squinted into the sun as the jet disappeared into the clouds over Brazzaville. "One of the toughest jobs I've ever had down here, believe it or not. You wanna know how tough it is to get the central bank to sell you five-thousand dollars' worth of brand new zaïre notes and ship them out of the country?" He held his hand over his mouth and belched loudly. "Damn tough, take my word for it, and damn expensive."

"What the hell does a PR firm in New York do with eight million z's?"

"Souvies. You send in a contribution to the missionary fund of Our Sisters of misguided Charity, and the PR firm sends you a ten z note as a souvenir. *Souvenir d'Afrique.* That kind of shit."

"And it works?"

"Damned if I know. Not my problem. Cashing the good sisters' fat check, that's my problem."

"What a way to make a living," Snead said.

"Beats some I know of," Sam said, reaching for another beer.

As the afternoon wore on, a cool breeze blew in off the water. Doris and Fiona, *Paris Match* spread over her bare breasts, slept. Snead and Wofford wandered off with the journalist to the middle of the island in search of a waist-high bush, and Josh and Jacques sat silently drinking beer and watching Sarah and Gussie swim out against the powerful current and float with the current back to the beach.

"I like a woman with slim hips," Josh said, as Gussie and Sarah came out of the water. "Bit of a dope, though, isn't she, this Sarah? Very pie in the sky. Doesn't have a sodding idea what Africa is all about."

"No," Jacques said.

The transistor radio of a group of Americans across the narrow channel sent out loud waves of static. Three beeps, and then *This is the BBC World Service,* loud and clear before being washed away in more static.

As their party headed back upriver to the yacht club, Jacques realized that he had had too much to drink and was testy. He was tired of the whole lot of them. It was too much to put up with for a little exercise on the water. And a chance to watch Sarah Laforge continuing her conquests. He was tired of Bika, grinning out at him over the rail before speeding away with Marceau. He was tired of trying to figure out how he could keep his company going and divorce Janine at the same time. He was tired of waking every day to problems that no one in Zaïre wanted to solve.

They ended up for dinner at Lola la Crevette, a seedy fish restaurant in a palm grove with four or five thatch and bamboo paillotes scattered at some distance from the kitchen.

"Aw right, gang! Party! Party! Slow night. We can make all the noise we like," Sam said, falling onto a bench next to Sarah.

"I should be doing interviews," Rick Riveira said, his head bobbing back and forth drunkenly. "I should be filing a story."

Propped on his elbows, he kept lunging a beer bottle past his mouth trying to drink.

"We'll do your story for you," Sam Wofford said. He threw a pellet of bread at Fiona, who looked pale and underfed in the garish light of the overhead lamp. "We know them all by heart, don't we, gang?"

"Oh, yes, Rick. You could do the one about the flower vendor at the cemetery," Fiona said in a tony British accent. "Terribly affecting."

"How about the one about the little kid and the crocodile and the sick mama?"

"That one's not bad. Made me cry. Once."

"The *Washington Post* guy got a lot of mileage out of that one."

"I think Gussie should go home," Fiona said. She was still drinking champagne. "Jacques, you think Gussie should go home, don't you?"

"The L.A. *Times* did that one, too," Snead said.

Riveira nodded thoughtfully. "Sounds good. Sounds real good. Human interest stuff, that goes over big. And then the terrible government . . ."

"You never have to sweat that," Jacques said. He was bored and irritable and could not understand why he had not cut out of the party as soon as they got back to the club. The car, that was it, there were not enough cars. And Sarah . . . more to the point. She sat quietly observing them all with her large, round eyes like a little child who has wandered into her parents' late-night party. Her aloofness irked him. "That's easy. You just type out *Zaïre* on your computer, punch Enter, and that hot story you have been looking for comes up ready-made. Just copy what's on the computer. It'll say all you want to say about kleptocracy, etc. etc., about Mobutu's five- billion-dollar fortune . . . "

"That's the Man's real problem, if you want to know my opinion," Sam said, "I think he's got the same financial adviser I have. He's had that same damned five billion dollars for the last ten years. Even at two percent he ought to have another billion by now."

"Josh, make Gussie go home. *Now*, I said, *now*, Josh," Fiona said and started to cry.

"Oh, dry up, Fiona. We're working on Rick's story," Snead said. "How Mobutu's personal fortune . . ."

"Equals the national debt!" The others sang out in unison. Sarah impassively watched Riveira. Josh Hamilton had put his Oxford blazer around her shoulders.

"You see? Everybody knows the hot story by heart. And nobody in the outside world gets tired of reading it," Jacques said. "Just write it up, and then you can spend all your time down here partying."

"Hell, write anything you want. Who gives a shit about Africa anyway?" Josh said. "Uh, sorry, Jacques. What I mean is—umm, how do I get out of this one, gang?—umm, this is not exactly the garden spot of the world, is it?"

"It used to be," Fiona said. "I ought to know. When the Belgians pulled out, this was one of the prettiest cities in Africa. Everybody called it *Kin la plus belle.*"

"Yeah, well, now it's more like *Kin la poubelle,*" Sam said. "This place gets more like a garbage dump every day."

"I can write a *good* story!" Riveira said, his sunburnt face screwed up as if about to burst into tears.

"Sure you can," Jacques said. "But that doesn't mean you can't party, too. All good journalists learn how to do that really well down here. Especially if they don't speak French in a French-speaking country."

"You were nasty to him," Sarah said as Jacques pulled away from the Hotel InterContinental. "What did you do with him?"

"I turned him over to the manager. He'll make sure that Riveira gets to his room safely."

"Well, you were nasty to him at the restaurant."

"I wasn't very nice."

At the gates of walled villas, guards in wool stocking hats sat warming their hands around bonfires made of dead palm branches.

"He was drunk, though, really drunk. They all were. I'm awfully fond of Gussie, and Sam makes me laugh, but those other people make me sick," Sarah said.

"Journalists like Riveira make me sick. They come down here with their big expense accounts, their canned stories, their clichés about Africa. They get drunk a few times with what they think are the right people, then they go back to America and spew out the same tired old stories. They're ignorant. They have no respect. These are real people here, goddamit. They're smart. They work hard. They deserve respect."

He lit a cigarette and inhaled deeply. "And—don't laugh. This will be a great country some day. You'll see. You'll all see. I believe that with all my heart."

"I'm not laughing, Jacques. I wouldn't laugh. I'm so cold I couldn't laugh at anything if I tried." Her shoulders twitched in a long shudder. "Can you turn on the heat?" She was still wearing Josh's Oxford blazer.

"It's not cold," Jacques said, turning on the heat anyway. "For Africans it's winter. Not for us. It's only the evening cool coming on. You've got a burn."

The glow of the instrument panel lit up the lower part of his profile, the finely shaped nose, the strong curve of his chin. His long fingers rested lightly on the steering wheel, and, a moment before, when his hand came near her as he reached over to turn on the heat, a suffocating wave of desire set off an alarm in her head: I am about to make a fool of myself, she thought.

"Come up," she said, "I'll make you a cup of good hot coffee." She pulled the blazer tightly around her shoulders and shivered, her teeth chattering. "I've never been so cold in my life."

Her apartment was uncluttered and tastefully decorated; wire sculptures from Kinshasa streets, masks and primitive wooden and soapstone figures, the usual tourist stuff, blending pleasantly with the American look of embassy furniture. The lights of Brazzaville glimmered across the river.

"We have the same view, or almost," he said, as she came in from the kitchen. "Oh, *merde!*" he groaned, "Look at yourself, you are as red as a boiled beet!"

He took the tray from her and set it down. "You will be sick," he said. "Look at yourself! You're burned, badly burned."

Sarah turned her head and gazed at a small, clouded mirror hanging next to the door.

"I told you to get out of the sun! You should have put on the hat."

She watched his angry face in silence. "It was so cloudy I didn't know. I really don't like hats," she said meekly.

He looked so furious that she shrank back instinctively as he reached for her. As he kissed her, he could feel the heat of her body, like a stone on a beach after a hot summer day, coming through her thin cotton shirt. They clung together, and they were both trembling so much that when he released her lips, he had to bury his face in the soft, springy curls of her hair to steady himself.

"I must be hurting you," he said finally.

"Yes. A little."

He began matter-of-factly unbuttoning her shirt. He removed the shirt and dropped it to the floor. The burn along her shoulders was a red so deep that it looked almost purple in the lamplight. The tiny diamond at her throat looked white against her red skin.

"So stupid. The African sun is very unforgiving," he said, running his fingertips lightly over her back. "Turn around. Poor, poor Sarah. Poor Sarah's back." He brushed her back with his lips, then turned her around and took her in his arms and held her lightly and kissed her for a long time.

"You have very gentle hands," she said at last.

"We shall see. Let's get some olive oil from the kitchen, and I'll rub you down. Maybe that will help you through the night."

Sarah sat on a kitchen chair while Jacques carefully spread oil over her burn.

"This is one of the worst I've ever seen," he said. "And I've seen some bad ones. Little Suzanne almost fried herself in the pool a few dry seasons ago."

"Little Suzanne?"

"My older daughter. She's almost seven. You're so fair. Why didn't you at least put on the hat when I told you to?"

"Because you were being mean."

Jacques drew back and looked at her. "Mean? To you?"

"Yes. All afternoon you were mean and cold and sullen. Hostile. As if I were spoiling the party. As if you wished I hadn't come along."

Jacques stood with his hand cupped, and the bottle of olive oil poised over his palm. Sarah stared up at him. The overhead light cast deep violet shadows under her eyes, and her lips had begun to swell. Jacques bent down and kissed her.

"You're beautiful," he said.

"Why were you so cold to me this afternoon?"

"You seemed to have plenty of admirers."

She dropped her eyes. "But I wanted you to pay attention to me."

"Why?"

"I don't know why. I just did, that's all."

With light strokes Jacques finished rubbing down her legs.

"I think I must have been jealous," he said.

"Jealous? That's funny."

"It didn't seem funny at the time."

She reached out and took his hand, and he lifted her to her feet.

"I look like a new traffic light. Shiny and red." She hesitated a moment, then said, "Stay with me tonight."

"No. Not tonight. You really are going to be in a lot of pain before the night is over."

"But won't you stay? Even if I put a sword between us in the bed?"

Jacques laughed and drew her into his arms. "Like a medieval knight and his lady?"

"Yes."

"Have you got a sword?"

"No."

They both laughed, and he pressed her closer. "Oh, Sarah. Dear innocent, lovely Sarah." He kissed her and held her face between his hands. "I want so much more than that. That's only the beginning. You'll see. I want so much more than that."

17

By noon the next day Sarah's face and body looked like raw meat. Fat blisters, puffy with fluid, spread over her back and chest and thighs. Phil Olmstead covered his face with his hands when he saw her and sent her off to the embassy doctor. That evening her lips were so blistered and sore that she cringed when Jacques kissed her.

At lunch and in the evening Jacques brought over meals prepared by Dieudonné. Only when he punched the button for the eighth floor in the rickety elevator of her building, did his life seem to take heart again, in those few hours, alone with her, on the balcony overlooking the river.

In the shadows of evening, as sugar bats swirled and chattered in the trees below, they sat close together and talked quietly, sometimes holding hands, sometimes searching each other's faces in the half-light of the terrace. Sarah listened as Jacques unfolded the story of his childhood in the then Belgian Congo, his unhappy school years in Belgium, sent into "exile," as he called it, by his father because of the tribal conflicts after independence, and about how he still felt like a foreigner in Europe. He spoke of his children, his little girls, but never of his marriage, never of his wife. In a rush of homely detail he recounted anecdotes about the little girls as if he had just tucked them into bed for the night before coming over to see her, and it was with a shock that Sarah learned, through an inadvertent question, that one of the girls was in fact dead, drowned in the swimming pool, her tiny foot caught behind the last rung of the poolside ladder.

One night a shooting star burst across the sooty skies trailing a spray of greenish gold and plunged into the darkness beyond Brazzaville. Jacques lifted Sarah's hand and kissed it gently.

"Make a wish," he said.

"I already have."

With a stab of pain she remembered Gussie's remark that all the terrific men in Kinshasa were married. A remark, like so many others, that she had dismissed at the time, smug, complacent, certain that it could never have anything to do with her or her life. And now it did. There was a steadiness about him, a goodness, a promise that he would protect her, though she could not imagine what she would ever have to fear in this sun-filled land. With Michael she had been the steady one, the responsible one, she who coaxed him out of his threatening moods, she who brought order and calm into their lives. She reached out and touched Jacques' face. Make a wish. Make a wish. Yes. She would not walk away from this kind of happiness. Never. She would take him any way she could get him. Any way at all.

On Wednesday Rick Riveira's girlfriend Sue, who worked for the *Wall Street Journal,* called him from Johannesburg to say that she had heard there was great surfing in Durban. Why not come down? she said. Riveira had slept late after a party at the Marine house of the American embassy and had spent the afternoon at the ivory market shopping for his mother and his aunt Tilly in Brooklyn. Several hundred words on Zaïre, that's why I can't come down, Riveira said. But before midnight Sue had faxed him everything on Zaïre that she could dig out of her database, and by six the next morning Rick Riveira had put together and faxed a long by-lined article that later appeared on page seven of the Sunday edition of the *Times.* He worked a long time trying to find a synonym for saying that Mobutu's fortune "equals the national debt" and finally came up with "amounts to exactly the national debt," but the copy editor thought that sounded clumsy, that it read better as "equals the national debt," and changed the text accordingly. At ten o'clock Riveira was having his first beer of the day on the continuation of Sabena's flight to Johannesburg, having paid a check-in clerk at the airport two hundred dollars to free up a seat by bumping someone.

Dieudonné had to come into the bedroom and shake Jacques awake. "*Téléphone, patron, téléphone.*"

It was Sarah, calling from an embassy radio phone in the Chevrolet station wagon.

"I'm flying to Lubumbashi," she said breathlessly. She sounded distraught.

"What?"

"Lubumbashi. I'm on my way there. The flight leaves in thirty minutes."

"What for?"

"I . . . it's kind of complicated, but I have to accompany a group of musicians out there. Bluegrass musicians."

"What's that?"

"Bluegrass singers. It's a kind of American music. They're giving a concert there at the cultural center."

"In Lubumbashi? Blue . . ."

"Bluegrass."

"Bluegrass singers in Lubumbashi? What for?"

"It's a cultural thing. I'll explain later. Uh, Phil managed them through the concert at the ambassador's residence on Wednesday, by himself, and now, well, he says he can't. I was scheduled to go, anyway, but I thought with the sunburn and all. Phil has a bridge tournament or something like that. It's very important, he says."

She sounded disconsolate.

"How long will you be gone?"

"Until the plane comes back. Wednesday."

Jacques rolled over onto his back and stared at the ceiling. "God, Sarah, *Wednesday!*" he said.

18

Guy Marceau was invisible behind a row of pots of flowering hibiscus. The *maître d'hôtel* led Jacques to his table.

"Thanks for joining me for lunch," Marceau said. He moved his cell phone to one side and knocked his cigarette in quick jerky movements against an ashtray.

"Sorry I couldn't take you up before. I've been in and out of town."

"I know. I keep an eye on you."

"Really? Why?"

"You interest me," Marceau said. His throat was suddenly dry and tight, and he realized his cigarette was trembling. "Nicole has told me a lot about you."

"Well, I've known Nicole and her husband a long time, since they came out here. Must be ten years now."

"Yes, she's told me all about it? *Enfin,*" Marceau said and sighed and crushed out his cigarette and lit another. "A drink?"

"No thanks. I'm in something of a rush. Have to get back to the office and then out to the airport."

"Then, let's get down to business, hein." Instead, Marceau talked aimlessly, mostly about his new boat, and smoked a great deal, explaining in passing that he had discovered a little shop in the Galeries Présidentielles that sold Gauloises cigarettes.

"Petro-France is very much interested in Boketsu Bika," Marceau said, finally, after the waiter had served them melon and prosciutto.

"I'm not surprised."

"Oh, not in that banal way," Marceau said. "Not in the way you're thinking. We're interested in Boketsu and . . . his ideas. *Oui, c'est ça*," he said, as if encouraging himself. "His ideas for the country, for Zaïre, for the future of this country, are very interesting." He was sounding like Guichard, and that was no good. He couldn't shovel the bullshit like that grease ball.

"What ideas are those?"

Etienne, the *maître d'hôtel*, a pale, hushed presence, stood at a discreet distance and surveyed the room, mostly filled with businessmen on expense accounts.

Perspiration stood out along Marceau's hairline. A cigarette drooped from the corner of his thin mouth, and he tilted his head a little, squinting away from the smoke. He was a small, dark man with a deep olive complexion. Jacques wondered if he might be Corsican. Sicilian, perhaps. His eyes were grey, glinting, shimmering like fish scales. Doris Snead was right, Jacques thought, there is something creepy about Marceau.

"What I mean is, we hope . . . that is, I hope you're going to cooperate with us."

"If I can. Cooperate in what?"

"In keeping Boketsu headed in the right direction. In these great ideas he has. You know, these African guys need encouragement. They need support. They need to be told they're doing a great job, and keep up the good work, and that kind of thing. Somebody like you, an old friend, that means a lot."

"Well, Bika has had these great ideas, as you call them, for a long time. Since he was a kid. He can be pretty determined. I doubt that he needs any encouragement from me, or from anybody else, for that matter."

"Care for another bottle of red with that steak?" Marceau asked.

"No thanks."

"Well, I'll have another. I'm not punching any time clocks down here."

Marceau pushed back his plate and lit another cigarette. Jacques noticed that he had barely touched his filet mignon. For a few minutes he sat smoking and nibbling French fries.

"I think you'll find that everybody needs a little help from time to time. Especially if the going gets rough," Marceau said, wiping his hands on a napkin. "Boketsu's going to need some help with his ideas. A man like that. And Petro-France is ready to stand behind you, for instance, because what you will be doing for Boketsu is a big contribution. *Et ça se paye,*" Marceau said, looking Jacques in the eyes as he pulled on his cigarette.

"What? I'm not sure I follow you. As a matter of fact, I don't follow you at all."

"What I mean is, *nous, les Européens,* we've all got to stick together, hein? I help you, you help me. In these countries," Marceau said with a sweeping gesture, "especially a place like Zaïre, if we don't stick together. We Europeans understand each other. We know how to get things done by sticking together. I know these are not the best of times for you, and with a divorce coming on top of all that." Delpech was looking at him coldly, a smirk spreading slowly across his face. "Hey, *croyez-moi,* I know what I'm talking about, I'm hitting that divorce trail myself," Marceau said, smiling weakly.

Jacques leaned forward and folded his arms on the table. "I guess I'm having a hard time understanding why a French oil company would be interested in my financial affairs. Or why a French oil company would have such lofty, humanitarian inclinations. Interest in the future of this country and all that crap. For years I've watched you people operating in Africa. You're greedy . . ."

"And we play hardball, Jacques Delpech," Marceau said, his fish grey eyes glinting. "Don't forget that. We play hardball."

Jacques folded his napkin carefully and placed it on the table. "Sorry, I have to go. Thanks for lunch," he said politely, getting to his feet. "I have to pick up someone at the airport."

He was still too stunned to be as rude as he would have liked.

Jacques stopped by a flower shop improbably named *L'Arlésienne* and bought a spray of pale nutmeg orchids with eleven flowers, one for each day since the Sunday on the river.

"Plenty of time, *patron*," Louis said, staring at the orchids. "No hurry. Plenty of time for the plane."

Ça se paye. Jacques still could not take it in. A bribe, the goddamned stupid shit was offering him a bribe. For what? What the hell was going through Marceau's head? Was he just a bumbler, pitching the wrong man? Stupid shit. Goddamned stupid shit. And what the hell was Bika up to now? Crazy fool was probably ranting about what ought to be done to bring down Mobutu, about all his politicking with tribal leaders, the same old stuff that he had got him into first-class trouble before. But shooting off his lip to a jerk like Marceau. It didn't make sense. Bika was too smart to do that. *Things have changed*, Bika had said on the telephone. What things? Later, after the afternoon on Marceau's boat, Bika had evaded the question, had spoken instead of his infatuation with his latest niece—"God! A sweet piece of ass!"—whom he was seriously thinking of making his *deuxième bureau.* And he had laughed, and Jacques had not insisted on what he wanted to find out.

Bika had always used that trick, making jokes, throwing Jacques off the track, keeping him away from things that he thought Jacques shouldn't know. Like when they were together in boarding school in Bruges during the *événements* in the Congo, before Mobutu came to power for the second time, when the newspapers and movie newsreels and magazines were full of pictures of the flyblown bodies of slaughtered Europeans in the streets, the nuns raped and mutilated and butchered, and in Stanleyville, the body parts of whites found in cold storage after peace came. Most of the time Bika managed to keep Jacques from thinking of his father still down there, stubbornly refusing to leave, and when Bika failed, they wept together, and Jacques believed that his fears for Monsieur Delpech were as real as his own. At school the other boys snickered and called Jacques a *colon* and Bika his *boy.* And they hated them both, especially Bika, because there was always a cousin or an uncle whose house or store had been looted, burned and destroyed by the Congolese, someone they knew who had lost a job and had to come crawling back to Belgium to start over again. In the middle of the night they crept to the foot of Bika's bed and left their shoes there to be polished by the *boy*. Coming off the field after a game of soccer, while Bika was in the infirmary with the flu, Jacques had taken them on, all of them, behind the scoreboard on the way to the gym. They beat him senseless. *Nous, les Européens*, we have to stick together. Stupid shit.

19

At the airport Sarah could not disentangle herself from her gaggle of bluegrass singers. One of the women, a large blond woman balancing on crutches, had twisted her ankle getting out of the consul's jeep in Lubumbashi, and Sarah had to take her to the medical unit at the embassy. The woman was chewing gum vigorously and blew a bubble of pale emerald green, exactly the same color, to Jacques' astonishment, as her eye shadow. Sarah looked harried, her peeling face disfigured with blotchy patches of reddish pink, and she stood explaining the situation to Jacques a little apart, stiff and self-conscious, as the Americans watched.

His spirits sagging, Jacques smiled ruefully at his frustrated lust as he walked across the dusty parking lot to his car. Just when he thought he could touch her without making her flinch with pain. Just when he thought they could move from the balcony to the bedroom. The orchids lay forgotten in the back seat of the car. He slipped into the driver's seat and tried to convince himself that his talk with Marceau would have soured the pleasure of being with Sarah again, even though he knew that nothing could ever do that. He drove back into town, dropping Louis in the *cité*, and, on an impulse, headed up the hill to Djelo Binza and Bika's house.

For the first time, he could not say for sure what Bika would do when he found out that Marceau had tried to bribe him—to keep Bika headed in the right direction? In the old days, before Bika's return, he would have known. *Ça se paye,* Marceau had said, a thin trickle of sweat rolling past his ears.

Out along the Matadi road dry season smoke hung in the air and turned the sunset skies fantastic shades of orange and purple, the rich, riotous colors of days without rain. The sky in a K-Mart painting, Doris Snead had said once, looking out over the river, and everyone had found this amusing, he could never figure out why. But, then, foreigners always found so much to laugh about in Africa. It was part of the fun of being there. *Nous, les Européens.*

There were no soldiers at the gates of Bika's house, only three ordinary guards in brown overalls sitting on the ground on pieces of cardboard boxes smoking cigarettes. *Patron* had left for the evening, they said.

For a moment he thought of going in and asking the cook to make him up something to eat while he waited for Bika. But it was half past six, still the drinks hour. He sat in the car and smoked a cigarette, then decided to drive across the crest of the hills to the Hamiltons'. He was afraid that if he went back down the hill and into town, he would let the moment pass, would lose his resolve to find out what Bika and Marceau were up to. And why it had anything to do with him.

Jacques drove inside the Hamilton gates, averting his eyes from Fiona's Jaguar, an ugly brown, a Simba beer truck brown, parked in the porte-cochère.

Surrounded by parrot cages, the Dalmatian bitches, and various cats, Fiona sat smoking with a drink in her hand on the untidy verandah that ran the full width of the front of the house.

"Jacques, Jacques, I'm delighted to see you," she rose to her feet and steadied herself against the back of her chair. "I truly am."

"Where is Josh?"

"At the riding club. Planning this year's ball. Gussie's there. Gussie's always there. So I came home."

She looked around distractedly for a chair that was not piled high with children's toys or books and papers and magazines. The Hamiltons were the kind of English who ran a house that was forever slovenly, dingy and unclean, no matter how many servants swarmed about the place. It was part of their carefree allure. Debris piled up in corners, the odor of birdcages and the urine smell from children, dogs, and cats clung to the nostrils.

Fiona dumped the contents of a chair to the floor and Monopoly cards and money spilled over it.

"Shit," she said. "Sit down, Jacques. Mawata will be along with the drinks cart in a minute. The boys are getting the children ready for their supper."

She was dressed in a pale blue silk dress that tied on one side, like a sarong. She wore a double strand of large pearls with a diamond clasp and her makeup was fading, and her face going slack with the whiskies.

They sat together and drank and smoked while darkness took away the garden until the servants remembered to turn on the dismal fluorescent guard lights. Mawata brought out a tray of hot samosas. At the back of the house Jacques could hear the sharp, bright voices of the children as the servants put them to bed. He yearned to join them, to laugh with the children, tell them a story with a happy ending, and smell the soapy fragrance of their hair as he bent over to kiss them goodnight.

A parrot in one of the cages beside the front door said "Lawdy, Lawdy," and uttered a prolonged sigh.

Fiona clutched at her temples theatrically. "You know she has set out to drive me crazy, Jacques."

Jacques knew that she was talking about her husband's mistress. Gussie Pearce had become the drama of Fiona's life. Gussie gave her something to talk about, Gussie gave her an excuse for drinking as much as she liked, as often as she liked.

Jacques sat and listened and thought of Sarah and the sweet tightness in the pit of his stomach when he saw her blond head as she stepped out of the plane and started down the steps.

"Crazy. Absolutely crazy. You don't take me seriously, do you? Neither does Josh." She poured herself another drink. "Did you hear that parrot?"

"Sure."

"It's not mine. Gussie gave it to Josh to drive me crazy."

Jacques laughed. "Stop it, Fiona."

"Laugh all you like. Gussie has set out to drive me crackers with that parrot." She leaned across Jacques and looked at the parrot. "Gussie named the parrot Lawdy, Lawdy, Miss Scarlett. She taught it to say 'Lawdy, Lawdy,' but not 'Miss Scarlett' so that every time the sodding bird says, 'Lawdy, Lawdy,' I keep waiting for it to say 'Miss Scarlett.' I can't help myself. I say it under my breath. I wait for that 'Miss Scarlett' to come out of the damned bird. Everybody does. It's not just me. The bird's driving me mad. She knew it would. She knows I'm like that." She looked at Jacques, her eyes indeed a little wild. "Did you wait for it to say, 'Miss Scarlett'?"

"No."

"Well, I did. I always do."

"Throw a cover over it."

"You don't understand me."

"Listen, go to bed now."

"Do you know what she told a crowd of us the other day?"

"What?"

"Gussie told us that when she was sixteen, she was voted The Most Inspirational Volleyball player in her school. Can you imagine? Being proud of that? The Most Inspirational Volleyball player? Who but Gussie would ever think of being proud of that? Would you?"

"I don't know," Jacques said. "I never played volleyball."

"I've noticed that Americans brag about some very strange things, haven't you?"

"It's late, Fiona. I have to go."

"Where? At this time of night? Is there a party I don't know about?"

Jacques got out of his chair and bent down to pick up the Monopoly game scattered on the floor.

"Jacques, . . . everyone's been wanting to know . . . is Janine coming back?"

The steady thuda, thuda, thuda sound of drums in the *cité* drifted up from below the hill.

"No."

Jacques started down the steps.

Fiona swayed to her feet and followed him. "Well, then, think of that," she said, pensively, as if to herself, "Silly ol' Janine will get exactly what she always wanted: all the money in the world and a big flat in Brussels. Humph. She wasn't as dumb as we thought."

20

In Bika's large living room six or seven men smartly dressed in dark *abacos* sat around in the unshapely overstuffed sofas lining three walls. The acrid odor of monkey skin rugs, thrown over the backs of the sofas, pervaded the room. Jacques recognized most of the men, some of them Bika's *petits frères*, men from the Mongo tribe who kissed Jacques and called him "*mon frère*." Now that Bika was an important minister, men like these would show up and hang around for days and weeks hoping for a word that would mean a job, money, even a new *abacos* or just a hot meal or a sack of rice or manioc.

Bika appeared in the doorway and motioned for Jacques to follow him out onto the terrace. It was close to midnight, and the whole house seemed to be full of hushed activity.

"Where have you been?" Bika asked, white teeth glowing in his round face. He sat down, but on the edge of his chair, and kept darting his eyes over the grounds and the rooms behind him. He seemed distracted, in a hurry. "I haven't seen you for over a week. Been back in Europe?"

"No. Are you in a hurry? I want to ask you about something."

The murmur of drums in the *cité* rose and fell. Someone dead, someone married.

"Sure. Fine." Bika slid back in his chair. "I'm just winding down, that's all."

"Look, I had lunch with Guy Marceau today."

"And I had dinner with him tonight. What's your impression? I get on with him, and—"

"I don't," Jacques snapped. Bika's back was to the light. Jacques leaned forward but could not catch the expression on his friend's face in the half darkness. "As I was saying, I had lunch with him today. Probably the most interesting lunch I've ever had in Africa. Yeah, I guess I can say that. Because it's the first time anyone has ever offered me a bribe. Flat out."

"Petro-France?" Bika eased a pack out of his pocket and shook out a cigarette.

"Of course."

"You're sure? Positive?" It seemed to Jacques that Bika's voice squeaked on a high note.

"No doubt about it."

Bika lit a cigarette and held the smoke for a long time before exhaling. "To do what? What did he want you to do?"

"Encourage you. Keep you headed in the right direction. You and your great ideas. There was also something about us Europeans having to help each other out in Third World countries."

Later Jacques would remember that Bika did not laugh. He had expected him to laugh. Instead, he asked, "How much did he offer you?"

"We didn't get to that."

Bika smoked silently for a moment. "So, you turned him down?"

"Hell, yes! Why should I get mixed up with Petro-France after all I've seen? So, what are these great ideas he was talking about? What does he want you to do for Petro-France?"

Bika raised his hands and clapped. "I want you to see my latest *fantaisie*."

"What does he expect to get out of you, Bika?" Jacques persisted.

"*Chérie!*" Bika called, and clapped his hands again. "Oh, Marceau . . . ," Bika said, lighting another cigarette. "Do you really want to know, my friend, I believe that he is a just a hot-head. Impulsive. One of those Mediterranean types."

At that moment a young woman, girl, stepped through the doorway out onto the terrace. The light was behind her, and she was dressed in a silky aquamarine European negligée. It seemed to Jacques that he had never seen a woman more voluptuously formed. The cool evening breeze fanned the gown around her legs. She was an erotic vision, and he was instantly aroused, watching her walk slowly toward Bika. She placed her hand on his shoulder, and he squeezed it and pulled her into his lap.

"What do you think, hein? Of my latest *fantaisie*?"

It was the girl on Marceau's boat, but, up close, she was nobody's dream girl. Her eyes turned so steeply upward that they exposed a broad half moon of white, giving her a stupid, doltish expression. She breathed noisily through thick, protuberant lips.

"Her name is Liliane," Bika said. The girl stared at Jacques. "And she thinks she is going to be my *deuxième bureau*."

"Liliane," Jacques said, smiling at the girl. "Is that your authentic name?"

"*Authentique*, my ass, what a load of crap," Bika said, pushing the girl off his lap. "That's some more of Mobutu Sese Seko Kuku Ngbendu Wa Za Banga's shit that we're going to get rid of one of these days." He looked up and caught a look of intense interest on Jacques' face. "Ah, well," he sighed.

"I do have *un nom authentique*," the girl said, as if her feelings had been hurt. "I just don't remember it. It starts with an 'm.'"

"Half the names in Zaïre start with an 'm'. Get back to bed, *chérie*," Bika said.

Bika was on his feet, and Jacques understood with a shock that he was being dismissed. With his arm on Jacques' shoulder, Bika walked him down the terrace to the front drive.

"Saturday they're burying my uncle in the village. He died last rainy season."

"Your uncle Kesa? I remember him. He couldn't be that old."

"No. Only five years older than the two of us. The usual African thing. High blood pressure and the rest of it. Anyway, I have to go because my father is still in the hospital in Geneva, but I want to go. It's been too long." He glanced nervously toward the three black Mercedes parked in the curve of the entranceway, which was flooded with powerful lights mounted along the walls and the roof of the house. It seemed to Jacques that Bika's stocky body jiggled with impatience. "I've got an idea. Come with me, you haven't been back to the old places in years. Hein? We'll stay at my father's place at Iyondo. Bring a girl. Liliane will need company."

"I wouldn't be able to leave until late Friday afternoon."

"That's fine. Fine."

"We could use my plane."

"Ah," Bika laughed, "I was hoping you would offer. More discreet." His eyes wavered. He realized that he had said too much and gave a short, edgy snicker. "Okay?" he said, loosening his grip on Jacques' arm, "We'll talk in the morning."

By the time Jacques slipped behind the wheel of his car, Bika had disappeared into the house.

"Bula! Where is Bula!" Staring straight ahead, Boketsu bellowed into the living room as he walked quickly through to the terrace.

A tall man with a neat round head and tiny ears and scraggly patches of beard along his jaw line sprang forward and followed Boketsu out of the room.

On the terrace Boketsu turned. "Get that bastard Marceau and bring him here. Right now!" he said, catching his breath. "Right now!"

"It's after one, *patron*," Bula murmured.

"*Je m'en fous!* Get the bastard over here!"

Under a streetlight near the crossroads Jacques pulled off onto the sandy shoulder and walked back to a woman selling cigarettes and matches and small packages of Omo laundry soap. The woman crouched down in the sand, a dirty Matadi flour sack pulled up over her head and around her shoulders. A candle burned in a broken drinking glass atop an overturned tin dishpan where she had arranged a pyramid of matches and five or six packs of local cigarettes and blue and white packages of soap.

He bought a pack of Okapi cigarettes and started back to his car.

A black Mercedes hurtled past and swerved left onto rue des Mimosas, narrowly missing a rain ditch. Jacques stopped and listened as the car, tires squealing with every turn, raced down the street. After a moment, in the silence, he could hear prolonged honking at the gates of somebody's villa far down the rue des Mimosas. It was late. The guards must be asleep, or having a cup of coffee at the back of the house.

It was Bika's official car, with green and white government plates, and Jacques recognized the small round head of the driver: Bika's *petit frère* from Mbandaka; Bula, his most trusted henchman.

21

A 747 angled down from the dusky blue mass of clouds over Charles de Gaulle airport, setting up a thin whine of vibrations in the windowpane. Marceau reached out and held his fingertips against the glass until the vibrations stopped. His fingers left foggy blotches on the glass, chilled by an air conditioning unit beneath the window. He watched the plane speed down the runway and fade away into the rain. KLM.

The narrow strip of grass in front of the hotel looked raw green in the sallow morning light. *Quelle saloperie!* Marceau said aloud. Summer not over yet, and it looks like November.

He coughed and placed his fingers on the pane again. His hand began to tremble, and he pressed harder. Another plane dropped down from the ashen clouds. Sabena. In L'Etrier Jacques Delpech watching him warily, his straight black eyebrows raised ever so slightly over cool blue eyes. Goddamn Belgians. Crash, you bastard, he muttered, crash, go up in flames! The jet settled down onto the runway, like a plump hen, and cruised into the distance. Suddenly dejected, Marceau stared gloomily down the runway as the plane disappeared from sight.

He lit a cigarette, turned from the window, and fell into an armchair. He was exhausted. He said to himself that he had to hold on just a little longer, an hour, maybe two, depending on Guichard's jibber-jabber, and then a quick flight to Geneva to pick up the Swiss Air flight back to Kinshasa. And Nicole. He groaned aloud. No more! No more! It was over! No more questions. Finished the all-night fights with Nicole that in the beginning had ended with good, hot sex, but lately sent him off, festering with jealousy into a separate bed. Over. Done with. He could not stand it any more.

At this point, after three months with Nicole, Marceau knew the exact size and shape, according to Nicole—the bitch probably exaggerated on purpose to drive him crazy—of Jacques Delpech's prick; the name of his favorite aftershave—Drakkar Noir, which every goddamn pansy waiter on the Right Bank in Paris used, for God's sake—he knew that he ordered his suits from Henry Poole and Company at 15 Savile Row where his fitter was a Mr. Meryan-Green, and his shirts from Charvet in the Place Vendôme; he knew his favorite champagne—pink Laurent Perrier, the same as his lordship Citoyen Président Mobutu, and Delpech's birthday—June 18th, the anniversary of the Battle of Waterloo; what was a Belgian born in the Congo doing with a birthday like that? He also knew that Jacques Delpech never wore pyjamas to bed. He also knew that he always went to sleep on his back. He also knew . . .

With a violent effort Marceau heaved himself out of the chair and went to the bathroom, where he splashed cold water over his face and stood for a long time drooping over the sink running cold water over his wrists.

He dried his face and hands and went back to the chair to wait for Guichard. He lit a cigarette, leaned back, and watched the smoke hesitate, then slide down unresisting toward the air conditioner. The diabolic dialogue itched at the back of his thoughts, pushing forward. Listen to me! it said. Again: And how many times did you go to his office, Marceau had asked. How many times, hein? Staring past him, Nicole sat cross-legged on the bed, her hands draped over her ankles. Not her best feature. Nicole's ankles were thick. Piano legs. From time to time she took a sip of champagne from a glass on the bedside table. Stubbornly, she pretended that he was not there. She picked up an emery board and began to file her nails. Where was Delpech's secretary all that time, hein? Hein? *Dis-moi, chérie*, he had asked finally in his best, sweet, shit-eating tone, Tell me, were his wife's ankles as thick as yours? Both legs flailing, Nicole shot off the bed and planted herself in front of him. Twice a week, she hissed, lowering her face to his. Sometimes three. If *I* wanted it! she said, and Marceau thought that he was going to burst into tears, right in front of her.

Marceau rubbed his eyes and sighed. The windowpanes buzzed like a beehive. He looked at his watch. Half past ten. He thought of Guichard coming through the door and what he was going to say and suddenly a great surge of joy overwhelmed him, so exhilarating that he had to get out of the chair and walk quickly into the bathroom to relieve himself. Every time he remembered the miracle—the *Miracle!*—the idea that had come to him, magically, when he awoke from a doze on the plane coming up, he had to go pee.

My God, Marceau thought, these past three days would have killed an ordinary man. Guichard ringing him from Angola to set up this meeting in Paris, then Jacques Delpech and his up-yours, buster smirk, and then Boketsu, our soon-to-be in-house *petit nègre* dragging him out in the middle of the night to rake him over the coals for getting down and dirty with his buddy Delpech. And Nicole. That torment. God, no wonder his body ached as if somebody had been twisting him by the short hairs for days. Marceau shook himself, and as he was zipping up, he thought he heard a knock on the door. He had a violent urge to pee again but restrained himself and walked to the door.

"Guy!" Guichard shouted as if they had just stumbled across each other at the North Pole. He stepped into the room and fumbled with the buttons of his raincoat. "*Mon Dieu*, Guy, you look like shit."

"I feel like shit."

"Are you sick? Malaria?"

"No. Hell no. I've been working hard. Contrary to what the big know-it-alls in the corner suites may think, it's hard work down . . ."

"I know, I know," Guichard said, scraping a chair across the carpet to a table. "We're anxious to hear what you've got for us. Sit."

"Be right with you. I was about to take a leak."

Guichard could hear the toilet swishing and gurgling as Marceau came back into the room.

"So," Marceau said, breathing heavily as he sat down, "What would you like to know?"

"Why, *everything!* my good man," Guichard said, baffled. "Start with Delpech. I imagine he was the tough recruit of the two."

"Delpech?" Marceau said, and he could feel that tight little coil of joy, the miracle idea, ready to spring. "Delpech tough? Well, I guess I may have a little more experience in these things than you, Bernard, I'm not bragging, I'm just saying I've had some experience with these things, men like Delpech, I mean, and you'd be surprised..."

"So?" Guichard seemed to be staring at him, those big, bulgy frog eyes, popping out of his head. "So Delpech is on board? No problems?"

"What?"

"Is Delpech going to play ball with us?"

"You bet," Marceau said, a little louder than he would have liked. He thought that Guichard jumped. "Sure he is, just as you said he would, Bernard, you said it right there sitting out on my terrace, you said. I believe it was you who said that he needed money, the bastard needed money because his business isn't going too good and his wife is suing him for divorce, or I think I heard that he is suing his wife for divorce, but whatever it is, he needs money, lots of money, and you were right all along about that, Bernard, so Delpech is ready to sign the ticket."

"Ticket?"

"Yeah, I mean, play ball... you know on our team. On board."

"Oh. Fine. Fine. Because you know, Guy, this operation is worthless without Delpech. Petro-France can't afford to paint itself into a corner where we're dealing only with some unpredictable African who can turn on us overnight."

Guichard took out a burgundy leather portfolio and laid it across his lap. "And Boketsu Bika?" he asked, looking up at Marceau.

"Well, there... ah, with Boketsu, it's complicated, because he's got in mind some pretty radical, I mean, some substantial, I mean, it's not your usual kind of kickback."

"What does he have in mind?"

"Ah . . . a coup. A *coup d'état.*" It seemed to Marceau that Guichard's frog eyes cranked out a little further from his face.

"A coup?"

"Yeah, a coup. And he's got it all worked out, which tribes will play along, which ones won't and why not, and how much money it will take to make them play along and all that shit. You ought to hear him talk. Says that Zaïre is going down the tubes, believe me, it doesn't take a rocket scientist to figure that one out, and he's the right man at the right time to step in and take over. Seems he's been working on this thing for years. Last time he tried out the idea, he wasn't so strong, and Mobutu wasn't so weak. And now he's got all his ducks lined up and all that's missing is money."

Guichard was breathing through his mouth, and his eyes had not moved. "Where will he get the hardware? Guns? Missiles? Whatever."

"He's got suppliers lined up in Libya. Maybe a big dealer in Brazil, he's waiting to find out."

"He's worked all this out on his own? A little hand from Belgium, maybe? It could be the Belgians. They hate Mobutu. Or the CIA. Mobutu is getting to be a real embarrassment for the Americans. And Boketsu speaks English. Studied somewhere in the United States. We'd better check that out. No need for us to bankroll a coup if the CIA is into this."

"Well, he never mentions any other parties. As I say, you ought to hear him talk. Gets really carried away." Marceau could feel fatigue creeping up his legs, over his body. He had to hold on a little longer.

"And who will fight? Who will pull off the coup? Take over the radio and TV station and those things they do in coups?"

"Mercenaries. He's got those lined up, too. South Africans, some Belgians, a few English and French. That's what the money is for. Good guns and good fighters. He thinks a thousand men ought to do it. Easily, he says."

Guichard sat back in his chair for a moment. "A coup," Guichard said softly, ramming his fountain pen into the breast pocket of his suit. "*A coup!*" he whispered, throwing aside his portfolio and getting up to pace the floor. "Do you realize what this means, Guy? Do you realize what you've handed us, on a goddamn silver platter, you fucking genius!" He slapped Marceau on the back and tried to pull him out of his chair. "I told them you were the man for the job. Robert argued with me, almost argued me down, but I held out. Fucking genius!"

Guichard pranced around the room. For a moment he stood at the window chewing on a fingernail. Then, he turned to Marceau. "Cabinda," he crooned. "Cabinda! Does that mean anything to you, Guy? Hmmn?"

"Another oil company?" Marceau queried half-heartedly.

Guichard laughed and sat back down. With both hands he smoothed back the hair at his temples and sighed happily. "Well, *cher ami,* Cabinda is a small triangle of land that fits like a puzzle piece into Congo, Angola, and Zaïre. Cabinda, unfortunately, currently belongs to Angola. Cabinda's oil is the main source of Angola's foreign exchange, in point of fact. The Cabindans want to secede from Angola. And take their oil with them. We know, or we have reason to believe, that Mobutu has been financing the rebel secessionist FLEC-FAC for years. Why? Because Mobutu wants those gorgeous oil reserves—as well as a few more miles of coastline to add to Zaïre."

Marceau could feel his stomach knotting again. Money, when was the bastard going to talk about the money? Cut out the goddamn geography lesson.

"So what does Boketsu's coup have to do with Cabinda?"

"Plenty," Guichard said. He smoothed his hair again and settled his shoulders against the chair. "Ah, *mon cher ami,* thanks to you," Guichard said, pointing a meaty finger toward the ceiling, "Somebody Up There is dealing us some terrific cards! Petro-France is about to pick up a royal flush!"

Guichard leaned forward, his clasped hands dangling between his knees. "Look at it this way, Guy," he lowered his voice conspiratorially, "Boketsu stages his coup, takes over Zaïre, and with the kind of money we're going to pour into this thing, he can do it, but I want to talk to him first, before we lose our heads over this. Anyway, with *our* man running the country, well, I think you can see for yourself what the possibilities are."

"That's what I've been saying all along. I said it to you before, get the top guy on the payroll, and you said no, Mobutu was too expensive."

"Ah, ah, ah, there's a big difference here, Guy. All the difference in the world. I said *our* guy, remember? We're going to give him the money to put him on the top. After that, *we* pull the strings, he belongs to us. We aren't coming in begging for handouts. If we put Boketsu in Zaïre, that'll make two—what I mean is, we've got President Sassou Nguesso across the river virtually under house arrest. The whole damn country is falling apart. So we had to pull the plug on him. Let's face it, there is only so much the natives can take. After a while, what the hell, they start fighting even if they know the next bullet is for them. Look at Zaïre. It's getting there. So over in the Congo we've picked out our guy, we're funneling the cash his way, and he's going to take over. *Sans problèmes.* We just have to let the Congolese get their national conference out of the way and blow off a little steam about democratization. Look at it, Guy, do you see the big picture now? *Our* man in the Congo and *our* man in Zaïre means Cabinda in Petro-France's pocket. Let Chevron have what's left of the oil in Angola. After we take away Cabinda, the Americans can have Angola."

Guichard reached over and shook Marceau's knee. "Hey, Guy, sure you're not sick? The last man I saw with eyes as glassy as yours died of black water fever a day later."

With great effort, Marceau mumbled, "Sleep. I haven't had much sleep lately, that's all."

"Why don't you go home? Get some sleep. What're you doing in a dump like this, anyway, an airport Ramada Inn, for Christ sake?"

Guichard threw his head back and looked around the room. The bed had not been slept in, but Marceau had obviously stretched out on one side of the bed, which was slightly rumpled; a corner of the spread had been pulled back and a pillow wedged against the headboard. His folded garment bag leaned against the wall next to the door. "What's the story? You going to spend a few days with Margot before heading back down?"

At the mention of his wife's name Marceau, with an effortful jerk, sat up straight.

"I can't. I know I should. You see," Marceau floundered, searching for an acceptable excuse. What the hell had got into Guichard, asking him personal questions like that? "I can't. Have to get back for a party. At Boketsu's place. He expects me."

"*Bien sûr.* Margot will have to understand. You're turning into a ball of fire, Guy. A real ball of fire. So. Write up a presentation for Robert and the higher-ups. Pump every detail out of Boketsu and get it down on paper." Guichard got to his feet and headed toward his raincoat.

"The money," Marceau said, "Boketsu wants details."

"I'll have to see him first, before we . . . ah, formalize things. But there's no problem. No problem. Reassure him. Keep him spinning. Has he asked for a specific amount?"

"Well, in a way . . . more or less. A minimum he needs, he keeps talking about that."

"We can manage. Everything should go on wheels from here on out. Smooth as smooth. Just don't let your friend get unreasonable. The company is not fond of pissing away too much money on the natives."

"And Delpech?"

"That's more straightforward. Work out the details with him down there. Damned good thing you nailed him down. He's too close to Mobutu to be left out of the loop."

"The money. What do I tell him about the money?"

"What?"

"Delpech is asking a lot. I mean, he expects a payoff up front, too."

"How much?"

"Five million."

Guichard whistled. "Greedy. Very greedy. The black man's white man usually doesn't cost that much." Guichard pushed out his nether lip and jiggled the change in his pocket. "In the long run, that's peanuts, of course. And a guy like Delpech, a European, helps keep the wild cards to a minimum in a deal like this."

Marceau's head ached, a steady hammer blow at the base of his skull, and he was so tired that his knees were trembling.

"But the money . . .," Marceau said, his voice little more than a whisper.

"The money?"

Marceau was afraid that at any minute he would grab Guichard's fat shoulders and start shaking the answers out of him. "The money! How does this fucking thing *work?*"

Guichard's moist, unctuous laughter resonated throughout the banal room. "*Ah, pauvre innocent!*" he said. "I had no idea what you were driving at. Well, it's very simple. Numbered Swiss bank accounts are marvelously simple. I fill out the forms, send them to you, Monsieur Delpech signs them, and you send them back to me. *Compris?*"

Marceau felt his heart stumble and skip, one, two, three; then a steady purr of contentment lapped through his veins.

When the plane landed in Kinshasa, Guy Marceau was so delirious that he had to be carried off the plane. For the veteran Swiss Air crew, Marceau's comatose state on arrival was an intriguing novelty. Given the absence of medical treatment available in most African cities, they had become accustomed to handling sick and dying passengers desperate to reach the hospitals of Europe and South Africa. Even after the airlines adopted stricter measures prohibiting those passengers unable to walk to board planes, determined friends and relatives could always manage to get on each side of the sick or injured person and "walk" him or her on board. So Europeans who went out of their heads and raved incoherently during the flight or who were dead on arrival in Zurich or Brussels or Frankfurt or Lisbon or Paris or Johannesburg were still more routine than the airlines and their crews would have liked.

After Guichard left the room in Paris, Marceau had fled to the bathroom to relieve himself. That was when the vomiting started. He stood over the swirling water of the toilet until the retching gave way to dry heaves. His whole body felt bruised and sore. Even the weight of his shirtsleeve against his arm was painful. The pain at the back of his neck radiated down his shoulders. He lost an hour collapsed in a feverish sleep on the bed. He woke in a panic, grabbed his bag, leaving his shaving kit behind in the bathroom, and boarded the plane to Geneva. In the first class Swiss Air lounge in Geneva the hostess was convinced that Marceau, shaking uncontrollably and mumbling to himself, was high on some drug and considered picking up the phone and calling the police to get him out of the lounge. On the plane en route to Kinshasa the young wife of a Citicorp executive returning from summer vacation complained to the stewardess that Marceau had pawed at her back and tried to crawl between her and her seat. To get warm, that's what he kept saying over and over, the woman told the stewardess. The indignant young woman moved to another seat, and the stewardess collected all the blankets she could find and piled them on Marceau. Before he became delirious, Marceau struggled to the bathroom where he stood weaving unsteadily over the toilet. Steam from his urine rose from the toilet bowl. Jesus Christ, he said, Jesus Christ Almighty.

Afterwards, he could not remember how he got back to his seat. He could not remember landing at Njili or the drive up to the Villa San Diego, where his cook took one look at him, lying in a soggy heap on the bed, and ran next door to borrow a bottle of quinine pills from the Minister of Transportation's cook.

Two days later when Nicole came back to the house, the worst of the malarial fevers had passed, and Marceau was so overjoyed to see her that he forgot to ask her why she had not been there when he returned from Paris.

22

Those who live in Africa think of bush pilots as down-on-their-luck drifters, a sophisticated order of bums, rejects from the modern technological world of Europe, and usually recovering alcoholics. Johann Verhaegen, Jacques Delpech's pilot, conformed to the cliché perfectly, although he would have had trouble qualifying as a recovering alcoholic. At some point during his forty-two years Verhaegen must have been a handsome man, for there was a vestige of refinement in the features of his tanned and weathered face. A typically blond and blue-eyed *flamand,* he pulled his long, graying blond hair into a thick ponytail tied with a leather thong at the back of his neck. Grog blossoms sprouted over the end of his nose and across his cheeks. He had turned up in Africa in the late seventies and flown for Baptist missionaries in eastern Zaïre until he crashed one of their light cargo planes after a late night at the Big Boss Club in Goma. In the dry season of 1980 Verhaegen drifted into Kinshasa shortly after Albert Delpech and his pilot had gone down in a rain forest twenty kilometers beyond the end of the runway at Kisangani, having for two hours failed to raise a response from the tower where the controller slept soundly after a heavy meal of cassava and fish head stew and beer. After his father's disappearance Jacques bought a Beechcraft A-200 and hired Verhaegen to fly it.

Jacques and Sarah stood with Johann Verhaegen in the shade

of the tin-roofed cement block building that served as a kind of terminal and watched the porters who hung around the small airport waiting for jobs load Jacques' gifts for the village elders into the plane. The day before Jacques and Sarah had made the round of the tradings, the local stores frequented by market mamas who came down river into town to stock up on everything from tin basins and tin dishes to hair straightener and school notebooks and crayons, coffee pots and bolts of wax print cotton and candles and matches to take back up river to peddle. The tradings occupied long, low buildings with tin roofs and cement floors where merchandise was stacked or piled on the floor. The merchandise was cheap stuff, mostly from China, and there were no fancy displays, few shelves, only a waist-high counter covered in cracked and patched linoleum where the customer displayed his purchases before paying for them. Broad flyspecked ceiling fans whirred overhead. A thick layer of dust covered everything, especially in the dry season. Cypric Jews who had lived in Zaïre for five generations and Pakistanis had grown immensely rich from the humble goods that cluttered the floors of their stores.

Amused, touched by Sarah's excitement over the trip, Jacques had lingered in the dusky mote-filled air of the tradings watching her wander through the maze of articles.

"Look at this," she had said, holding up a pair of eyelash curlers. She studied the curlers solemnly. "Think of it. One of these days, these lash curlers will have traveled all the way from China, up hundreds of miles of the Congo River into a primitive village." She made a face suddenly and put the lash curlers down.

At the end of the day Jacques had bought two fifty kilo bags of rice and four cases of tinned mackerel, and as they stood waiting for Boketsu and his entourage, a Simba truck arrived with cases of beer.

Verhaegen pulled a cigarette from a black John Player pack and slowly swept his sleepy eyes over Sarah. She was wearing slim cut khaki slacks and a white linen blouse. As a joke she had borrowed a cream-colored straw Panama hat from Phil Olmstead. To her surprise, with her thick crown of hair, the hat, slanted slightly over her right eye, was a perfect fit.

The Simba truck pulled away, and Jacques started back toward the hangar.

"What time did you set?" Verhaegen asked him. The rutted tarmac, weeds pushing up through potholes, had begun to shimmer in the heat.

"Eight," Jacques said.

"Zaïrian time?"

"Yeah."

"We can always hope. Might as well start my final check," Verhaegen said.

"He looks like Willie Nelson," Sarah said, as Verhaegen headed toward the plane. His dark blue uniform with gold epaulettes was immaculate, his captain's hat cocked smartly at an angle over his ponytail.

Jacques smiled blandly as if he knew who Willie Nelson was. A bit of hypocrisy, a habit he had acquired while growing up with foreigners who passed through his life as they drifted in and out of Africa. He was suddenly aware of Sarah's foreignness and worried that she would be disappointed with the trip. After all, she had never seen an African village. Movies and books passed over the dirt and sickness and ugliness there. It would be a privilege to go, she had said, to meet your friend Bika, to see where you and he grew up. A quaint idea that he found endearing, in spite of himself. A privilege. He looked at her—her face was still blemished by peeling, patchy skin with shiny pink spots—and he was overwhelmed with such love for her that his right hand flew unconsciously to his heart, as if some simpering, fat cartoon cupid had suddenly flung a handful of arrows into it. They would make love for the first time in Iyondo, he had decided as soon as Bika proposed the trip, and he was not at all embarrassed by the idiotic romanticism of his idea. It was perfect. In every way.

"I hope you won't be disappointed," Jacques said.

"Disappointed? Why should I be?" She looked genuinely surprised, even affronted by the question.

"The dry season. It's not ideal for flying," and as he said it, he thought for the first time of the dangers of the flight, which he was so accustomed to that he never gave them a second thought. "You won't be able to see much. It may be boring up there."

"Don't worry," she said.

Boketsu did not apologize for arriving at the airport over an hour late. "In a little over two hours, we are in Mbandaka," he said. "We have all the time in the world."

He was accompanied by his *petit frère* Bula and three other kinsmen and Liliane, in native dress, who stood twisting and tightening her *pagne* nervously as her four pieces of Louis Vuitton luggage were taken from the car to the plane. At first, Bika seemed startled at the sight of Sarah. Then, in a flurry of mannerisms, he introduced Liliane and flirted with Sarah in a genial African way.

"I knew you would handle the rice and beer," he said to Jacques. "You always remember, and I always forget."

In the plane Jacques sat in the co-pilot's seat to assist Verhaegen with the navigating. As soon as they cleared the runway and circled over the corrugated iron roofs of the huge, sprawling central market of the city, the small plane disappeared into the clouds.

Liliane sat to one side with Bula, who was trying to teach her to inhale cigarette smoke. She was more interested in watching Sarah, who sat just behind Jacques with Boketsu. Liliane wore a green and orange wax print with a large cameo picture of President Mobutu in a leopard skin hat scattered at intervals over the material. At the seams on the back and front of the bodice, the two halves of Mobutu's face had not been matched up evenly and were sewn together so that his face was unusually thin and his eyes very close together, one higher than the other. The Mobutu staring out from the dress looked thin, distressed, and slightly cross-eyed.

"You like Liliane's patriotic dress, don't you?" Boketsu asked, grinning at her, somewhat nastily, Sarah thought.

"It's very nice," Sarah said. "That's the symbol of Zaïrian independence, isn't it?" She pointed toward the large yellow circles with a brown fist holding a flaming red torch. "The flaming torch?"

Boketsu inhaled deeply and studied her face for a moment, his broad nostrils flaring. "Hardly," he said. He stared out the window and seemed temporarily to have forgotten her. "It's the emblem of the President's party. The MPR," he said, turning to her. "The MPR," he repeated, with a nasty smile. "*Mort Pour Rien*. Dead for no reason at all."

Boketsu shrugged and turned back to the window. "Liliane's a little patriot," he said.

Jacques had been right. It was impossible to see anything below; a murky, yellowish light surrounded the plane. Sarah grew restless, and it was awkward sitting there next to Boketsu, who was smarmy one minute and cold and withdrawn the next. Sarah unbuckled her seat belt and leaned forward and squeezed Jacques' shoulder.

"Bored?" he asked. Verhaegen, too, had turned and was looking at her. The radio crackled and emitted a short burst of static.

"Not really. A little, maybe."

"Fasten your belt. We'll go down for a minute and let you have a look at the rain forest."

Verhaegen brought the plane down so fast and so low that Sarah thought that at any moment Jacques would yell or pull up or do something that would keep them from piling into the lurid green jungle rushing up to meet them. Instead they came down very low and leveled off for a few minutes over a mesh of green, as blank and unvarying as the chalky clouds above.

Then, suddenly, in a modest circle of cleared ground alongside a stream, the jungle below came to life. Children came running out of a large low mud-brick building with a thatched palm roof, sitting off to one side of the clearing next to a compound of mud huts with pens of chickens and goats and pigs. At the edge of the clearing, on lines of wire and vine, manioc, like freshly laundered clothes, dried in the sun. Two women with nursing babies sat in the shade of a tree. Heads bent back, the children flailed their arms and waved, their mouths open wide. The plane flew so low that Sarah thought for a moment that she could hear their shouts. As they swept skyward, she saw a tall white man come to the door of the low building. With one hand on his hip, he leaned against the doorway. He did not look up. He watched the children as they waved and shouted at the plane. A solitary white man leaning against the crude doorway.

"A mission school," Boketsu said. He seemed bored. He yanked frantically at his small ears as the plane gained altitude.

"Are there many mission schools?" Sarah asked, to be polite, thinking of the man in the doorway, the tilt of his lean body. He looked like a young man. It could have been Michael. Michael would do something like that. Michael would have done something like that. Michael, too, could be idealistic, especially if the cause seemed hopeless and had more than a possibility of self-destruction involved.

"Enough. Enough to teach a few to read and to write." After a while, he said, "I went to a mission school myself. Before *les évènements,* before the fighting broke out and Jacques and I left for Belgium."

"The President did, too, that is, he was educated by the missionaries, I believe I read that he was. Anyway, it was interesting to see what's down beneath this murky stuff."

"It's the smoke. That's why you can't see anything. In the dry season the people clear and burn the land to plant crops in the rainy season. They burn the trunks for potash. To fertilize the soil. It's the smoke from the trees burning."

"Slash and burn? Isn't that bad for the land? I mean, aren't the people told . . ."

"The people have to eat. You won't find many supermarkets in the bush," Boketsu said.

"Of course not. I know that. I didn't mean anything so ridiculous. I only meant that it's very destructive to the land. Slash and—"

Boketsu yawned and looked at his watch. "Twelve thirty. We'll be landing soon."

From the quiet, dilapidated airport in Mbandaka, the capital of Equateur, they raced in two Mercedes sedans down a rough laterite road, throwing up thick mauve-red clouds of dust behind them. Marshlands with only here and there a black pool of stagnant water lay off to one side of the road. Occasionally a clump of four of five mud huts crouched in the distance in a grove of banana trees. Farther out from the city huge stands of bamboo, squeaking dryly as the cars sped past, and sparse clumps of desiccated tall grass lined the road.

Bula, his small round head hunched down between his shoulders, drove with intense concentration, stomping on the brake and sending up a shower of laterite when he caught up with the dust of the front car carrying Boketsu, his three cousins, and Liliane. In the back seat, absent-mindedly holding Sarah's hand, Jacques said little and stared watchfully out the window, as if a moment's inattention would mean losing forever something precious, something vital. Sarah, still irritated by Boketsu's remarks, sank into a resentful lethargy as the sage-green landscape whirled by. Jacques was in a distant, inaccessible place: his African childhood with Bika. She was jealous, and she knew it.

"Hey, you look cross," Jacques said finally in English.

"Do I?"

His smile was broad and generous, his hands were dry and warm and firm as he took her hand in both of his. She wondered how she could ever have been so lucky, finding her way from Lincolnville, Maine, to the center of Africa, to this car, to this strong man whose simple touch made her happier than she could ever have imagined. "I'm like the eyelash curlers," she said.

"What?"

"Nothing. I'm not cross."

"Good. I don't want you to be cross, my darling Sarah," he said, taking her in his arms.

23

Some forty minutes from Mbandaka the two cars pulled up near a clump of towering rubber plants where two adolescents sat waiting in Land Rovers smeared with dried mud. Scrub bush, blanketed in purplish gray dust, stretched on either side of the road as far as the eye could see. Their arms running with sweat, the men loaded the gifts of rice and beer and tins of mackerel into the Land Rovers, straining and pushing the heavy sacks of rice onto the roof. Then, they turned off the road and jolted across the cracked and parched fields.

"We're heading toward the river," Jacques said, as they jerked and bumped through the bush. Sarah could only nod.

They climbed in and out of dried-up ditches, skidded down banks, and almost turned over when a rotten bridge gave way under them. Boketsu's Land Rover soon disappeared, and at some point, halfway to their destination, a little boy of six or seven came running out of the bush, swung onto the side of the car, and directed the driver as the woods became deeper and taller. Soon they were engulfed by the forest, following rudimentary trails past waterfalls and over shallow streams. They crawled along in a green gloom reverberating with raucous noise. Parrots screeched and screamed, branches crashed and popped, tangles of orchids dragged across the windshield. A pair of monkeys stopped picking at each other's heads and stared down gravely as the Land Rover ambled slowly through an alleyway of hanging liana vines.

Jacques had withdrawn again into blissful silence. The Africans laughed and bantered in their language, grinning, slapping each other, pushing at each other playfully. Whenever Sarah caught their eye, they would glance bashfully away.

"Ah, smell that," Jacques said suddenly, his face radiant. The Land Rover jolted and bucked up a soggy bank. "The river. Can you smell the river?"

Sarah steadied herself and inhaled deeply. She could not honestly say that she smelled anything, except perhaps Bula's spicy aftershave overlaid with a soupy smell of sweat.

"I think so," she said, and miraculously, it seemed, the forest wall fell behind them and they rolled onto well-trodden sandy paths that led to an extensive clearing with huts and pens and palisade fences up ahead.

Surrounded by a group of people, mostly men, Boketsu and his cousins stood waiting near their Land Rover under a great baobab tree.

"Where is Liliane?" Sarah asked.

"She's a Luba. Bika must have sent her on to Iyondo."

"Oh."

"She might feel out of place here with Mongos. They're not her people."

They climbed down stiffly from the vehicle and waited as four men rushed up with a crude stretcher made out of peeled saplings and plaited hemp. After a great deal of arguing and angry spitting, the men loaded the rice, hoisted the stretcher onto their shoulders, and started toward the village. Jacques and Sarah fell in behind them.

"I should tell you what's it's going to be like. There'll be a lot of eating and drinking and dancing. It's a funeral ceremony, but it's happy. No tears. No lamentations. Just celebration. When it's over the dead man's spirit will be freed, on its way to happier . . . uh, places, I suppose. Until this ceremony takes place, his spirit is trapped down here, with us."

Boketsu saw them coming, disengaged himself, and strode forward to meet them. The men turned to look at the strangers, and, as soon as Boketsu had walked away, a flock of small children rushed up to the men and, hanging on to them as if for protection, stood gaping at the white man and woman.

"So?" Boketsu said, beaming at Sarah, "That wasn't so bad, was it? You look terrific, *formidable*." He brought his fingertips to his lips and blew her a kiss. His fingers were short and stubby and the palms of his hand a soft coral pink. "So many of them remember you, Jacques. You'll see. They haven't forgotten the summers you spent here in my father's court."

He took Sarah's other arm and they walked past the group of men and boys toward the village. "Did you know, Sarah, that Jacques and I are blood-brothers? See?" He straightened his left arm and pointed to the crook of his elbow. "Show her, Jacques. Show her your scar."

In the crook of Jacques' elbow the thick kernel of an opalescent white scar stood out against the dark tan of his arm.

"You see? Here's mine. We cut ourselves, cross arms . . . like this," Boketsu placed the inside of his arm against Sarah's. "And we exchange blood. Like this. Blood brothers. For life. Nothing, no one can separate us or come between us."

Sarah laughed. "Not even me, Bika?"

"Ah, but you are only a woman," Boketsu said coldly.

Jacques pressed her arm hard against his side. "First we'll palaver with the village elders, pay our respects, and drink some ceremonial wine."

"Make sure she knows not to drink the wine," Boketsu said. He had dropped her arm and plunged his small hands into his pockets.

"Yes, you mustn't drink the palm wine. When they pass the bowl, just hold it up to your face, making sure that you get a good white mustache from it, pretend to drink, to swallow. Put it down and pass it along. But don't swallow anything. Got that?" He bent down and buried his nose in her warm, fragrant hair. "And put on your hat. You look like Ingrid Bergman in *Casablanca* in that hat."

They stopped in front of a compound with palisade fences made of bamboo and thatched with palm leaf. They sat down on low stools in the shade of a tree to wait until the elders had finished greeting visitors from a neighboring village.

One by one women with babies on their backs and toddlers clinging to the women's ragged and dirty *pagnes* came out into the yard to steal a look at the strangers sitting under the tree. Boketsu nodded and murmured a greeting to one of the women, who ducked her head and shyly turned away. The women were all barefoot and bare-breasted. Their breasts, like large, flat pancakes, sagged down below their waists.

Three or four chickens scratched in the hard red earth of the yard. A child idly threw stones against the side of a black kettle precariously balanced over a fire. The earth was bare and pounded to a hard, glossy finish.

A naked toddler cried and pulled at his mother's skirts. She hoisted him onto her hip and the child picked up one of the long, floppy breasts and sucked on it, his large round eyes staring at the strangers.

Suddenly, the child spat out the breast. "*Bidimo!*" he squalled, kicking at his mother's stomach. "*Bidimo!*"

Jacques and Boketsu laughed and said something in Mongo to his mother, who smiled tentatively, showing purple gums.

"The child thinks we're ghosts, you and I, because we're white," Jacques said to Sarah. "*Bidimo,* that means 'spirits.'"

The little boy squirmed away from his mother and slid down her legs to the ground. As if entranced, the woman stood with legs spread, staring at Sarah. From time to time, she raised the flap of one of her breasts to fan away a fly from her face. For a while the other women made a pretense of milling around the yard, but soon they, too, shifting children from hip to hip, came to stand at the fence and stare at the white woman sitting down with the African and the white man. Boketsu bantered and flirted with a short, thin woman sucking on a piece of sugar cane. With visible effort the woman responded grudgingly to Boketsu's teasing questions with nasal grunts and *ay-ah's*, as if trying to chase away a pesky fly, darting her eyes back to the white woman whenever she could.

A half-dozen men, some with their bodies painted a grayish white, emerged from the mud hut.

Instinctively, Sarah reached for Jacques' hand. "Don't be afraid," he said.

"No," she said, leaning against his warm body. Her heart full of dread, she watched the ghostly Africans move off slowly down the narrow pathway. Suddenly she remembered the glinting snow flanks of Mount Kilimanjaro. "It's just so different," she said. "From the city, I mean."

"You'll like the village better," Jacques said.

Boketsu rose first, and Sarah and Jacques followed him into the hut, which was dim and cool and smelled of smoke and something decaying, fermenting. Six men sat cross-legged on woven rush mats along the wall, and at the feet of the gray-haired man in the center sat a large calabash bowl filled with a white, foamy liquid. Boketsu and Jacques passed along the line of men, shaking hands and laughing. One of the men grabbed Jacques' hand and pulled his face down and kissed him on both cheeks. The others laughed, a high-pitched squeal that trailed off into a contented sigh.

They pointed to Sarah and tipped their heads and smiled and motioned for her to sit. She knelt down and sat back on her heels between the two men and put on an attentive expression, though she could understand none of the exchange. For a long while the grizzled man in the middle talked to them, sometimes in a thin, wheedling, hectoring tone, and sometimes he joked, for the tiny space in the hut kept filling up with boisterous laughter. Sarah's ankles began to ache. A smell of boiling fish wafted through the door and blended with the fruity odor of decay in the hut. Her stomach twisted with hunger, and she remembered that she had eaten nothing since a croissant and a banana with a cup of coffee at breakfast. Once she thought that Jacques reached out and touched her elbow to steady her, and just when she was about to move her cramped feet and legs, Boketsu began to speak. There was a noisy burst of clapping, and the gray-haired man raised the calabash bowl, drank, and passed it to his right. Now everyone seemed to talk at once with short pauses of silence for drinking from the bowl.

The third time the calabash bowl made the rounds, Sarah tilted back her head, brought the large bowl clumsily to her mouth, and, before she realized what she was doing, swallowed a large mouthful of palm wine. The wine sent a powerful charge through her body, a pleasant shock, and she felt better, more honest, for it seemed to her that the Africans had watched her closely as she lifted the bowl to her face. It was hypocritical to make a show while in reality shunning their offering. When the wine came around again, she drank lustily, staring into the eyes of the shriveled little African sitting opposite her, proud of herself. Then, guiltily, she wiped her mouth with the back of her hand and glanced quickly at Jacques. But he was bowing and laying the calabash bowl at the feet of the old man and then his hand was under her elbow helping her to her feet.

They stumbled out into the sunlight where two young boys stood next to the hut holding gifts for them. One boy, his face painted a deep yellow with red stripes down the nose and across the cheeks, held a dirty biscuit-colored goat by the horns. The other boy dangled four hens by their feet, the hens straining away from the ground, trying to keep their heads out of the dust. Boketsu giggled and clapped his hands and sent the boys running with the presents to the Land Rovers under the tree.

As soon as they left the hut, Boketsu, his spirits high, was encircled by relatives and friends.

"Bika," Jacques said, "Let's eat together under the baobab tree. Like old times."

"Yeah. Sure. I'll find you around." He lifted his hand in a half-salute and wandered off with the men toward the tables that were laid out with food.

"Listen. The dancing's started," Jacques said. In the distance they could hear the thump of drums and the high ululating of women.

"Let's eat! I'm starved," he said, taking her arm and setting off at a run along the worn path, past empty huts and bushes festooned with tattered pieces of clothing drying in the sun and primitive pens where scrawny hens scratched and scrounged for food.

As they came around a bend in the path, Sarah could see people milling about a long plank table and smell the smoke and tangy odor of burning animal flesh.

Jacques stopped, catching his breath. He seemed to be listening for something. "Wait," he said, pulling her off the path behind a spreading mimosa. His pale blue shirt was wet with sweat.

"What is it?"

"This," he said, kissing her, his mouth sour with palm wine.

"I think you're drunk," she said. The wine was strong. She could remember the rush of lassitude throughout her body after she swallowed.

"Yes. And hungry."

He made no move to go. He stood there holding her with a dopey grin on his face.

Around her head the pink and white flowers of the mimosa tree tossed and bobbed with the weight of burrowing bees.

"You must be a proper Bacchus. Bacchus needs flowers for his hair," she said, reaching out to pick a blossom. Bees swirled up from blossoms, and her hand brushed against the tiny dark leaves, which shrank together at her touch. Sarah's eyes clouded with melancholy fascination. She had never seen a mimosa tree before. She held her breath. Almost against their will, they both watched as the leaves cringed and pulled tightly in on themselves as Sarah's hand moved slowly from flower to flower.

"There are other flowers," Jacques said at last. "Come."

By the time they reached the table, it was tended by only a few women who stood about, talking loudly, stirring pots and turning the crudely made spits on which a goat and several small bush pigs roasted over open fires. The villagers, some eighty or ninety people, had already taken their food and gone to the fields to watch the dancers; from time to time children flitted back with battered tin bowls and basins to fetch more food before racing away. Boketsu was nowhere in sight.

From the looks of the pots and platters heaped with food on the plank table several villages could have eaten themselves into a stupor. One of the women spoke harshly to a little boy who soon came running back, grinning ecstatically, with two tin plates, washed, but still greasy, which he held out to Sarah and Jacques. The women clucked and fussed over Jacques in their timid way, giggling, ducking their heads, avoiding his eyes. Bowls and platters were black with flies, like a burnt crust covering each dish.

Sarah tried not to look at the table as she followed Jacques, who was serving both of them. "Let me do it, you must be careful what you eat," he said. Deep bowls crawled with live grub worms next to a basin heaped high with fried worms and caterpillars. Jacques dipped his hand into the basin and sprinkled the worms and caterpillars over some kind of stewed dark green leaves. A smoked monkey, black and rigid, lay on one side, its tiny hands tucked up under its chin, like a baby coiled in sleep. A young girl leaned forward from the other side of the table and wrenched off one of the monkey's legs with a casual, deft twist. Sarah swallowed nervously. The heat and the smells made her dizzy. Ropes of guts were draped over the ends of the spits, like wet stockings looped over a shower rod. Sarah took a deep breath and looked away, at the bland white sky.

Jacques, on the other hand, was exuberant, talking, gesticulating, sending the women into giggles. His own plate was heaped high with food while Sarah's contained only a lumpy white piece or two of something she did not recognize and a pile of fried plantains, and the women were teasing him about the difference in the two plates now. Sarah watched him, the flash of his fine white teeth in his smoothly tanned face, his dusty blue eyes crinkling playfully, his tall, healthy body, and felt the thrill of losing her heart to a stranger. That sudden burst of infatuation for a handsome stranger fleetingly glimpsed, on an escalator, at a traffic light, in the next row at the opera. He looked boyish, and happy to the point of silliness, thoroughly unlike the serious, somber man, sitting in the shadows of her balcony, his voice outlined in sorrow and mourning.

There was a lull in the dancing, and when Jacques and Sarah reached the fields, the villagers were quietly talking together, waiting for the masked dancers to emerge from a small hut on the other side of the clearing. Two women balancing buckets of millet beer on their heads swayed to a stop and emptied their buckets into a large tub. Many of the men and several of the women were already drunk, staggering into people and stumbling their way to the tub of beer.

The air was hot and still and the gamy stench of food hung in the air. Everyone seemed to be in movement. Sarah wiped her brow and fought back nausea. She was appalled with herself, feeling weak-kneed and queasy when she should be full of anticipation. How many foreigners ever got a chance to see masked dancers? Maï-Mati dancers in their own village? It was a privilege, just as she had told Jacques when he asked her to go. She leaned against Jacques and concentrated on the hut across the field, a dun-brown blur in the heat-dazzle of the afternoon.

They stood alongside a hollowed-out tree propped up almost waist high at one end with a skin stretched and bound over the raised end. Jacques was trying to explain to her that this was a talking drum that could call across the forest or the fields and from village to village. "They have different sounds for their names, you see, so when they're working out in the fields, and they hear their name on the drum, they come back to the village." The only thing that Sarah really understood was that here was a place where she could sit down. As if he knew what she was about to do, Jacques said, "Oh, no, you mustn't," and pulled her upright again.

At that moment there was a piercing sound, either of a flute-like instrument or a shrill drawn-out cry, and in a confusion of red dust the masked dancers, in single file, came across the fields, stamping, dancing, chanting. The villagers drew back into a broad circle, which was closed as soon as all the ten or twelve dancers had pranced into place.

The dancers were covered entirely in tight-fitting red and black striped woven raffia from head to foot, great shaggy manes of cut raffia flowing at chin height from their head mask, dense cuffs at their wrists and ankles, and, around the holes for their eyes, wide round thick layers of raffia like goggles painted white. They danced back and forth and around the circle, some punctuating their chants with the shake of roughly hammered metal bells and gourds filled with seeds. The crowd silently watched the swirl of bushy arms and legs. Suddenly, one of the dancers whipped through the air a wooden slat on a string that bellowed and roared like a beast being slaughtered. The dancers whirled and jumped out of the circle and ran back to their hut.

They were followed immediately by six unmasked men naked except for the furs of small bush animals hanging from leather thongs at their shoulders and waists. Carrying a sharpened *panga,* a machete, each man wore, fastened to each side of his head, the blade and handle of another machete, fashioned to look as if the blade of the *panga* had been thrust through the man's head. Blood had been dribbled down each man's face, onto the furs, and down his body. Dust, blood, straw, and feathers clung to the men's hair. They danced around the circle in a one-legged crouch, shouting, chanting, and slashing the hot, dusty air with their machetes. Their eyes were fierce and their breathing as shallow and harsh as a dying animal's.

Now the spectators, too, swayed, stomped, and shouted encouragement to the dancers. Women rolled their eyes and ululated. A drunken woman, naked except for a thick roll of rags clotted around her stomach, wandered into the circle and shuffled around the slashing machetes amid the huffs and shouts of the crouching men. Her worn, flat dugs flapped against her stomach like weathered leather bags.

It seemed to Sarah that hours had passed since the raffia-masked dancers had come and gone. Another group of men with bloody *pangas* fixed to look as if they passed through the men's heads danced into the circle, crouched down and wailed and flailed about with their *pangas.* Now both men and women wove drunkenly in and out of the path of the slicing blades. One man, nicked at the waist and bleeding profusely, clapped his hands wildly and stamped his feet. Sarah closed her eyes and willed her nausea away.

From time to time a child sidled up to Sarah and timidly stroked her arm. She could not help flinching, instinctively drawing her arm into her side.

"They've never seen a white person," Jacques said. "They don't mean any harm." He reached across her and patted the boy's head.

Proud of his courage, the boy promptly turned and scampered back to his sniggering friends who had not been bold enough to find out what white skin was like.

"Sarah. Are you all right?"

"Fine," she said, wondering how she could remain standing if she weren't leaning into him.

"You look pale. We ought to leave soon. They're getting too drunk to be fooling with those *pangas*." He tightened his arm around her waist and looked over the crowd. "I don't see Bika. He must be off somewhere with his *petits frères*. We'll go on to Iyondo without him."

Later Sarah would be unable to remember when Jacques noticed the girl standing directly behind her, or when he grabbed the girl's wrist and forced open her hand. She remembered only that the Africans nearest them suddenly grew quiet and turned to watch Jacques and the girl. When Sarah turned around, she noticed first the determined look on his face, the angry white knuckles of his hand, and, then, the girl's face contorted with mute pain. He was muttering something in Mongo to the girl, harshly, his right hand twisting the girl's wrist, the nails of his other hand digging into her fingers. With a small *aiiee* of pain, plump tears sliding slowly down her face, the girl released her hold. In the palm of her hand lay a raggedly cut blond coil of Sarah's hair. "It's okay, Sarah," he said, breathless, "It's okay." Still gripping the girl's wrist, Jacques swiftly picked the hair from her sweaty palm, turning her hand to the light to make sure that a strand had not stuck to her hand. He thrust the hair into his pants' pocket and dropped the girl's hand.

"We'd better go," he said, "It's best to be out of the forest before the light fails."

The boy who had guided them from the Mbandaka road through the forest, was asleep on the hood of the Land Rover when they got back to the baobab tree. The air was thick with flies drowsy from the heat, and the sun had slipped to an orange smear near the horizon. Boketsu had left with *ses petits frères*, the boy said. The goat and the hens, trussed up with strips of torn rags, lay behind the backseat. The goat languidly raised his head and dropped it with a muffled clunk to the floorboard when Jacques and Sarah climbed into the vehicle. In the heavy air, the Land Rover reeked of the moist excrement of the frightened goat and hens.

"You don't have another cigarette, do you?" Sarah said. She had not smoked in years, had given them up to set some kind of example for Michael, an intense smoker.

"Of course. Sorry. I didn't realize you smoked." He shook out a Dunhill and lit it for her.

Sarah inhaled hungrily. Her spirits lifted, and as they pulled away from the baobab tree, the air stirred and the clean smelling smoke from their cigarettes made her feel friendlier toward the miserable goat and hens bouncing and soiling themselves behind the backseat.

"For God's sake, what kept you?" Bika asked. He was leaning against the headlights of the Mercedes drinking beer with Bula. The car door was open, and Kinshasa music, low and sensual, played on the radio. "We came back for you. Hours ago."

"We had trouble finding another bridge. And Sarah was sick," Jacques said.

"Sick?"

Darkness had collapsed over the bush, and Bika could see little beyond the headlights of the two cars as Jacques helped Sarah into the car.

"Sick?" Bika said again.

"She drank the wine," Jacques said. "She'll be okay."

"Christ!" Bika said.

24

In the early seventies when Mobutu Zaïrianized virtually every business in the country, Boketsu's father had taken over the coffee plantation at Iyondo from a Belgian named Cellier who had come out to the old Belgian Congo as a White Father missionary and, when he lost his calling, had begged and borrowed enough money to buy six hundred hectares which he turned into one of the richest coffee plantations in Equateur. The former missionary married a plain young woman from Liège and built for her a sprawling white stucco bungalow situated on a hillock overlooking coffee groves that spread over the countryside as far as the eye could see and rubbed their branches against the wide verandah of the house. Zaïrianization took Cellier and his sons—by that time he had four—completely by surprise. From one day to the next, it seemed to him, all that he had accomplished in thirty years had to be handed over to Boketsu Lokumba, the chief of the Mongo tribe. Back in Belgium he suffered from the damp and the cold and from not knowing, as soon as he slid his foot into his slippers in the morning, exactly what he would be doing every hour and every minute of that day. When he committed suicide seven months later, he tried to make the automobile crash look like an accident so that he could be buried in consecrated ground.

Jacques led Sarah to one of the high-ceilinged guest rooms at the back of the house. A generator thrummed nearby, and the servants had turned on lights and hung mosquito netting over the large bed in the center of the room.

Sarah was sick again in the bathroom, and Jacques held her as he had in the forest while the young Africans stared and the goat bleated and kicked and scuffled behind the seat. The cigarette had been a mistake. A big mistake. The wine an even bigger mistake. She saw again the grayish white foam in the calabash bowl, and her stomach rose.

"I'm being a nuisance," she said.

"No. Just a little silly. Don't say that."

"Bika doesn't like me," she said.

"Bika never likes any of my girlfriends," he said.

Girlfriends. Jealousy ricocheted through her. She smiled wanly at him in the vague hope of making herself more agreeable, and was sick again, a retching, shuddering sickness.

"Why is he so angry? Bika?"

Jacques thought for a moment. "Because he is betraying his dreams."

He wrung out a washcloth and held it to her face. "Can you manage?" he said. "I'll go look for a Coke or an Orangina. Something to settle your stomach."

A pastel translucent gecko slipped down the tile wall and froze into place as if sent by a community of geckos to find out what she was doing. Weakly, Sarah washed her face and quickly showered in the none-too-clean shower stall with rusty, red water stains spilling down the dingy white porcelain tiles.

Later, when Jacques came back to the room with a lukewarm bottle of Orangina, he found Sarah sprawled across the bed, fast asleep, one slim, shapely foot sticking out from under the mosquito netting.

Jacques could not remember ever being awakened in such a gratifying way.

For a long while he lay passively in a half sleep, prolonging the dream, afraid to open his eyes, afraid that what was going on was happening only behind his closed lids, only in a wanton dream, the puerile fantasy of an adolescent. Then Sarah moaned and shivered against him and his whole body arched upward. He dug his hands into her thick curls and startled himself fully awake when he groaned or gasped aloud her name.

She slid down at his side and nuzzled her face into his neck and closed her eyes. Immediately, he could feel her deep, even breathing.

He lay for a long while trying to catch his breath. "Hey," he said finally, "I want you to wake me up like that every morning for the rest of my life."

He pushed back the net and reached for a cigarette. "Sarah? For the rest of my life, Sarah. Did you hear what I said?"

"Mmm," she said, and yawned.

"Well, goddamn," he said, "Want a cigarette?"

She inhaled the smoke deeply, closed her eyes, and slipped down beside him once again.

"You okay?"

"Hmm." She turned over onto her back and flung her right arm upward over her head. After a moment, she burrowed her head snugly into his neck once again.

"Sarah?"

She was asleep.

Cautiously, he turned onto his side and lay quite still and smoked, listening to Sarah's peaceful breathing. Beyond the netting the windows looked like ghostly gray boxes stuck into the dim walls. Small animals skirmished in the ceiling overhead, but otherwise the house was silent. Some time during the night the generator had been shut down. Jacques gazed at Sarah's long, slim body and imagined its goldenness when all traces of the ugly sunburn would be gone. Gently, he followed the outlines of her bikini with his fingertips, the thin spaghetti straps crossing from the side of her breasts to her neck, the half moon cups at her breast, the skimpy triangle below her navel.

He crushed out his cigarette in a shallow metal ashtray with the logo of the Hotel InterContinental Kinshasa and took a deep breath and closed his eyes.

Down in the coffee groves, he heard the laughter of women,

on their way to fetch water probably. He opened his eyes. The windows had turned a pale lemon. The day's heat had begun.

Sarah stirred slightly, and he bent over and kissed her lightly on the lips. He ran his hands over her body, and waited. Little by little, he increased the pressure of his caresses. After a moment Sarah sighed and he could feel her nipples hardening against his chest.

Then he said softly, "Wake up, Sarah. My turn."

"You look like a woman who has just been most satisfactorily laid," Boketsu said, as Sarah sat down at the breakfast table on the terrace. He was wearing a white Georgetown Hoyas sweatshirt and shorts.

"Jacques is shaving," Sarah said.

"I didn't ask what Jacques was doing," Boketsu said. Liliane looked up from *Elle* magazine. "So, as I was saying, am I right, was it a good lay?"

"*The best*," Sarah said levelly, looking him straight in the eye.

Immediately after breakfast Boketsu withdrew to the room that old Cellier had called his office with three men whom he introduced vaguely as "superintendents" on his father's plantation, but Jacques noticed over the noon meal that none of the three spoke Mongo and that they were wearing tailor-made *abacos* instead of the ragtag assortment of tee shirts and pants usual in the bush.

After the men had left, Boketsu seemed unusually restless, lighting a cigarette, then laying it down in an ashtray and forgetting to smoke it, twirling the transistor radio dial through tunnels of static in search of Radio France International, snapping at Liliane, ignoring Sarah, pointedly referring to her as "she" and "her."

"Come, let's walk down to the river," he said finally, and both Jacques and Sarah got to their feet. Liliane, her lips parted, was still poring over the photographs in *Elle*.

"She can't go," Boketsu said to Jacques. "Those shoes, she can't go down to the river with those shoes."

Sarah was wearing sandals, which would have been perfectly all right, as Boketsu knew very well, but this was the chance Jacques had been waiting for to corner him again on the Marceau business.

"That's true." He kissed Sarah on the forehead. "Stay here with Liliane. Do you mind? Be back shortly."

Liliane brightened, laid down her magazine and came to Sarah's side and shyly took her hand. They stood side by side and waved as the men disappeared under the low arch of the coffee trees.

They walked along in silence for a while. Jacques lit a cigarette. The trees at the end of each row were either dead or dying. He looked down the slope and could see the path of whatever disease had stricken them.

"So, how do things look? Any changes in the government coming up?" Jacques asked.

"Can't say. The Man seems to be letting me sit. That's as much as I know."

"Where is he this weekend?"

"Up river. On his yacht. Dispensing largesse. Doing his chief's thing. Lisala is getting a generator. He's giving the Catholic mission fifty thousand dollars and the Baptists thirty."

The air was close in the paths of the grove, and Jacques' shirt clung damply to his back.

"Tell me, I'm curious, what did your friend Marceau have to say when you sent for him the other night?"

"What are you talking about?"

"I'm talking about the night I came to tell you that Marceau had pitched me. Wednesday night. After I left."

"You know, Jacques, I've never seen you like this before. What is it with you and this guy? He's just some dimwitted French businessman who doesn't know his way around in Africa."

"Then why did you send for him at one o'clock in the morning? If he's just a dimwitted French businessman."

"What?"

"You know what. You sent Bula to get Marceau. After I left. I saw Bula turn into the rue des Mimosas and heard him sounding his horn at Marceau's villa. Villa San Diego. Rue des Mimosas."

Bika dragged on his cigarette and stared straight ahead. Great beads of sweat stood out on his rounded forehead. "So." He exhaled slowly and picked at a piece of cigarette paper stuck to his lower lip. "So. My best friend. My brother. You've turned into a regular spy, hein?"

Jacques whipped around and faced him. Bika was still staring into the distance, smoking. His black eyes were filled with tears.

"Oh, Bika, no," he said, embracing him. "No. That's not it at all."

Bika said nothing. They stood together for a moment longer, then Bika slowly drew away and brought his cigarette to his lips again. His hands were trembling.

"Then what is it?" Bika said finally.

"I don't want you cutting any more deals, especially with Petro-France. I don't want you putting your trust in people who can't be trusted. Who are out to screw Zaïre. And who will use you in the process."

Bika dropped his cigarette and stood slowly grinding it into the dirt with his foot. He did not look up at Jacques.

"Remember Bokamba? Accepted a million-dollar bribe from Sodac and they put down a hundred thousand in a Swiss bank account and never paid another cent and Bokamba running around asking everyone whether he could sue for the rest of the money?"

Bika gave a short, derisive snort. "Bokamba is a jerk. A typical African jerk."

They left the coffee trees and the bungalow far behind and followed worn trails through the high grass toward the forest bordering the river. Scores of monarch butterflies rose and fell in the high grass like orange and brown fans.

"Oh, yeah, the deals, the deals. Plenty of those. The government is finally going to do something about the Matadi road. In a few months Mukata and Joe Snead will have their couriers with heavy bags shuttling back and forth to Geneva. Mukata and Snead, they're a matched pair. Snead's one low bastard. He offered to put in a paved road up here on the plantation." Bika turned and gestured toward the house. "From the Mbandaka road to the house. Eleven kilometers. No strings attached, he says."

"I know," Jacques said.

"*What!*" Bika's voice squeaked when he was excited. Or angry.

"He told me. Said that he had offered and you had refused. That's all."

"Well, *mon frère,* it appears I have no secrets as far as you are concerned."

"So? Is that a problem? We've never had any secrets from each other, you and I. Do you suddenly have something to hide?"

Bika did not answer. They had reached a point in the forest when they could pick up the peaty smell of the riverbank up ahead.

"Let's get back to the house," Bika said, turning abruptly on his heels.

"What about the river?"

"Fuck the river," Bika said.

Even though they walked back through the coffee grove at a fast clip, it took almost an hour to reach the house. Bika did not seem in a mood to talk further, responding when he had to with accommodating grunts and monosyllables. Jacques could not understand the hurry to get back to the house: Bika could do no business by telephone because the phone no longer worked. Perhaps he was expecting more visitors like those in the morning.

Sarah and Liliane were sitting at the far end of the verandah, and when Sarah heard their footsteps, she jumped to her feet and ran to the steps to meet them.

She was dressed in Liliane's Mobutu print dress with the president's anxious, cross-eyed stare in the middle of the bodice, which had large puffed sleeves and a boat neck. The *pagne* was pulled tight around her middle and knotted on her left hip and fell in a straight line to her ankles and made her look tall and extremely curvaceous. Liliane had braided Sarah's blond hair into short, thin, spiky braids that stood out all over her head, the popular native coiffure called the "Sputnik." Liliane sidled up beside Sarah and took her hand and, grinning proudly, her strange eyes turned up into her lids, glanced back and forth between the men and Sarah.

"You look ridiculous," Boketsu said.

Jacques could follow the traces of his remark, like a stinging slap, across Sarah's open, smiling face.

"Wait for me inside, Sarah," Jacques said. His mouth had the same thin, hard look as when he pried the girl's fist open. He put one foot on the steps leading to the verandah and turned to face Boketsu.

"Lay off Sarah, Bika. Leave her alone. I mean it. And I'm not going to say it again."

"*D'accord! d'acc!* I only said that she looks ridiculous. All white women look absurd when they dress like Africans. What's the big deal? I've never seen you act so ridiculous over any woman. I just don't like her, that's all."

"Naturally."

"No, not *naturally.* I tried to be nice to her. But I don't like American women. I never have."

"That's absurd and you know it. What about Betsy? You were pretty far gone on Betsy for over two years, and a long time after you finished Georgetown. Don't say you weren't because I remember it only too well."

"Betsy was different. This one is your typical American, always lecturing, telling us poor folks in the Third World what we should or should not do."

"Well, maybe you should listen. For a change."

"We don't have to listen to anyone any more."

"Good for you."

"I mean it, Jacques. Cut the bullshit, will you? Americans play with us and use us when it's convenient. Look how they've cut their aid to us. For American politicians, Africa means photo ops with starving children while their wives try to buy out the ivory market and meet at four o'clock for cappuccinos in the atrium of the InterCons. When they can get some good publicity, play the savior, they throw us a bone. Otherwise, forget about it. They won't give Africans a measly dollar."

"Why should they? Why should they give you anything?"

"Why? For God's sake, because they're rich. And we're poor. They've got it, and we don't."

"Well, you had it once, didn't you? And now you don't. My God, Bika, have you any idea how you have changed your tune? Do you have any idea how far you've fallen from the man you used to be? Remember when you used to rant about Mobutu and his foreign dependence saying that this country is so rich that it can tell the rest of the world to go to hell? Remember that before Independence this country exported food by the ton? And now, God help us if the cargo planes from South Africa stop flying in. Just look around you. Look at this place. I remember the days when old Cellier and his boys ran this plantation. Now what have you got? Trees that are diseased and dying, generators that are patched together with pieces of old tire and kitchen forks, shutters that are rusted out and falling off the windows, broken faucets, broken window panes. No one on this continent gives a damn about maintenance or repairs. It's use it up, tear it down, throw it away. You saw all this before you went away, I know you did. I'd like to know what's happened to you. Your ideas have certainly changed since you left here seven years ago."

Bika, his hands in his pockets, stood placidly gazing over the coffee trees. "Good old Betsy. I haven't thought about her for years. You know, she ended up marrying a linebacker for the Redskins. What do you think," he asked, turning toward Jacques, "Do you think Betsy just liked dark meat?"

"Yeah. Probably," Jacques said, starting up the steps.

"Where are you going?"

"To find Sarah."

"What are you going to do? Screw all afternoon?"

"Maybe," Jacques said.

25

It had started off as a joke: Carter Everett had promised Kowalski that he would bring Sarah to watch the "graduation" performance of Kowalski's team of Zaïrian anti-terrorists. Then, when the day for the exercises arrived, Carter had his own reasons for finding a way to spend time alone with her.

Carter's driver arrived to pick her up at the American Cultural Center at three o'clock, and Carter was waiting for them on the steps of the embassy on the Avenue des Aviateurs. When he saw the car pull up, he picked an enormous hibiscus blossom from a bush next to the gate and presented it to Sarah as he got into the car.

"God, at last, a gallant Yale man," she said, tucking the flower through a buttonhole of her green linen suit.

Carter laughed and settled in beside her. "I take it you didn't enjoy Yale and Yale men that much," he said, and as soon as the words were out of his mouth, he remembered. "I'm sorry, Sarah, I had forgotten." But he noticed, as Carter Everett would, that she was no longer wearing her thin gold wedding ring.

The car pulled up behind a *fula-fula* jammed with people. "Yale was long ago," Sarah said, staring at the tangle of black arms in the *fula-fula*.

"And far away, of course," Carter said, covering her hand with his. "Jesus Christ, one of Hitler's escaped madmen must have dreamed up those buses. Look at them jammed in there, worse than animals. Jesus."

The *fula-fula* belched a cloud of black smoke and downshifted gears with a grinding smack as it started up the hill to Kitambo. *Fula-fulas,* covered trucks converted into buses with no windows, had only a two-feet wide strip cut out of the metal side of the truck with a bar across it for ventilation. Passengers stood inside, packed tightly together, holding each other up. Most *fula-fulas* were painted a dismal dark green or black, and from the outside, only the arms, belts, midsections of passengers were visible.

"*Doublez,* Justin. *Allez-y,* go ahead and pass," Carter said quietly, and Sarah squeezed the armrest as their car, horn blaring, shot around the struggling *fula-fula,* into the path of an oncoming car, which braked and, impotently, blinked its lights.

At Camp Tshatshi where the exercises were being held, Carter left her in the care of General Lucola's aide.

Bending over her, Carter looked into her eyes, squeezed her arm and winked. "I'll be right back," he said, then turned and walked away toward the General's waiting Jeep. Carter, it seemed to Sarah, was one of the most naturally seductive men she had ever met, his smallest gesture laden with intimacy. Unlike Jacques. Who wasted so little, who saved it all for wave after wave of passion when he made love.

Sarah and the General's young aide joined the other spectators, about forty men (Sarah was the only woman there), African and European, in uniforms she did not always recognize. They watched as Carter, looking like a movie star graciously smiling despite the fact that he has stumbled onto the wrong set, and General Lucola circled the field in the open Jeep and saluted the troops.

When Carter joined her, they went to stand with a dozen or so other observers on a raised platform overlooking the exercise field, which consisted of a mock-up of a high-rise building, a reinforced cinder block front with windows, and a mock-up of a Boeing 747 made from stacks of old tires. The point of the graduation was to show how swiftly and efficiently the trainees could rescue hostages and liberate buildings and aircraft as well as manipulate the sophisticated hardware of anti-terrorist maneuvers: stun grenades, M-16s, and fifty-caliber machine guns.

It was a deafening affair. The trainees rappelled down the face of the mock high-rise, kicked out windows in a flash, tossed stun grenades inside, and after a burst of machine gun fire, heaved themselves through the windows and subdued the "terrorists" inside.

In the rescue of the 747 hostages, which took place immediately below their platform, the trainees first threw a series of stun grenades, then from above to the right, came a sustained burst of machine gun fire meant to keep the "terrorists" down while the rescuers moved in to complete their mission. "Goddamn that Kowalski!" Carter said. "Where the hell is he? I can't see him. Who's commanding that fire?" Carter had given Kowalski specific instructions about controlling the machine gun stations. Unconsciously, he reached out and pressed down on Sarah's shoulder. "Goddamn Polack! I'll kick his ass all the way back to New Jersey. Goddamn! Goddamn!"

Unaware of the potential danger, Sarah couldn't help laughing, and the Mossad officer standing on her right with his hands behind his back and an amused look on his face, turned to look at her.

The Mossad officer, grinning broadly, shouted across Sarah. "Carter? Is there a problem?"

There was a burst of whining pings, and the machine guns stopped.

"Let's go," Carter said, steering Sarah off the platform. "Got to get you some champagne. Goddamn that Kowalski!"

Thirty minutes later, at the end of the exercises, Kowalski strolled into the green and white striped tent where the General and his guests were drinking pink champagne.

"You're a hero, chief. I watched you. Never once did you bend your knees or duck your head. An inspiration."

"Shut up, Kowalski," Carter said.

"He's going to kick your ass all the way back to New Jersey, Kowalski," Sarah said, and Carter and Kowalski laughed.

Kowalski was short and muscular and young, and his deep-set black eyes sparkled in his ruddy face. Melodramatically, he slapped his hand over his heart. "I love you, Sarah," he said. Kowalski was known to be thoroughly married, the father of two youngsters whose photographs at play in a backyard plastic wading pool he scotch taped to the walls of the villa he shared with five other men sent over on the same mission. "Did you like the show, Sarah? You must have. I wanted you to see it, and when your ears stop ringing, Sarah, promise that you will think of me."

"I promise that I'm going to kick your ass all the way back to New Jersey, Kowalski," Carter said. "To the New Jersey Turnpike. To Exit 12, where you were born. How's that? Let's go, Sarah." His eyes were smiling as he punched Kowalski's shoulder, and Sarah could tell that he was in a good mood.

Carter's invitation to stop for a cappuccino at the Kilimanjaro seemed so casual and spur-of-the-moment that Sarah never suspected that it had been carefully planned and that Kowalski's graduation exercises were merely a pretext for this tête-à-tête over coffee. It was after five o'clock, no sense getting back to the office now, Carter had said, and besides, it would be pleasant to sit out in the courtyard under the rubber trees and talk and watch Madame Hulbert's neurotic monkeys.

There were few customers in the Kilimanjaro at this hour. Carter chose a small table in a spot midway between the sidewalk and the terrace of the café, and they talked aimlessly about books and movies and the way the video committee at the American Club ordered witless TV sitcoms instead of decent movies.

"Though I shouldn't complain," Sarah said, "I never have time to watch anything really."

"So I gather," Carter said, and smiled. "How was your trip up to Iyondo?"

"How did you hear about that?"

"I don't remember . . . Jacques must have told me. So? A Mongo funeral ceremony, was it interesting?"

"Yes. What I remember of it. Which isn't much. Masked dancers. Maï-Mati dancers. I'm afraid it wasn't my finest hour."

"What happened?"

"I got sick."

"Sick?"

"I drank the palm wine."

"My God."

"As I said, I didn't exactly cover myself with glory."

"And Boketsu. The minister, Jacques' buddy? He's an unusual person, terrific education. Georgetown Law School and all that. Always shown a lot of promise. What do you think of him?"

"We don't exactly get on."

"Boketsu? That's odd. I would have thought Boketsu would be all over you. He's got a reputation. Likes good-looking women. Especially blondes."

"I guess I'm not his type." Sarah removed the wilted hibiscus blossom, its edges now curled and outlined in deep purple, and laid it on the table.

"Well, anyway, how did he strike you? Everyone's curious about how he and Mobutu are getting on. Boketsu was up to his hips in trouble when he skipped out in '82. What would you say? Is he a happy camper?"

"I don't know. We didn't exactly talk politics. We didn't exactly talk, period, if you really want to know the truth. Everything I had to say seemed to irritate him. One way or the other." Sarah remembered the veranda and Liliane's dress. You look ridiculous, Boketsu had said, and Jacques' mouth had gone hard and mean.

Sarah sprinkled more cinnamon over her coffee. "A happy camper? I wouldn't exactly say that. He sounded pretty cynical to me. Sometimes. He made a sarcastic remark about the President's party, the MPR, standing for *Mort Pour Rien.*"

Carter's eyes registered a quick spark before he nonchalantly half turned from the table. "Christ, look at that monkey." One of Madame Hulbert's monkeys had one long arm looped over the bar of his cage and was gazing pensively at Sarah while he scratched his armpit. "If he had black hair and a red face, he'd look exactly like Kowalski."

Sarah laughed. "Leave poor Kowalski alone, Carter. He's adorable. Even Gussie Pearce thinks so."

"Gussie Pearce never met a man she didn't want to know— Biblical sense—and love. And I'm not going to leave Kowalski alone until he pays for scaring the hell out of me. I didn't wet my pants, but I added a few more of these out there on that platform this afternoon." He ran his hand through his voluminous shock of silver hair. "So, did the funeral celebration turn into a kind of pep rally for Boketsu?"

"He disappeared as soon as we came out of the elders' hut. Where I drank that witches' brew. I think Jacques was disappointed. I know he was. We didn't see him for the rest of the afternoon. No great loss as far as I'm concerned."

"Does Jacques know how you feel about his friend?"

"More or less. I can be pretty obvious. On the other hand, I realize that with Jacques there are two sacred territories. No criticism or complaints tolerated. I know that and pull back because whatever I say would only hurt him. Boketsu—Bika is one of them."

"And the other?"

"Zaïre. I always thought that I was a pretty ardent flag-waver until I met Jacques. But he makes my feelings for America seem tepid in comparison. He gripes and grumbles about things here, but I can sense that he wouldn't put up with hearing the same remarks from an outsider like me. Anyway, why would I complain? I have a wonderful life here in this flat-out beautiful country with the man I . . . Well, anyway, it can be discouraging. I'm not making any more progress with my linkage program. Everything seems to be unraveling on me. Just as Phil Olmstead said it would. It's getting me down. But Jacques is the most idealistic person I've ever met. He has such faith in these people, Carter, you'd never believe it. "

"Well, for Jacques, this country is home. It's all he knows."

"It's all he wants to know."

"And yet, the fact is that Jacques, whether he likes it or not, is an outsider here, too. And will always be an outsider because he's white. He can never change that. He'll always be Belgian, never Zaïrian."

"Well, I don't see how anyone could be closer to the people than Jacques. Bika is in and out of the house all the time. Less since I've been around, I guess. They flock to Jacques."

"They know Jacques respects them. And their culture."

"He certainly has plenty of friends."

"In these countries, that can be a problem sometimes. If your good friends happen to be on the wrong side when the shooting starts."

"Anyway, he loves this place. This country. Up in the bush he was beside himself. I don't think I've ever seen anyone so happy. It made me jealous. It's a funny feeling, being jealous of a country." Her eyes swept around the small world of the courtyard, the metal tables with flaking green paint, the enormous rubber trees, drooping, pendulous, the sulfurous white sky, cloudless and still, the air fragrant with wood smoke. "Carter? A girl up there at the village slipped up behind me and cut off a piece of my hair, and Jacques got very uptight about it. He took it away from her. He forced her hand open and took the hair. Why would he do that?"

"Oh, to keep the girl from giving it to a *féticheur*, I suspect. Jacques doesn't want anyone putting a spell on you. Except himself, of course. So, otherwise, it was a quiet weekend, then? Just the four of you? No visitors?"

"Visitors? Yeah, as a matter of fact. Three men. Bika said that they worked on the plantation."

"Did they stay very long? The three men, I mean."

"They were there for lunch. I remember Jacques trying to speak Mongo with them. Later, he said that they didn't speak Mongo, and he thought that was odd."

Slowly, Sarah put down her coffee cup and for a moment seemed to be studying it. She picked up a pack of cigarettes from the table and shook one out. Carter struck a match and leaned forward with the light.

"We're not just having a cup of coffee, are we, Carter?" she said finally, searching his face. His long face was solemn, but in his eyes, Sarah caught that familiar seductive gleam, watching, waiting.

"No," he said. He held the match to her cigarette and waited. "Does that make a difference?"

"No, I suppose not." She smoked for a moment without saying anything. Then, she said, "But I do have some sacred territory of my own now."

"Jacques?"

"Yes. Jacques. Don't ever expect me to dig information out of him, Carter. Because I won't. I won't ever do that."

"I wouldn't expect you to. Jacques is a friend. I would always go to him if I needed certain information. Which he might or might not give to me."

The three monkeys started to squeal, biting and pulling each other's tails. Madame Hulbert, inside the café, slapped her fat hands against the counter and shouted, *"Sales bêtes! Arrêtez!"* The monkeys slunk off, each into a corner, and turned to stare at Madame Hulbert.

"For instance. This is the sort of thing I'd like to know. The kind of thing Jacques might not tell me. Maybe just because he doesn't want to think about it in these terms. What would you say, Sarah? Just from what you've seen. If Jacques had to choose between Mobutu and Bika? What would happen to his sacred territories then?"

"He would choose Bika."

"No hesitation. You sure about that?"

"Sure. He would support Bika."

"Well, he didn't in 1982. He stuck with Mobutu then."

Sarah shrugged. "All I know is, whenever I or anyone else criticizes Mobutu and the way he runs this country, Jacques either laughs or he agrees. He doesn't seem touchy as far as Mobutu is concerned." She stood up. "Let's go, Carter. The ambassador is giving a birthday party for his little girl, and he's asked me to help out."

"Oh, Sarah, *gently*, please! I wasn't invited."

"Well, I wasn't that lucky. Come on, I have to pick up some things at my office before I go home. Can you drop me off?"

Traffic had picked up on the Avenue des Aviateurs, and the embassy parking lot was almost empty. On the corner, close to Carter's car and driver, a woman crouched in the sand and roasted ears of corn over a fire, which hissed and threw up thick spirals of smoke as she dipped her fingers in a bowl of coral red palm oil and flicked drops of oil over the corn.

While Carter held the door for her, Sarah slid into the back seat and smoothed her narrow skirt around her legs. "Carter?

Those questions about Bika. They don't have anything to do with Jacques, do they? I mean, what Bika does or does not do won't affect Jacques, will it?"

"No," Carter said. "Why should it?"

26

It was the first time that Guichard had ever set up a dummy bank in a foreign country. He had fudged the details a little when the job in Gabon came up, and being very senior to the staff lawyer who had been working on the project for six months, Guichard got the nod. He remembered with fondness the sea breezes at Le Relais, the European style hotel where he liked to stay, the raffish hedonism of the nightlife, and La Toulousaine restaurant just off the main boulevard, which served a cassoulet he could never resist even though he always had a *crise de foie* afterwards. He had therefore pressed a little to get the assignment so that he could make this sentimental journey back to Libreville and its lazy tropical pleasures before taking a flight to Geneva, where he was to meet with Boketsu Bika.

Setting up a dummy bank had been almost as easy as Guichard had persuaded himself that it would be. Fortunately, in the interval since Petro-France had sent him to Gabon for six years in the seventies, Guichard had maintained contact with the government types who flowed in and out of President Omar Bongo's various governments. He knew what he had to know about the various tribes and their political weight and had never, *ever*, referred to pygmies in Omar Bongo's presence or made jokes about the president's high-heeled shoes.

The work itself had gone smoothly—Guichard was well known in the company for getting things to "run on wheels"—he had put a deposit down on three ministers who did all the necessary paper work, including registering the name of the bank: *Banque d'Union Commerciale*. Guichard thought that the name had a definite ring to it, and even the acronym, B.U.C., had, well, a certain *je ne sais quoi*.

The sole purpose of the bank was to receive funds from Petro-France operations in the Congo and Zaïre and to funnel these funds to France to maintain Petro-France's political interests there. One of said interests would eventually be taking his pants off every night in the Elysée Palace.

Shortly before midnight, Boketsu Bika stepped inside the cabin of the vedette motorboat that he had hired to take him across the river to Brazzaville. In a small bag he carried a dark blue business suit that he planned to change into as soon as the boat left the dock. He would have ten to fifteen minutes, depending on the level of the water, to get out of his *abacos* and into the suit so that he would not stand out as a Zaïrian when he checked into the hotel and the airport. Outside, he heard shouts, a scuffle, and a woman's drunken curses. The one-armed young man who had reserved the boat for him opened the door to the cabin. "*S'il vous plaît, patron*. This woman says she paid the captain. A lot of money she says. Just to get to Brazza tonight." The woman slithered down the narrow steps in a clatter of high heels and, grinning, stood watching him.

Boketsu felt the blood drain out of his face. If he refused to allow the woman to cross with him, she could make plenty of noise and people would ask questions. Ordinary people would remember seeing him. The one-armed young man would recall Boketsu's generous tip. Too generous.

The woman was clearly a prostitute and definitely very drunk.

"Okay. *Ça va*," he said quietly.

From the windows of the Citicorp office in Geneva Guichard had a fine view of the lake, where anchored sailboats bobbed in the water and two young couples in down jackets and scarves chased each other round and round in pedal-boats. The cold autumn wind kicked up white caps across the water, and the leaves of the plane trees along the lake had already turned and were falling into dispirited heaps of blotchy brown and yellow.

Guichard sat strumming his fingers impatiently on the polished mahogany conference table. Boketsu was late. Forty-seven minutes late, to be exact. Guichard straightened the portfolio of papers on the table and took out his agenda book and wrote "*Hermès pour Claire!*" and drew heavy bars around the note. He added another exclamation point. An Hermès scarf, Guichard believed, was the traveling executive's best defense against a guilty conscience over a bit of dalliance in the course of a business trip. Much better than perfume. Classier.

Guichard took a deep breath and sighed. The tranquility of a Swiss bank, he thought, impossible to find its equal anywhere. The discretion of the whole process, exquisite! The way you were met personally and led through corridors and conference rooms without seeing anyone. And, more to the point, without being seen. Privacy. Discretion. The Swiss might not know a damned thing about making wine, but they did know exactly when a man needed privacy most: when he had to talk money. The old *notaires* of France knew that, and the offices of the good ones still had double doors, both doors thickly padded on all sides and covered in leather with heavy brass studs. Guichard would no more think of doing his financial business with a *notaire* in one of those modern buildings with a single, thin door where anyone sitting in the waiting room could overhear every word being said in the *notaire's* office than he would think of wearing an American tee shirt on the beach at Deauville. Privacy. Who could do business without it? The young *notaires* in France, regrettably, were losing that insight into the human heart.

While Guichard sat reflecting on the serene satisfactions of dealing with Swiss banks, Boketsu Bika was still trying to shake the tail that had started following him as soon as he hailed a taxi at the Holiday Inn near the airport. He was not altogether surprised. The prostitute on the vedette had turned out to be not so drunk after all, unwrapping her *pagne* and inviting him to take off her black lace panties, which, he noticed, with growing apprehension, were expensive and probably French, not the sort of cheap underwear sold at local markets. When he declined her invitation, she abused him obscenely, like the loud, aggressive whores in Nigeria, calling him names. As the vedette docked at the beach in Brazzaville, she spat to one side, and said, "You can do something besides pee with that thing, you know."

So when the gray Volvo pulled away from the hotel and fell in behind his taxi, Boketsu was ready. He asked the driver to drop him off at Le Grand Passage, a large department store on the rue du Rhône. He paid the driver, surreptitiously noted the gray Volvo hanging a few cars back in the traffic, and walked, without haste, through the revolving doors of the department store. Once inside, he headed immediately at a brisk pace for an exit on the other side of the store, out onto the rue de Marseilles, and into the W.C. of La Petite Chaumière, a corner café. He stayed in the W.C. for over twenty minutes, ignoring the knocks and rattling of the door. From La Petite Chaumière he crossed another street and went into a newspaper shop from which he could observe the people and cars passing along two streets. He bought the *International Herald Tribune, Le Monde,* and a pack of John Player cigarettes. After a half hour of appearing to browse through magazines, Boketsu left by a side door and climbed steep sidewalks to the old part of the city where he wandered around in a crowd of housewives at an open market before descending the narrow steps leading down to the boulevards around the lake.

When Boketsu entered the Citicorp building on the Quai Général-Guisan, he was clean: there was no sign of the gray Volvo anywhere.

There was something about the way Boketsu walked into the room that immediately irritated Guichard. Something about his long stride that ate up the distance between the door and the table in not more than four or five big steps. And his gait, shoulders back, his body relaxed and settled into the swing of his hips. Most unusual, Guichard thought, for a none-too-tall, portly man. He strolled in, no apologies for being over an hour late, hurried through a handshake, avoiding eye contact with Guichard, briskly pulled out a chair and sat down.

Boketsu was dressed in a smart blue European suit with a red silk tie. Smart, but not Savile Row, and very little jewelry, only a gold link bracelet. A good one, probably 18 carat. No diamond rings. No Rolex oyster watch. No ostrich leather shoes. Or briefcase. Not your ordinary, run-of-the-mill African politician, Guichard said to himself as he ticked through his inventory, then took his seat opposite Boketsu.

Guichard had prepared some fairly lofty and inspiring remarks about partnerships and common goals and the good of the people and the future of Zaïre, but Boketsu was already leaning back in his chair with his eyes on the portfolio of papers. Besides, their meeting, thanks to Boketsu, was already running behind schedule, and if Guichard wanted to hit the Hermès duty-free before the noon flight to Paris, they had better get down to business.

"Marceau has already gone over your ideas with me. Petro-France, however modestly, wants to share in your . . . ah . . . vision of the future of Zaïre. What we have to do now is iron out some specifics and, of course, get some signatures from you for your account," Guichard said, opening the portfolio and separating the documents into three stacks. "I need more detail about the operation itself, the men you are going to use, your suppliers and their reliability. That kind of thing. As well as your timetable. Your ETA, as we say." Guichard took a deep breath and smoothed back his hair. "Your estimated time of arrival. Things mustn't drag. As I assume you realize."

Almost mechanically, as if Guichard had punched the correct button, Boketsu began citing figures for men, equipment, provenance of hardware, the schedule for taking over the radio and television stations, closing the airport, all of which key positions were, according to Boketsu, already penetrated by his partisans. He lolled, rather lazily it seemed to Guichard, in the spacious chair, his head tossed back a little as he spoke. His French was excellent, and his *tournures de phrases* were surprisingly elegant and slightly pedantic. Guichard could not bear to hear patent foreigners speak French effortlessly like that, as if it were their native language. Especially Africans—and Americans. It enraged him to hear Americans speak fluent French with a proper accent. Once Claire had dragged him to see an American movie dubbed into French, and he had spent two hours listening to Burt Reynolds speak impeccable French. Burt Reynolds! It was unbearable.

Guichard pushed a sheaf of papers across the table to Boketsu. It would be premature to bring up Cabinda at this point. The best approach would be a meeting with Delpech, who would be quicker to understand the logistics of the situation and could then get it across to Boketsu.

"I notice you didn't mention costs or money, Monsieur Boketsu. Ah, *pardon*, Citoyen Boketsu, I believe it is. But I imagine you won't be unhappy to discover that we've set up an account for you with five million dollars in it." Guichard chuckled. "Our little joke."

"Five million dollars? Is that all? I can't pull off an operation with a piddling five million dollars! It's ridiculous!"

Boketsu sat forward and put both hands on the table. He did not look at or touch the papers that Guichard had pushed in front of him.

"We realize that, *cher Monsieur.* We are well aware of that. But we can't very well toss fifteen or twenty million dollars straightway into your pocket, can we? Mmm?"

"Why not? Fifteen or twenty million is what it's going to take. To do the job. To make it a success."

"Why not? Why, because, *cher Monsieur*, there are too many paradise islands around this fair world where one can go and live quite nicely on twenty million without ever having to bother with the dirty, no doubt stressful business of pulling off a successful coup. You'll get your millions. But not today. Not right now."

"Then, what the hell am I supposed to do? Send you a bill for a thousand South African mercenaries?"

"Something like that. You send us a request, as the arrangements, as it were, proceed, and we make the necessary deposits into your account."

"Did your wisemen ever stop to think that I can't just pick up a phone and say, Hey, send me another million for some ground to air missiles. Someone else interested in the 'future of Zaïre' might be listening in? Ever think of that?"

"Of course," Guichard said, leafing through the papers and pulling out three pages that were stapled together. "Communicate with us by all means. Using the codes we've worked out." Actually, Guichard loved codes and secrets and had compiled the three pages of code names and places and materials himself. He had struggled to find a suitable code name for President Mobutu and had finally hit upon Monsieur François Hyun, the name of an obscure French military painter whose major achievement was a series of snowy visions of Napoleon's retreat from Moscow. Of course, the code name was a bit of arcane trivia that no one would appreciate except Guichard. Which, to Guichard, made it all the more delectable. He handed the pages to Boketsu. "For example, when you need another installment, you wire us something like this: 'I have not yet received my copy of *Le Monde* and would appreciate receiving it by such and such a date, at the latest . . .'"

"I don't read that rag," Boketsu said. "I don't trust the French press."

"Ah, *dans ce cas-là.*" Guichard was shocked, speechless. In the company they were in the habit of joking that Gabon was Petro-France's *chasse gardée* and the Congo their *plantation.* Boketsu didn't talk as if he were going to become another of their genial plantation hands. Guichard thanked his lucky stars that he had been smart enough to sign up Delpech, a European, someone on his own level with whom he could deal without unpleasant surprises that made his ulcer kick up. Africans could be impossibly arrogant, capricious. Unreliable, in a word.

They sat in silence for a moment. Boketsu stared moodily out the window at the lake.

"I'll say I am expecting the arrival of my niece on such and such a date," Boketsu said finally, a faint, lopsided smile twisting his face.

"Your niece?"

"Yes. And when you've deposited the money, you wire me that my niece will be arriving. You specify the time."

"*Très bien,*" Guichard said. He was miffed. He had worked hard on the codes and found them perfectly ingenious. When Boketsu took the time to look at the list, he was sure to agree. "Then we can get started by having you sign these forms for the bank."

Boketsu removed a pen from his inside coat pocket and signed. No Mont Blanc fountain pen, Guichard noted. Boketsu passed the form back across the table.

"The same form. They want it in triplicate," Guichard said, handing Boketsu more papers.

When Boketsu had finished signing the forms, Guichard collected them and tamped them together into straight-edged stacks.

"And now all we have to do is add my signature," Guichard said.

"Your signature?"

"Yes. Of course," Guichard said, raising his eyebrows in surprise and staring over the top of his reading glasses. "*My* signature. As joint tenant of the account." Guichard lowered his voice to a whisper. "So that I can get to my paradise island before you get to yours."

Boketsu was coldly searching his face.

"My little joke," Guichard said, bending over to add his signature below Boketsu's.

Boketsu had drawn back from the table and sat staring at the papers as Guichard signed them and meticulously set them aside, one by one. When he had finished, Boketsu sprang from his chair and extended his hand.

"That's done, then," Boketsu said, looking somewhere to the left of Guichard's right shoulder. "We'll be in touch."

With that, he turned, gathered up his briefcase, his newspapers, which included, as Guichard observed, *Le Monde,* and strode across the room.

"Here. You're forgetting the code names." Guichard held out the papers, which Boketsu took without a word, slapping them inside the folded newspapers.

Guichard stared after him. No *politesse*. Nothing. A merest handshake. And that insolent saunter.

Suddenly, it occurred to Guichard why Boketsu's walk galled him so much: Boketsu swaggered exactly like a Texas oilman.

27

Jacques thought that he would never get used to sleeping with her. To begin with, Sarah was a sprawler: in the middle of sleep she would fling out an arm, swat, right across his chest or throat or face, or a long leg would suddenly swing over his hip as he stealthily prepared to roll over away from her. Her arms and legs seemed to anticipate his every move, and if he inched away from her as far as he could go without falling off the bed, she pursued, little by little, until finally arms and legs enfolded him in a loose, amorous embrace and her curly head burrowed into him. In the mornings she sprang out of sleep like a child, clear-eyed and happy, her breath when she kissed him as sweet and minty as a cold summer drink. Then, finally, after a month or so of waking up to stiff necks and unexpected sensitive spots on his face and body, of interrupted sleep and hours of lying still in the darkness, smoking a solitary cigarette, listening to the tranquil rhythm of her breathing, he found that he could no longer sleep without her and the tender, entangling warmth of her naked limbs.

In December when he had to make a trip to Brussels to meet with Janine's lawyers and to celebrate Saint Nicholas Day with Suzanne, he thought the loneliness of the hotel bed would drive him mad. He paced the floor of the dimly lit room, smoked, had another whisky, worked out a dozen financial scenarios on his calculator, and finally sat morosely in front of the television and watched street vendors selling pieces of the Berlin Wall on CNN and protest riots in the capital of Romania.

In Kinshasa their domestic arrangements were haphazard. During the week, Jacques spent most nights at Sarah's apartment, and on the weekends they were together in the house on the river. Malu, Sarah's servant, developed a possessive streak, pointedly removing all evidence of Jacques' presence from the bathroom, carefully stowing his toilet articles and shaving gear in a cabinet as soon as Jacques left the apartment in the morning, and rearranging Sarah's things on the bathroom counter as they had been before—when Madame Sarah lived alone.

Under Sarah's care the beauty of old Albert Delpech's house on the river came alive again, the marble floors polished to a gleaming finish, the dramatic flowers of the tropics—birds of paradise, orchids, poinsettia, plumbago, Angel's trumpets—in sparkling crystal vases, and the kitchen clean, orderly and well stocked with supplies. Sarah could not imagine a life filled with more tranquility and beauty. The house servants kept their white uniforms immaculate and stiffly starched, and Dieudonné gave up his hashish in favor of the Dunhill cigarettes in malachite cigarette boxes scattered around the house.

Dieudonné was happy again. A Madame in the house! In the mornings Sarah, wearing a long robe, fresh from her morning shower, her hair still wet and clinging to her head, would come out to join Jacques on the terrace overlooking the river, and Dieudonné would hold her chair back, beaming as she took her seat. For a moment, he would stand watching the two of them, a silly grin on his face as if he had just that moment stumbled upon a great secret. As a boy, before he left his village for the city, Dieudonné's front teeth had been filed down to sharp points so that when he smiled, he looked like a euphoric vampire, eager to get on with his feeding. After serving them breakfast, he would excuse himself and let Alphonse take his place. Later, they would hear him in the far-off living room, playing his Simon and Garfunkel tape and humming and singing to *99 Miles from L.A.* as he mopped the marble floors. The only word he could understand well enough to repeat was "L.A.," which he sang out loudly at brisk intervals, like an ecstatic holy roller shouting "Amen!"

In October the rains had come back, and in the night Jacques would waken to the drumming on the roof and the roar of water in the rain ditches and the smell of wet earth, and his heart would lift as when he was a child. In the mornings the air would be pure and clean, expectant, waiting for the sun to release the heady fragrance of the garden.

Late one lazy Sunday afternoon, as Jacques and Sarah lay reading on lounge chairs on the terrace, the distended white clouds over the river swelled together and turned dark and the winds soughed despondently through the palm trees and tossed soft pink and white frangipani blossoms, like tiny Easter eggs, across the lawn. They closed their books and, with their toes, hunted under their chairs for their sandals. Down the river, near the rapids and the cliffs where Mobutu's residence overlooked the river, they could see an opaque gray wall of rain moving over the waters.

"Not yet. Don't go in," Jacques said, reaching out and taking her hand.

The wall of rain kept coming closer, picking up speed; the reeds along the shore rattled and cowered under the wind. Silently, they waited. To Jacques, the loud, lashing sound of the approaching rain was exciting, like the roar and crash of the rapids on the river. The rain seemed to have spotted them on the terrace; it suddenly turned slightly and raced toward them. On it came, faster and faster. Then, abruptly, the rain stopped at the edge of the terrace and pounded away, like a jogger running in place. They could feel the cool spray on their faces. Behind the wall of rain they could see nothing—the river, the reeds, the garden, rained into nothingness.

They stood together, holding hands, watching, ready to scurry into the house, should the rain come forward. Instead, after a pause, as if its curiosity had been satisfied, the wall of rain seemed to shrug and turn its back on them, veering rapidly across the river toward Brazzaville.

Sarah laughed in delighted surprise, and he laughed because she had. Many times before, he had seen rains in Africa behave in peculiar ways, but something about the wall of rain troubled him, and he gazed after it long after the banks of Brazzaville had disappeared from sight.

28

They had their first real argument over Jacques' trip to Angola. A few years before his death Albert Delpech had sold off a brewery and some beach property in Angola. After Independence and the turmoil of the civil war between MPLA and UNITA this sizable sum of money had been frozen by the government. Jacques had never made much of an effort to recuperate the money because he thought, vaguely, that one day, once the civil war ended and the socialist government was expelled, he might be able to start up a profitable business in Luanda, the capital city. Now with the divorce settlement and zooming inflation in Zaïre and the plummeting value of the local money, which complicated every financial step he took, he needed the money badly. In the past, he had never been able to make a contact on a level high enough in the government to get the money out. Then the Belgian firm that handled his legal matters hired a young lawyer, Paulo Pena, who not only spoke Portuguese but also had very reliable contacts in President Dos Santos' government. Pena had worked out a deal with the Angolan foreign minister who would free up Jacques' assets in dollars for a twenty-five percent cut. It was an expensive deal, but Jacques knew that he would never get a better one. And Pena assured him that the foreign minister would come through. "It's a done deal," Pena said.

Jacques had no idea that Sarah, with her round, guileless blue eyes and sweet manners, could be so stubborn. She was determined to go to Luanda with him.

"There's a civil war going on there, Sarah," he argued. "A fucking *civil war!*"

"Then *you* shouldn't be going."

"I have to go. You don't."

"Angola is not on the restricted travel list. If the U.S. government says it's safe, it must be."

Jacques knew better than to touch that one. "And there are all kinds of shortages. Angola's had a Marxist government for years. There's nothing in the stores, I mean, ordinary things like toothpaste and soap and toilet paper. The hotel might not have toilet paper, how would you like that? And the water will almost certainly be cut off for hours during the day and the electricity, too. Besides," he said wearily, "They sometimes fire on incoming aircraft."

"I don't care," she said, "If you go, I'm coming with you."

Then one day she came home with an Angolan visa in her passport, and Jacques shook his head and groaned, a *pro forma* groan because he had already started remembering the sleepless nights in the lonely hotel bed in Brussels.

In packing, he tried to anticipate everything that Sarah might need and might possibly forget, including a box of tampons, which Dieudonné scrutinized quizzically before slipping it into the corner of Jacques' bag. At Pena's suggestion he took along a case of beer and several cartons of cigarettes to use for tips and small expenses since most of the local people refused to accept Angolan money.

The ease with which the three of them passed through immigration formalities at the airport in Luanda buoyed Jacques' spirits and convinced him that Pena did indeed have excellent connections. They had to go through a metal detector frame before entering the terminal, and when Sarah's belt set off the machine, a soldier with the *de rigueur* black reflecting sunglasses grinned at Pena and waved them on. They waited for their luggage next to a worn old conveyor belt and watched stacks of automobile parts come off their flight: tires, batteries, an occasional windshield, and spare parts that Jacques could not identify creaked past, along with a few pieces of luggage, cases of shelf milk, tomato paste, shampoo, and Jacques' case of beer.

Pena had arranged for an Avis rental car, which he drove into the city, slowly skirting the cratered potholes resulting from fighting around the airport during an aborted coup in the seventies.

Alongside the road, naked children with rounded bellies and large staring eyes played in open sewers, rising from the filth to gaze at the white people in the car. Filthy streams oozed down to the road from a shantytown of lean-tos made out of cardboard and tin scraps and old, rusted and burnt-out derelict cars.

"Sarah? What's the matter?" Jacques said.

"It's appalling," Sarah said.

"Yes."

"Worse than Kinshasa. Ten thousand times worse than Kinshasa. No one could ever imagine this."

Pena kept his eyes on the road and said nothing.

"It will be better. Someday," Jacques said.

"You always say that," Sarah said.

"Because it takes time, Sarah. Democracies aren't like machines that you can plug in and push the start button."

"These senseless tribal wars all over the continent, isn't there just one leader in these countries who has some civic sense? Who wants to do something to help his miserable people? Give them just one or two of the basics. Like clean water and some food. Angola has been playing killing games for almost thirty years. Why isn't there some leader to stop it all? I'll never understand it. Never."

"Well, for one thing, there's a lot at stake," Jacques said.

"You mean things like oil. And diamonds," Sarah said.

"I think she's got it," Pena said. "Welcome to Africa, Sarah."

As they neared Luanda, they passed in front of dirty white stucco shops, most of them empty and boarded up, with scabrous orange pockmarks of bullet holes scattered over their facades.

They had rooms at the Hotel Presidente located near the middle of the great horseshoe esplanade overlooking the port and the immense white sand beach across the bay. Handsome baroque colonial buildings built by the Portuguese in the nineteenth century lined the broad avenue where ancient palm trees swayed patiently in the soft sea breeze.

They unpacked, and while Pena went off to dinner with a distant Portuguese cousin, Jacques and Sarah ate shrimp scampi and noodles, the only item on the menu that night, and drank scotch and sodas with their meal. Afterwards they sat in the hotel bar and listened to a bossa nova tape of João Gilberto playing guitar and singing *Só Em Teus Braços* and *The Girl from Ipanema* over and over while four Cuban soldiers in dirty camouflage uniforms quarreled over a poker hand.

When, a little woozy with drink, Jacques and Sarah went upstairs to bed, the electricity shut down, suddenly plunging them into darkness and silence; they undressed by the light of the moon over the bay. They opened a bottle of tepid champagne that Dieudonné had shoved into Sarah's hands as she ran out of the house that morning, and stood on the balcony drinking from the bottle in the warm night air, surrounded by the moonlit darkness. All the lights in the quartier had gone down. But from the tiny balcony of their room, they could see the fires and kerosene lamps and hear the drums from the *cité*.

"I'm resisting telling you how beautiful this night is," Sarah said.

"Why?"

"Because you might find out that I've never in my life been this happy before," she said. "Happy simply because I'm here, with you. I do miss home, though."

By "home" she meant the house by the river, and the gentle harmony of the life they led there. She thought of the beauty of the back terrace where Jacques, after shedding his business suit and tie, would join her in shorts and tee shirt for drinks at sunset. His head in Sarah's lap, he would stretch out on the long rattan sofa, and they would talk quietly, and sometimes, as Sarah stroked his hair, he would fall asleep. For Sarah, he was the courtliest, gentlest man she had ever met. His quirky American tastes amused and delighted her. In the gathering darkness, he would listen to Nat King Cole songs by the hour, and when especially amorous, or tipsy, would sing "Blue Gardenias" with what he fancied was a Nat King Cole accent.

"Sing 'Blue Gardenias' for me," Sarah said. Someone had set a bonfire down on the beach, and the smell of kerosene swept across their balcony.

"I'm not that drunk."

"Then have another swig of warm champagne."

"All right. But come to bed."

"Don't forget. You promised to sing."

"Remind me," Jacques said.

After they made love, Sarah closed her eyes, flung out one arm, and, as usual, fell into a deep sleep, her left leg still coiled around Jacques' middle. Jacques lay awake, contentedly finishing his cigarette, when suddenly the ceiling of the room exploded with light as a searchlight from somewhere down along the beach beamed through the open French doors. A minute or two later a tank slowly clanged down the esplanade, its gun turret whirring and snapping as it rotated position. *Merde,* he thought, *merde alors.* He drew the sheet up over Sarah and held her tightly against him and waited.

He could hear the noise of the tank fading away, toward the *cité,* and then the street was quiet.

He lay rigid, struggling to stay awake, until, at last, sleep overtook him, and he drifted down into unrestful dreams in which Sarah called his name in a ragged sob before disappearing behind a curtain of rain.

29

"He's already made the transfer. Made it yesterday. I've just had confirmation from your bank in Zurich. So. It's a done deal. A piece of cake," Pena said. He was a man who spoke little but who took comfort from the catchy phrases and clichés that surrounded dicey business deals such as this one.

"He's expecting us in his office at one. Sarah had better come with us," Pena said. "As your secretary or mine. You choose."

Jacques had never stopped to think of what Sarah would be doing while he and Pena completed their business with the foreign minister. After last night and the tank rolling past the hotel, leaving her alone was out of the question. To be separated if fighting broke out was unthinkable.

"Mine, of course. You'd never be that lucky, Pena."

Pena laughed. "I know, *patron*, I know."

It was still the siesta hour, and all of the offices in the grandiose building were closed. Sarah's heels echoed along the long marble corridor.

"Oh. Important detail," Pena said, lowering his voice, "The minister has a bodyguard who never leaves him. Sticks to him like glue. A South African. A white chappy. Speaks no Portuguese, so he says, but who's he trying to fool? He's Irish. Jeremy Flanagan. So be careful about anything you say in English."

"A *South African*?" Sarah said.

"Yes," Pena said, shrugging his thin shoulders as if to say, There is always so much to explain in Africa. "*C'est l'Afrique.*"

The foreign minister was thumbing through a Mark Cross catalogue when the three of them were ushered into his office. He was a tall, robust man with light brown skin and pale gray eyes that had a puzzled, nearsighted look. Jeremy Flanagan sat far off to one side in a leather chair, his elbows resting on the arms, his fingers steepled over his stomach. The foreign minister came round from behind his desk, shook their hands, and welcomed them with courtly ducking bows and lingering handshakes. Jacques responded to the minister's courtesy in rudimentary phrases meant to suggest that he spoke some Portuguese but not enough to carry on a conversation. Which, to some extent, was true: his Portuguese was weak but entirely sufficient for the business at hand. He wanted Pena to handle the meeting.

Back behind his desk again the minister appeared reluctant to turn his attention to the portfolio of papers that he withdrew from his desk drawer. He carried on in Portuguese with a few generalities about their hotel, the weather, and the rains that had stopped the fighting in the south. "And the protests, the riots, the looting," he said, "The rains put an end to that. No one likes to protest and throw stones in the rain. Better than a firing squad, the rains."

Pena smiled politely, while Jacques and Sarah did not respond at all. Perhaps they had not understood.

The minister's chair squeaked as he tilted back in his chair.

Pena clicked open his briefcase and brought out a folder of documents, which would transfer the Delpech assets to the foreign minister. The foreign minister then produced his own set of documents, which needed Jacques' signature. The minister raised a finger, and without a word the South African bodyguard came forward to witness the signatures.

"Thank you for your hospitality, *Monsieur le Ministre*," Jacques said, shaking his hand.

Two uniformed soldiers in black sunglasses and white motorcycle helmets and heavy combat boots were leaning against the rented Peugeot that Pena had left a boy of about ten in a Michael Jackson tee shirt to guard. The boy sheepishly watched them approach, doodling in the dust with his big toe. Jacques put his arm around Sarah's waist and drew her tightly against his side.

"The President of the Republic of Angola wishes to speak with you before you leave the capital," one of the soldiers said, glancing nervously from Pena to Jacques, uncertain now as to which man was the object of the president's request.

"We will escort you," the other soldier said. "Follow us." They walked away toward their motorcycles, left in the shade of a large trailer truck with a flat tire.

"*M'sieur,*" the boy said, holding out his hand. Jacques gave him two packs of John Player cigarettes, and the boy clapped his hands and whooped and danced away toward his friends lying in the shade of an oleander hedge.

Pena looked at Jacques. "You could be in for another slice of the pie."

"It looks like it. What the fuck, it's only money. Then, we get the hell out of here."

With only a few minutes delay, they were ushered into the president's office, an enormous space with heavy, ornate gilt furniture and mirrors and deep green velvet draperies trimmed in gold.

President Dos Santos knew immediately which of the two men was Jacques Delpech. "Monsieur Delpech," he said, extending his hand first to Jacques, then to Pena, and, with only a slight, but clearly discernible, flicker of interest, to Sarah, who was again presented as Jacques' secretary. Three unidentified men who did not come forward to be introduced sat to one side in elaborate burgundy velvet chairs.

A handsome, fine-featured man with a complexion the color of toasted almonds, Dos Santos took it for granted that his visitors spoke Portuguese. He offered them cigarettes, and an aide brought in large glasses of whisky, with no ice, on a silver tray with small, snow-white beautifully embroidered napkins of fine linen. "Cheers," he said in English, lifting his glass.

"I wanted to meet you, Monsieur Delpech," he said finally, "Because you are a close friend of President Mobutu, I am told."

"Yes," Jacques said.

"As was your father."

"Yes, as was my father."

"Umm. Your father, I believe was more than a friend. An adviser, too. Especially during the early years."

"More of a friend, I would say. Though my father was apt to give anyone advice. Anyone who would listen."

Dos Santos laughed genially and took a healthy drink of the whisky. Jacques noticed that his nails were carefully manicured and polished with a clear gloss.

"Anyone who would listen," Dos Santos repeated. "Ah, very good."

Jacques could not tell whether Dos Santos was referring to the whisky or to what he had said about his father. He sipped his whisky and waited. He was suddenly, anxiously aware of Sarah, and of Sarah asleep in his arms, her leg around his waist, when the tank rolled by the hotel. He glanced at her. She was watching the president, her lovely face composed, absorbed in the situation.

"Well, a president needs friends. Friends who will advise, too, you see. Presidents need that, I can assure you, Monsieur Delpech."

He then embarked on a long-winded, digressive account of his youth, his rise to power, with frequent references to associates and friends and advisers, several of them Soviets, who had assisted him along the way. Jacques struggled to keep up, to follow the rambling narrative.

"So that is precisely why I wanted to meet you, once I learned that you and your associates were in the capital," Dos Santos said in what sounded like a summary statement. Jacques had a moment of panic, wondering exactly how much the president knew of the deal that had just been completed in his foreign minister's office. And if he knew, exactly what he would do about it.

"You know, I will say even more, Monsieur Delpech," Dos Santos began again after staring for a moment at the ceiling. "A good friend has the duty, the obligation, to advise his friend, the president. Otherwise, what kind of a friend is that, hein? No friend at all, if you want my opinion. And I will tell you how you can be of service to your president. How you can show him that you are his friend."

"How is that, *Monsieur le Président*?"

"I will tell you how. You are familiar with Cabinda? Of course. Anyone in this part of Africa knows what Cabinda means. Cabinda is the black pearl of Angola. The black pearl of oil. You understand? A precious jewel, the black pearl. No one throws precious jewels away. No one allows these precious jewels to be stolen right out from under his nose. Instead, what do you do? You fight to keep your black pearl. And that's the message I want you to take away today, Monsieur Delpech: Angola will fight to hang on to her precious black pearl."

"Which you think President Mobutu is trying to steal."

"Of course."

"Not the Congo?"

Dos Santos straightened his shoulders and took another drink. "That thought has not escaped me." He narrowed his eyes and studied his glass.

"Nonetheless," he said and paused again. "It is the president of Zaïre who has supported the rebellious FLEC-FAC for years now."

Dos Santos frowned, his elegant features crumpled into a harsh scowl, then he smiled and said, "It's quite simple. Your President Mobutu must not be greedy. He would be terribly mistaken if he thinks that Angola, that old crocodile, has no teeth. We are vulnerable, yes, very vulnerable, weakened by this civil war that never ends. But," he pointed his finger toward the ceiling, "this old crocodile has plenty of teeth left. The president of Zaïre needs to know that, Monsieur Delpech."

One of the three men sitting outside the circle coughed and excused himself in a whisper. Dos Santos' attention strayed to the civil war and his rival Savimbi's hold on the people in the rural parts of the country. He leaned back in his chair and warmed to his subject, ignoring Pena and Sarah, while addressing all his remarks to Jacques.

Time passed and still Dos Santos talked on, more and more animated about the civil war and Savimbi. Pena shuffled his feet to get Jacques' attention, then tapped his watch and with his head motioned toward the door.

"You see, Monsieur Delpech," Dos Santos said, leaning forward confidentially, "Savimbi is making a classic mistake. The bush does not represent government. The cities, the urban areas, they are the political power in Africa today."

"Interesting, very interesting," Jacques said, happy that his limited Portuguese meant that he was not expected to make profound comments. "And it has been a pleasure meeting you. As well as a great honor. But we mustn't keep you from your work. I shall bear in mind all that you have said today. Please be assured of that." He rose to his feet and held out his hand to the president.

"Oh, why should you rush away like this? Sit down. I'm enjoying our little chat."

"I'm afraid that we have to catch the flight to Kinshasa this evening."

"I know. I assumed that was what your friend was trying to remind you of," he laughed and looked over at Pena, who had also risen to his feet. "Oh, but sit! Sit! What's the hurry?"

"You're very kind. And generous with your time, *Monsieur le Président*," Jacques said.

"What time is your flight?" Dos Santos asked.

"Five o'clock."

"Ah, you're right. You're not going to make it. You need time to get to the airport." He turned to the men sitting near the wall. "João."

A tall, thin young man in a dark brown suit came forward.

"Let's see, it's Thursday evening. Sabena, isn't it?" Dos Santos said.

"Yes, Sabena," Jacques said.

"Sabena, João," Dos Santos said to the young man. Then, to Jacques, he said, "João will take care of everything. Sit down."

In a few minutes the man called João returned and nodded toward the president, who stood up to shake their hands. To Sarah he said, with an earnest, warm squeeze of her hand, "I hope you will carry away a beautiful memory of our country."

In the presidential Mercedes as the lead car, to which João had transferred their luggage, and with a motorcycle escort of six—three in front and three to the rear—they sped to the airport, sirens screeching and wailing. The limousine did not once slow its speed, no matter what appeared on the roadway. Whenever the convoy met another vehicle or a group of people walking along the highway, the outriders on motorcycles made a fist with their white leather gloves and motioned toward the sandy shoulder, swinging their white fists back and forth, out and downward from their sides. Drivers jounced clumsily off the road and waited, wide-eyed, sometimes stonily resentful, particularly if they were white, until the ear-splitting convoy raced past.

At the airport they veered off onto a narrow dirt track that led to a gate opening onto the tarmac. Once on the tarmac the motorcycle escort slowed, turned, and circled back, sirens still shrilling, leaving the two black Mercedes alone to cruise up to the nose of the plane.

Even before they got out of the limousine, Jacques could see that the doors of the DC-10 were closed and that the plane was ready to taxi to the runway. The ground supervisor for Sabena, a middle-aged Belgian whom Jacques had met once or twice when the man managed cargo loading at the airport in Kinshasa, was intercepted by João and the two other men in the rear car, when he came running, his arms waving, out of the airport. They talked for a while, the three Angolans crowding close to the Belgian.

Then, João broke away from the group. "Make yourself comfortable in the V.I.P. lounge," he said with a smile.

The lounge was full of shadows and deserted. A huge picture of President Dos Santos dangled crookedly over the empty bar.

Jacques stood at the dirty paned windows and watched the Sabena supervisor arguing with the Angolans and holding one hand over an ear, speaking on his walkie talkie to the DC-10.

"They're not going to open the door," Jacques said. "Costs too much. If they open those doors for us, they'd have to refuel before taking off. They'd be out of their minds to do it." He could see the Belgian pilot in the cockpit looking down at the men wrangling on the tarmac.

Suddenly, the Sabena man threw open the door to the lounge. While he caught his breath, he nervously pushed his glasses back on his nose, which dripped with perspiration.

"Can you help us out?" he said in French, panting, his chest heaving. "Look, we just can't do it. We can't open those fucking doors. To put up the stairs, we have to shut down the engines. Then start them up again. We do that, and there goes our fucking payload. Come on, you gotta understand."

"We need to get back to Kinshasa tonight," Jacques said, feeling obliged to hold out a while as some sort of polite gesture to Dos Santos.

"I'll get you back. Don't worry. I'll get you back there. Can I tell the president's guys that you agree? Help us out on this."

"There's no other plane out tonight."

"I'll find you one. Chevron has a Learjet prepped to depart for Kinshasa sometime this evening. You'll be on it. Promise you that."

"All of us?"

"All of you. I know the Chevron guy myself. Nice American."

"*D'accord,*" Jacques said.

"Goddamn! Thanks! I'll call the tower to release." He ran toward the door. "Hey," he said from the half-opened door, "Do me another favor, will you?" He pushed his glasses back up. "Explain it to those goons out there."

30

"Sarah, Sarah, Sarah!" Phil Olmstead said, swinging his head dolefully from side to side. He was sitting slumped forward behind his shining, immaculate desk, where only a pen and pencil set commemorating his twenty-five years of service to USIA disturbed the bare surface. Behind him on six-foot staffs hung the flag of the United States on the right side and on the left the green, yellow, and red flag of Zaïre. On the wall directly behind Olmstead was placed a formal picture of President George Bush, his right eye squinting almost shut and the left corner of his mouth lifted, as if he were aiming a golf ball down a fairway.

Through the black strips of his hair, Olmstead's scalp gleamed, a rosy pink. "What in God's name could you have been thinking of?"

"Look, Phil, you're making a big fuss over nothing," Sarah said.

"*Nothing!* Do you call it nothing when an American diplomat, a member of the staff of an American embassy, is seen by a whole planeload of people stepping out of a presidential limousine? Oh, my God, I can't believe you did this to me . . . the limousine of the President of Angola! Well, let me tell you, Sarah, the ambassador is fit to be tied! I can't believe you did this to me."

"Did what? And who reported seeing me there?"

"Sarah, won't you ever understand that you live in a *village* down here? A village. Everyone knows everything. You can imagine how fast that little piece of gossip flew around town." He sighed and flicked at a speck of dust on the polished desktop. "The political officer saw you, if you really want to know."

"Bill Donovan?"

"No. The *real* political officer."

"Well, there was nothing to see. I was incognito. No one even knew that I was an American. I was introduced to President Dos Santos as . . . a . . . a secretary. He barely knew that I was there. He was interested in other things."

"*Sarah!* Barely knew that you were there! How naive do you think I am? Listen, Sarah, a girl with your looks, in Africa and a blonde to boot. What I mean is, that incognito stuff doesn't really apply as far as you're concerned."

"So. The ambassador's nose is out of joint. What exactly did the Peacock have to say?"

"*The Peacock!*" Olmstead shot to his feet, then aimlessly moved the pen and pencil set slightly, and sat down again. He looked furtively at the closed door.

"Sarah, sometimes you scare the hell out of me, you really do, you talk just like one of those pinko sixties radicals. Honest to God. *The Peacock!* Where's your respect? You are referring to the personal representative of the President of the United States." He hiked his head backward toward the picture of George Bush hanging on the wall, still optimistically sighting his golf ball. "We all gotta remember, the ambassador is going through some pretty tough times these days. He's bound to be touchy. It's rough being a single parent, knowing that everybody on post has heard the story of how your wife ran off with a sous-chef at the Hilton in Greece. A sous-chef, can you believe it? Oh, she was a big eater, that Mrs. Peacock. Still, you don't run out on your husband and kid for somebody else's chocolate mousse, for God's sake!"

Olmstead fell silent, a musing calm settling over his face. He placed his clasped hands on the desk. Sarah sat studying the forest green carpet at her feet. She had a heavy load of work to clear up before leaving for the day, and she had promised Dieudonné that she would go by the medical unit to have blood drawn for his ten-year-old twin daughters suffering from sickle-cell anemia.

"Listen, Sarah, I don't like hauling you over the coals like this, believe me, it's not my style, and I admire your work here, I really do, God, every single one of the foreign nationals working here thinks that you walk on water. One of these mornings I expect to come in to the Center and find that they've canonized you over the weekend. Put up one of those little saint statues in the foyer where people will come by and drop their pennies in there and make a wish or something like that. They worship you already, these Zaïrians. And you deserve it, let me be the first to say that. You're a hard worker, and you know how to get results. I admire that, Sarah, I really do."

Olmstead lowered his voice and again placed his clasped hands before him. "So, let's talk seriously, Sarah, because you ought to know that with your background and your looks . . . just a minute, scratch that, forget I ever said that, Sarah . . . what I mean is, Sarah, we're looking at a great career for you farther down the line, you've got a tremendous future, and I know what I'm talking about. You hear what I'm saying? If you just toe the line, and follow my advice. Will you do that, Sarah? Will you listen to what I have to say?"

"Sure, Phil, sure. You know I will."

Olmstead gazed at her for a moment, then leaned forward over his desk. "I've said it to you before, and I'm going to say it again, Sarah. Because you have no idea, absolutely no idea, how your career could take off if you follow this one little piece of advice."

"What's that?"

"Learn to play bridge!" he whispered dramatically.

"Phil? Bridge? When do I—"

"Find the time, find the time, that's what I say. Make the time. All right, you're going to say, hey, what the hell, give me some specifics, Phil, on how this is going to change my future. Well, hold on, I've got a pretty terrific specific right here. You know the congressional delegation due in here next week? Well, guess who is going to be their escort officer, hmm? Guess who is going to fly out to Lubumbashi with them in the embassy plane, hmm? Guess who is going to spend five days and four nights holding their hands and making sure that they go away happy? Well, you're looking at guess who, Sarah." Olmstead jerked a thick thumb toward his chest. "And you wanna know why the ambassador picked your boss to escort these VIPs. Simple. The ambassador's smart. Because I play bridge, that's why! They needed a fourth. And *voilà!* Philip Winslow Olmstead at your service."

Sarah laughed. "And is this congressional delegation going to give you a medal because you make up a fourth, Phil?"

"Maybe not a medal, but an ambassadorship someday maybe. Hey, listen, it could happen. That's the way the system works. One of these Capitol Hill types gets to know you, remembers your name, remembers that he made a seven no-trump hand when you were his partner out there at the consul's house in Lubumbashi. It's happened, listen. I knew a guy, name of Joe Watkins, great bridge player, got to know a senator from Nebraska on one of these swings, played bridge with him, and five years later ended up as ambassador to the Bahamas. Not a bad post, the Bahamas. Kinshasa with a seashore."

"So that's how the system works. I don't know, when I was in Washington, I figured out that promotions must come from the cesspool system," Sarah said.

"The cesspool system?"

"Yeah," Sarah said, bending toward him, "The cesspool system: all the shit rises to the top."

"*Sarah!*" Olmstead said, his face stricken, "For God's sake! The cesspool system." And then his shoulders started to shake and his hands shuffled on the immaculate desktop. "The cesspool system. Patty and I could name a few of those!" He began to laugh, rumbling and snorting and snuffling like a pig in a turnip patch. "*The cesspool system,* wait until I tell Patty. Sarah, you crack me up, you really do. So classy Park Avenue blond with those innocent blue eyes, and then you say something like that . . . Cracks me up!" He snorted and snuffled again, back to the turnip patch, took off his glasses and wiped his eyes.

"Oh, my, my, my," he wheezed, putting his handkerchief into his pocket. "Okay, Miss Laforge, I know you're going to say that your boss has gone soft in the head, but I'm going to make it all right with the ambassador for you. Okay? And I'm going to throw you a plum that just might spark your own career. Listen, the congressmen's wives, I want you to look after the wives, it's getting near Christmas and they'll want to do their Christmas shopping while they're here. Some of the congressmen may want to pick up a few gifts for their girlfriends. So I want you to bring some of the best ivory vendors from the *cité* to the InterCon, discreetly, don't bring a pack of them in at one time, so that the wives can make their purchases. Ask Gussie Pearce, she knows the best ivory workmen in the *cité*. She'll be glad to line them up for you."

"Ivory? Phil, nobody can take ivory into the United States any more. It's illegal, in case you haven't heard. Against the law."

"Sarah. Pay attention. You didn't hear what I said. These are *congressmen!* Okay? Do I have to draw you a picture? So, make sure the ladies see some nice stuff. Okay?"

"Okay," Sarah said, getting to her feet. "I'll do what I can."

"Good girl!" Olmstead said. It was true. He did have a soft spot for Sarah, there was no doubt about it. As a matter of fact, because of Sarah, he was beginning to change his mind about the job Stéphane at the InterCon was doing with Patty's hair, which had always been such a source of pride to him. Lately, looking at Sarah's short, burnished curls, the kind of hair that a man could run his hands through without worrying about a thing, had started him thinking. Patty's hair, well, it was different, it was always, careful, don't touch my hair with that thing, or get Pierre to close the French doors, my hair is beginning to droop, or don't get too close, I've just had my hair done. Patty's hair had become something more like a fragile family heirloom that required constant care and protection, an anxiously guarded, delicate piece that might tip over on its nose and smash.

"I'll see you Monday, Phil," Sarah said, turning from the door. "Have a nice weekend."

"You, too. And no more hobnobbing with African heads of state, you pinko sixties radical, you," Olmstead said, wagging his finger at her.

31

The American consul's residence in Kinshasa was so large that it occupied almost an entire floor of the Sozacom Building, a modest high-rise of fifteen stories with the usual undependable elevator service, on Avenue 30 Juin, named for the Zaïrian independence day. As a single woman Gussie Pearce preferred the huge apartment on the main street downtown to a villa along the river or up in the chic quartiers of Djelo Binza, though there she would have been closer to the Cercle Hippique for her daily rides and, of course, to Josh Hamilton.

Gussie Pearce had just finished taking her bath when Sarah and Jacques' driver Louis arrived with flowers for Josh Hamilton's fortieth birthday party. She's giving Josh's party to spite me, Fiona told her friends, and Gussie told the same friends that she was giving the party because you never could tell what you were eating at the Hamiltons' any more: bird droppings or cat hair, it was all the same to Fiona's cook after all those years of living in a zoo.

Gussie announced that it was going to be the best damned party of the New Year, and everyone believed her because they knew Gussie's parties.

Sarah and Louis brought in bucket after bucket of flowers that Dieudonné had cut fresh from the garden after the heat of the day had passed. They placed the flowers on the long white tile counters of the kitchen while Gussie and a servant hunted for vases in the pantry, and Louis left to bring up another load of flowers.

"Is Fiona coming?" Sarah asked.

"Of course, she's coming, hon, you can't keep Fiona away from a good party. And this one's going to be good, and she knows it. Capricorn. Josh is a Capricorn. Do they have a special color, Capricorns?"

"Doesn't she mind? I mean, doesn't it bother her a little?"

"Mind what? Me and Josh?" Gussie's thin black eyebrows pushed her forehead into undulating furrows. "Why should she mind, hon? That'll be the day. When I was posted here nine years ago, Fiona Hamilton never got up off her back. She'd start to spread her legs if a man so much as smiled at her. So why should she mind, answer me that? Jerome, bring me that champagne bucket in the side cabinet."

Gussie tightened the sash of her robe and stuck a vase under the sink faucet. "You see, it's like this, Sarah: women in the tropics either do alcohol, or they do other women's husbands. Fiona does both. And that's a no-no. You gotta have limits, hon, you gotta know how far is too far. Thanks for the flowers. You'd better run along and get dressed. And don't wear blue because that's my color tonight."

"I don't know, Gussie, I think I'm coming down with something. We may not—"

"Oh, no, you don't. You can't sick-out on me tonight. You and Jacques stick too much to yourselves. You've got to get out and around more. Hon, we're a messy, foul-mouthed bunch, but we're all you've got. Face it."

It was a large, boisterous group, made noisier by the Elvis Presley and Jerry Lee Lewis CDs that Gussie's houseboy kept feeding into the player.

Despite the billowing drafts of night air from the open windows the women's faces had started to shine and coarsen with wine. Expatriate women with nowhere to go except round and round in a repetitive circle of clubs and living rooms seized any occasion, however casual, to display their trophy jewelry and costly clothes. Except for Sarah Laforge, who wore only a plain watch and a thin gold necklace with a tiny diamond, and Gussie herself, who favored large, chunky ethnic costume jewelry because she thought that it enhanced her high color and dramatic looks—which it did—the women around the table had taken advantage of this dressier than usual occasion. They sparkled like Christmas trees laden with gold and diamond baubles.

Doris Snead, her dark eyes wreathed in thick black eyeliner, held her diamond-encrusted fingers across the top of her low-cut dress and leaned across the table. "Did you see that ring Nicole is wearing?"

"Goddamn headlight," Sam Wofford said. "Marceau must have called in some points from his Lebanese friend Chehab."

"How many carats? What do you think, Sarah?" Doris said.

"I don't know," Sarah said.

"Ten. Must be ten. Gotta be ten. What do you think, Gussie?"

"I think she's already disappeared into my powder-room with Marceau. She's trying too hard. Sets a high standard for the rest of us girls."

Sam Wofford barked with laughter and squeezed Gussie to his side and gave her a loud, wet kiss.

"'Bout time you got back up to Geneva, hon," Gussie said, wiping her mouth.

"Just got back."

"Then you better troll the Avenue de la Justice before you go to bed tonight."

"Well, I wouldn't wear a diamond like that out on the streets," said a very thin, very young, and very pretty woman named Gabrielle, married to a fortyish Italian coffee exporter. The woman had a high, metallic voice, and she had spent most of the meal smoking Marlboro cigarettes and watching Jacques Delpech, seated down the table next to Fiona Hamilton. "The other night, there was this Belgian couple on their way to the Cercle de Kinshasa, and right in front of our house, at Thieves' Corner, when they stopped at the corner, two men attacked the car and stole all their money and jewelry, and when the woman's diamond ring wouldn't come off—her fingers had swollen with the heat—well, one of the men chewed off her finger and took the ring."

"Ugh," Gussie said.

"They should never have stopped at Thieves' Corner," Sam said. "Run the stop sign at Thieves' Corner, that's what you have to do."

"Good Lord," Doris said, "An African chewed off her finger. She could get AIDS. You know that? She could get AIDS. Joe? Joe, can you get AIDS if somebody chews off your finger?"

"What?" Joe said.

"If somebody chews your finger off, can you get AIDS from that? You can, can't you?"

"Jesus Christ, Doris. How should I know, I'm no fucking doctor."

"We saw it all from the balcony of our bedroom," Gabrielle said. "We can stand there every evening and watch them do it. One car after another. And our sentinel just sits there with his bow and arrow across his knees and watches. Never moves."

"Well, you can't count on a sentinel for anything," Doris said. "A sentinel's just the man who sleeps in the chair at your gate."

"So Dino went to the gate and told them to come into our house to radiophone their embassy. The woman's hand was a mess. Blood all over her dress. A two-piece Yves Saint-Laurent. Silk."

"Good lord," Doris Snead said. "She'll never get it out. Blood on silk. Forget about it. What color was it?"

"A kind of pinkish purple. Really pretty. With that new look short jacket. Fitted at the waist."

"What a shame. A two-piece Yves Saint-Laurent," Doris said. "Maybe she could save the jacket."

"But wear it with what?" Gabrielle said.

"Well, my houseboy Jerome can get stains out of anything," Gussie said.

"Not out of silk."

"Jerome soaks the stain with lemon juice, sprinkles it with salt, then puts it out in the sun. Works every time."

"Not silk. Silk would—" Doris leaned forward again and lowered her voice. "Here they come. Gussie, please for heaven's sake, stop that spooky little man from speaking English until he can learn to pronounce *th*. Tell him he can speak French all he likes."

"Oh," Sarah said, "He's trying. He's making a big effort to speak English."

"Well, all I know is, I am *not* going to sit here through dessert and listen to him go on and on about the *Turd World*. I've had enough of that for one night," Doris said. "Gussie, please, not with dessert."

"Well, we missed you," Gussie said to Nicole. "Having fun?"

Without answering, Nicole, looking sullen and out of sorts, resumed her seat next to Joe Snead and lit a cigarette. A between-courses lull, a stupor of the well-fed fell over the table. Joe Snead tried to explain the football pool at Americo to Guy Marceau, and everyone sat back lethargically and listened. Then Marceau began a long and complicated story about some boating accident that had recently taken place in France at the "mouse of the Seine."

"The *what?*" Doris Snead asked crankily.

"Ze mouse of ze Seine," Marceau said carefully.

"Is that somewhere in the *Turd World*, Guy?" Josh Hamilton said.

"The *mouse?*" Doris said, raising her voice harshly as if Marceau were hard of hearing. "You mean 'mouth'. Mouth of the Seine."

Marceau stared at her dumbly. Nicole gave a short, strangled laugh and inhaled deeply, blowing the smoke across the table toward Marceau.

"Hey, Marceau, you wanna know why Africans have sex on their brains?" Joe Snead asked, his large head sunk between his shoulders. "Ya' wanna know why?"

Marceau was watching Nicole. Snead ran his eyes around the table. On the tape a man sang *They Don't Make Jews like Jesus Anymore* with a nasal Texas twang.

"So. You wanna know why Africans have sex on their brains?"

No one said anything. Josh Hamilton shook his long blond hair back from his pocked forehead and yawned.

"Because they have pubic hair on their heads," Snead said, his round shoulders shaking with thin, snickering laughter. "That's a pretty good one," he said.

"Oh, *Joe*," his wife said.

Sarah tried to meet Jacques' eyes, but he was staring down at his plate, attending to his own thoughts. After all these years he's learned to tune out, Sarah thought, and I haven't. In her more charitable moments she could persuade herself that back in Europe or in the United States the people around this very table could be quite nice, ordinary folk with a decent set of values. But here, pampered, privileged, with servants to clean up their messes and ease the pain of hangovers, they all ended up Joe Sneads, in one way or another.

"Darling Gussie. Where's the champagne?" Josh Hamilton said, yawning again. He was wearing a navy linen blazer and a stark white shirt with a deep burgundy paisley silk ascot, which he arranged and rearranged nervously with twitchy, womanish gestures.

"She didn't say you were going to have champagne," Fiona said. Her head, heavy with drink, listed toward her shoulder, like a sleepy bird nodding on a perch.

"Well, I can't very well have a birthday without champagne, can I? Where is it, Gussie?"

"Go to the kitchen, birthday boy, and light a fire under Jerome. I'm exhausted," Gussie said.

The table came to life again when, preceded by Josh, Jerome wheeled in an enormous birthday cake with forty candles and a magnum of Dom Perignon. They rose to their feet, relieved to get out of the chairs where their limbs had stiffened since the dinner had begun two hours before, and, with revived enthusiasm for the party, toasted Josh's forty years.

"A little late, but Happy 1990, y'all," Gussie said, lifting her glass. "Make it a good one."

"Ah," said Joe Snead, draining his glass and smacking his plump lips. "I wonder what poor people are doing tonight?"

"Oh, *Joe*," his wife said.

"So you live at the house on the river with Jacques now?" Nicole said.

"I…well, I have my own place. My own apartment," Sarah said.

A moment before, Sarah had been standing alone with Jacques on the balcony. He had wrapped his arm around her shoulder, an index finger resting under her chin, and she leaned back against him, following the direction of his finger as he pointed out the house, her apartment, the embassy and all the familiar landmarks of their daytime world. Then he had gone off to the kitchen to ask for a glass of soda water for her.

"I know that," Nicole said with an impatient nod of her head. "Funny. Jacques never liked American women before."

Sarah said nothing. She had turned so that her own face was in darkness and Nicole's in the light from the living room.

"He always preferred European women. Particularly French women."

"And you? I gather you prefer French men," Sarah said.

"Not necessarily." She turned and stepped quickly into the living room, and Sarah saw her weave rapidly across the room until she intercepted Jacques on his way back to the balcony with her glass of water.

They left the party early and stopped at a beer garden in the *cité* to dance, to listen to the music, and to drink a few beers before going home to the house on the river.

"That woman Nicole," Sarah said finally, "What exactly is her problem?"

"Her problem?" Jacques asked, even though he already knew what Sarah was about to say.

"Her problem as far as you're concerned. She gives me the impression that she thinks I've muscled her out of her territory."

"I don't honestly know what she's dreamed up. I've known her, off and on, more or less well . . . depending. Over the years. Like every other man in that room tonight."

They were sitting side by side, very close together. Jacques reached out and stroked Sarah's bare shoulder. He suddenly felt worn out. He leaned his forehead wearily against her shoulder and let his arm fall loosely along the back of her chair. Something had gone wrong tonight, something that he could not put a name to, or isolate the moment, but it had to do with Marceau and Nicole. He could not figure out why Nicole, with an eye half-cocked, or so he thought, in Marceau's direction, had accosted him so provocatively in the living room. Why him, and not Wofford or Snead or Hamilton or Fratelli or any other man in the room that she had screwed for whatever reason since she had arrived in Kinshasa? There was a long list, and he would have placed himself somewhere near the bottom.

Jacques jerked his head up and dropped his cigarette. "Damn," he said, "I burned my finger."

"So. Is there anything special I ought to know?" Sarah said.

"About Nicole? Nothing except that she seems to have landed exactly what she's been looking for all these years in Africa. Marceau's the answer to her maidenly prayers."

"Then I won't worry," Sarah said. "Those two have nothing to do with us."

"Nothing at all."

"Want to dance? I can finish teaching you the Electric Slide."

The band, three young men with patched instruments, was playing Kinshasa music now. The air, soft and warm and ingratiating, smelled of the rain that would shortly begin. Jacques gazed at the three or four couples, standing facing each other, not quite touching, the movements of their hips subtle and controlled.

"Not tonight." He stood up and put a handful of bills on the table. "Come. Don't make me wait," he whispered, lifting her out of the chair.

32

Marceau thought that the goddamn ring with a diamond so goddamn big and bright that it would make a goddamn blind man see would have put an end to his misery. He sat smoking on the terrace of the master bedroom. At the end of the rue des Mimosas a funeral wake for a black bwana had been going on for three days, and at two in the morning the live band had left and guests were dancing to Stevie Wonder tapes. *I just called to say I love you, I just called to say I care . . .* A dilapidated car farted past the house.

Marceau slid back the doors of the bedroom. "Nicole? You going to stay in that damned bathroom all night?"

There was no answer. He went back and sat down and propped his feet on the railing of the terrace.

"What is it?" Nicole said. She was wearing a white satin dressing gown and her dark, lank hair fell down her back. In the half-light of the terrace, her broad features looked harsh and masculine. "*Tu te fais du mauvais sang pour rien,*" she said and waited at the threshold of the door. "Why do you always have to make such a fuss?"

"Let's get back to the time I called you from Geneva. Sick as a dog, not knowing whether I was dead or alive, shaking so bad, I can barely make the call, but, by damn, I kick ass and get a call through to this house. This house, *tu entends?* I didn't pay a fortune for a cell phone for nothing. *Madame n'est pas là,* Gaston says. Now. *Mon petit ange,* why the goddamn hell would Gaston say you weren't at home if you were?"

"I have no idea. Besides, Gaston doesn't even remember that you called. You were feverish. You got confused." They had had this conversation so many times that she could have done it in her sleep. Sometimes she thought that she had.

"Okay." Marceau said. "The fact remains that for two days . . . two days, got that? . . . after I got back, lying up here in that bed raving with malaria, you are nowhere to be found. That's a fact."

"You didn't look for me. I told you. Jacques Delpech called me to hostess a small party with him, and then the power went down in the morning and Dieudonné refused to do the dinner. He's like that, Dieudonné. Temperamental."

She knew that he hated it when she showed how familiar she was with Delpech's household.

"So your ex-lover Delpech . . . ex-lover, got that? . . . cancels the party and takes you out for dinner, a pizza at Chez Nicolas. And then you go back to your own apartment for the night and the next night. Right? While I'm lying up here in that bed in there not knowing whether I'm dead or alive. Okay. So why doesn't Nicolas remember seeing you two ex-lovers in his restaurant that night? *I* would remember it if I saw you two lovey-doveys in *my* restaurant."

"Nicholas drinks too much of his own vino fino to remember who's been in his restaurant. Can we go to bed now?" She hesitated a moment before going back into the bedroom. Marceau was so zeroed in on Delpech that she felt certain that he would never find out where she had been while he was making his business trip to Paris. Which should have lasted four days and instead took barely two. When Sam Wofford invited her to come along with him and a man who said he was Adnan Khashoggi's brother-in-law on a deep-sea fishing trip to Mombassa, she was sure that she could get back before Marceau returned from Paris. Nicole had seen this man who claimed to be Khashoggi's brother-in-law several times in L'Atmosphere and had even danced with him one night, though later he had not remembered her. He was a not too unattractive Arab, a little too fat, too oily, but he had terrific jewelry and a private jet that would take them to Mombassa. She had jumped at Sam's invitation. She was bored. Life with Marceau was heavy. Marceau was heavy. Moreover, he was not the best lover she had ever had. He was too wet. He sweated copiously during lovemaking and slobbered into her mouth so that in the morning she woke up with foul breath as if she had been chewing stale cigarette butts all night long. It had not been a dream trip, though. The Arab had rubbed up against her a few times on the flight to Nairobi, but there he had picked up a sixteen-year-old Swedish blond with short hair and a flat chest who looked exactly like a boy with freckles and, after a late lunch the next day, Nicole had fellated an Englishman named Reggie who led safaris, in the cabin below while Sam and Khashoggi's so-called brother-in-law drank beer and talked business deals on deck and the blond Swedish girl who looked like a boy sunbathed in the nude. Marceau would never find out where she had been. He was so obsessed with Jacques that he never raised his head to look around and see what was really going on. So what if Marceau hated Jacques like a lunatic? No harm in that. Jacques looked so smug these days, mooning over his American girl, unable to keep his hands off her. The point was to keep a man like Marceau off guard. Keep him dangling. She could tell that a man like him, once he was entirely sure of his conquest, would get cocky. His eye would start to rove. And there were too many stray women on the loose in Africa who would give anything to step into her lucky shoes. Nicole slipped into bed and turned out the bedside lamp. In the dark, she rubbed an index finger over the splendid diamond on her left hand. She had worked too hard to get lazy now. Yes, the point was to keep Marceau walking the floor at night, wondering whether she loved him. A little? A lot? Not at all?

33

Mobutu was waiting for Jacques in the large reception room that opened out onto the terrace. The residence seemed unusually quiet. Off in the distance Jacques could hear women laughing. No one was on the terrace. Only a handful of people waited in the front antechambers when he came through the foyer.

They shook hands, and Mobutu sat down again at his accustomed place in a large armchair that faced the double doors of the room.

"Coffee, Jacques?" Mobutu asked.

"*Non, merci.*"

Mobutu looked tired and preoccupied. He had gained weight since Jacques had last seen him. He sat a little to one side in the large chair, leaning on the arm, one hand cradled in the other.

"Thank you for coming."

"I had planned to see you anyway. I hadn't realized that you were back from Gbadolite," Jacques said.

Mobutu brightened a little. "What's this I hear about your new *amour*? Hein? When are you going to bring her to see me? I have to give my approval, you know." A rueful grin spread fleetingly across his face.

There was a swift patter of knocks on the door and a pause, then the door opened and Mama Bobi Ladawa, the president's wife, came into the room, followed by Mobutu's official photographer, a slight, pale Belgian with dark horn-rimmed glasses named René Staline.

As his wife's heels tapped across the floor, Mobutu leaned back in his chair and lapsed into sullen silence. He had the look of his usual photograph in the world press: a stiff, dour expression, unsmiling, downturned lips, thick gray lips outlined in a deep grayish purple. The expression of an arrogant black man, Jacques thought, and that was the way Europe saw him, one of the many reasons they had no use for him. An uppity black man. Mobutu had never been a bullshit artist like Nyerere or Kaunda or Nkrumah who knew how to smile and posture for the white man. Mobutu rarely smiled in public, and certainly not for photographs.

Jacques stood up, and as he raised Mama Bobi's hand to his lips, she swayed a little on her high heels and murmured greetings, breaking into a dimpled smile. There was something eternally girlish about her, in her voice, her mannerisms, her surprisingly small, even teeth. She was much shorter than the president, for Mobutu was a tall man, and rotund and sturdy with that obligatory embonpoint of wealthy African women. Her color was golden brown—she had told him once that her grandfather, or was it her great-grandfather? was Italian—and she had slightly hippopotamus-like eyes whose swell she emphasized with pale pink iridescent eyeshadow. Mama Bobi Ladawa had been Mobutu's mistress for years before his first wife's death, had given him several children, and fully expected to become his legal wife after Mama Marie-Antoinette's death. Instead, Mobutu had dallied, and the marriage took place only when an official visit by the Pope was imminent. On the advice of a *féticheur* consulted before the marriage took place, Mobutu was to keep with him at all times for a full year, under the same roof, the identical twin of Mama Bobi. Jacques, who had been among the swarm of people accompanying them on their wedding trip, still associated tight rushes of embarrassment with the president's wife because he had so often on that trip mistaken her sister for the new bride. He had never been able to tell the two women apart.

She bent over slightly and said something in Ngbangi to her husband, who did not reply but stared gloomily at the floor. She smiled nervously and glanced first at Jacques and then at Staline, who was gazing out the French windows to the terrace, his back slightly turned to them. Staline had been King Baudouin's photographer and had first come to the Belgian Congo on a royal visit. When Mobutu took power, Staline materialized at his side and had never left it, traveling the world with him. Jacques assumed that at some point Staline must have been a Belgian plant in Mobutu's entourage. A discreet, self-effacing man who wore inexpensive polyester suits of ambiguous hues, Staline was the sort of man that you had to look closely to see, even in a small group.

Mama Bobi played with a gold bracelet on her wrist and waited. She was wearing a wax print with row after row of primitively drawn tiny fish in green and white. Her jewelry was less ostentatious than usual, three or four Cartier gold bracelets on her left arm, and a Cartier beaten-gold necklace with a cluster of diamonds at the center.

Mama Bobi traced a bracelet lightly with her dainty fingers; she smiled and spoke to her husband again. As far as Jacques could make out, it seemed to be a question of a photographic session that had been scheduled. Mobutu had not yet looked at her. Finally, he muttered something gruffly in his low raspy voice, and she smiled again, her tight apple cheeks arching away from her cupid's-bow mouth, nodded briefly to Jacques, and left the room with Staline.

Mobutu sighed and raised his gaze to the closed door.

"Do you see much of Boketsu Bika?" he asked suddenly and turned to face Jacques.

"Not as much lately," Jacques said. "My amour, as you say, there's been that," he said, attempting a light note, but Mobutu's face remained flat and grim. "Some traveling. A few days in Brussels in December. I went by the clinic to see your daughter, but she had already checked out." Four years before, one of Mobutu's daughters had combined alcohol and pills in a suicide attempt because of her marriage to a man many believed to be homosexual. She had lost consciousness while smoking a cigarette, had set fire to the bed, and had suffered extensive burns. She survived but had to have an arm amputated in the first of many operations.

"Thank you, Jacques. That was a great kindness." He fell silent again. "It never ends, these operations." After a long pause, he said, "Such a pretty girl."

"Yes. She was."

"It never ends. I will lose Nyiwa, too."

Nyiwa, Mobutu's oldest son by his first marriage, was rumored to be dying of AIDS. One Sunday afternoon, long ago, in the concrete circle in front of the terrace, Jacques had taught Nyiwa to ride a bicycle. The little boy, barely tall enough to reach the pedals, had fallen again and again, tearing the knees out of his nice trousers, and so intent on learning to ride that afterwards he could not imagine what had happened to his clothes.

"I've been in Angola, too. Briefly. On business."

Mobutu looked at him steadily but said nothing, waiting.

"President Dos Santos sent for me while I was there. That's what I was referring to when I mentioned that I had planned to come to see you. He wanted to talk about Cabinda. Basically, he believes that you are funding FLEC-FAC rebels with the intention of taking over Cabinda and Cabinda's oil. He sends a warning that Angola is not about to give up Cabinda. They will fight back with all they've got, the civil war notwithstanding."

Mobutu swung his gaze away from Jacques' face back to the floor. They sat together without speaking again for almost a half hour. Jacques was used to this African way; there was nothing uncomfortable in the silence. He and his father had spent many hours like this, in the dust under trees and on shaded verandahs, the talk dying away, and starting up again. He was relieved that Mobutu had said nothing about the trip to Equateur with Bika. He was certain that the *sûreté* would know about it, despite Bika's idea of slipping in and out of Ndolo unnoticed.

When Mobutu did speak again, he said, "*Intéressant*," articulating every syllable, then fell silent.

Finally, Mobutu said, "And that was it? That was what Dos Santos had to tell me? Sent for you to give you that message to me?" The two neighboring presidents hated each other.

"That was the message. The rest was extraneous talk about the war. Savimbi. That sort of thing."

"Ah, Savimbi. Dos Santos said nothing about the Congo?"

"He gave me the impression that he has discarded the idea that the Congo could be supplying FLEC-FAC."

Jacques thought that Mobutu murmured "So have I," but he could not be sure.

Mobutu scratched the back of his hand thoughtfully and studied the floor. Suddenly, he looked up and said, "Does Boketsu see much of the Petro-France man here in Kinshasa? The little man with the mustache?"

"No," Jacques said, instantly aware that he had been too quick with his answer. Mobutu cocked his head a little to one side and studied his face, and Jacques realized that Mobutu knew that he was lying. It was the first time that he had ever lied to him. He felt suddenly as if he had taken a careless step forward and a door had shut forever behind him. "Boketsu is not likely to see as much of Marceau as I do, for instance. I don't see Boketsu around much in the expatriate crowd. Where Marceau circulates."

Mobutu leaned back against the chair. His eyes had not left Jacques' face. "*Intéressant*," he said. "You see, Jacques, I am picking up the pieces of a puzzle and looking them over very carefully. Very carefully."

Jacques fingered a pack of cigarettes in his coat pocket. Since Mobutu did not smoke, no one ever smoked in his presence.

Abruptly, Mobutu jerked himself upright and slapped his right hand rapidly against the arm of his chair, a flat, angry sound disturbing the solemn silence of the huge room. "There it is. The missing piece of the puzzle, Jacques."

Slowly, moving his fingers gently back and forth, he began to scratch the back of his hand again. "Petro-France, that's the missing piece, Jacques. Petro-France."

He inhaled deeply, nostrils flaring. He sighed and slumped back against the chair.

"You mean . . . supplying FLEC-FAC?" Jacques said.

Mobutu leaned forward and said slowly in a low voice, as if he were explaining a situation to an obtuse minister, "I mean, Jacques, that FLEC-FAC hasn't picked up a dollar from me in months."

Jacques' chest tightened and he felt chilled, as if he were plummeting down a long, interminable chute. Bika's deal. So that was the deal Bika had cut with Petro-France. Not just a few Dupont lighters and a million or three or four on the side. Jacques remembered the lunch at L'Etrier with Marceau, pushing his cell phone back and forth nervously across the white linen tablecloth, *nous, les Européens,* we must stick together, and all at once he was thinking of his father and the way his *colon* Belgian friends had ostracized him and ridiculed him for his friendship with the idealistic young Colonel Joseph Désiré Mobutu, and Sarah at the airport, and the pale beige orchids wilting in the back seat of the car, and Bika's *petit frère* Bula, his small head hunched low into his shoulders, tearing down the rue des Mimosas at one o'clock in the morning. The missing piece of the puzzle. That was Bika's goddamned deal.

After a long while, Mobutu said, "Is it too early for a whisky, Jacques? No, of course not, why do I even bother to ask, hein?"

Mobutu rose and poured out two stiff glasses of Macallan's scotch. They tossed the liquor down in a kind of morose torpor.

"I must go, *Citoyen Président,* you mustn't let me keep you from your work," Jacques said in the old, familiar formula of leave-taking.

"Work? I've already done my day's work. I've found the piece of the puzzle that has been missing all these months. Don't worry. I would have found it. Sooner or later." Then he added sarcastically, "Even without the warning of *mon frère* in Angola."

He clapped his hands on Jacques' shoulders, and they shook hands.

Jacques could feel Mobutu's eyes on his back as he walked the long distance to the double doors of the room. At the door, he turned around, and Mobutu, his head tilted a little toward one side, was still standing, watching him, his hands tucked into the pockets of his *abacos* jacket. He looked lonely and faraway. Yet tall and strong, a solid pillar standing alone in the grandiose room. They stood and looked at each other. Bika would never have that grandeur, that strength, Jacques thought bitterly. He would never be able to do what Mobutu had done, bring a sprawling mass of tribes hell bent on chopping each other to pieces into one nation, under one flag, so that even a cab driver or a houseboy would say first, without thinking, that he was Zaïrian, and not a Luba or a Lulua or a Mongo or whatever other tribe. Bika could never have done that. Bika did not project that personal strength. He did not have Mobutu's legendary bravery, either, his fearlessness. Bika had no sense of how a national identity could be created by a strong leader. Mobutu had that. He knew the value of symbolism in creating a sense of national identity. Knew the value of creating a national dress so that Zaïrians on the streets of Paris or London or New York were recognized, not merely as Africans, but as Zaïrians. *A bas le costume.* Down with suits! Bika laughed at all that. But it had worked. Just as Sarah's Benjamin Franklin in Paris had dressed in a Quaker suit and a coon-skin frontiersman's hat so that people would know that he was different, an American and not just an Englishman who happened to have been born in the New World.

Jacques stepped into the hallway. At the end of the hallway René Staline, grey-suited and deferential, stood next to a window, waiting. Mobutu had not moved. Jacques looked at him one last time. Without warning, his anger flared. You goddamn fool, Jacques thought, you grasping bastard, you had it all, it was all yours. And you threw it away, you tossed it all away so that you could preen and crow like a rooster on a garbage heap. A great, golden, stinking garbage heap. Well, just stick around, *Citoyen Président, Citoyen Maréchal, Président fondateur, Notre Seul Guide.* Chaos will come again. Bika and Petro-France will see to that.

34

In the weeks following his meeting with Mobutu, Jacques watched and waited, and heard nothing from Bika. There were no more casual stops for late afternoon talks on the terrace, no more invitations to Saturday night parties in the garden.

In mid-March riots broke out in the central market when the price of manioc tripled overnight and the local currency went into a free fall. Along the rue du Commerce gangs of looters pillaged the shops owned by Indians and Pakistanis and Lebanese and beat and killed several Congolese before they could climb aboard the ferry to Brazzaville. On his way back to the *cité* on his night off Dieudonné was attacked by a roving gang of young hoodlums and the money he had so carefully hidden away in his shoes stolen. Downtown, the cars of expatriates were stoned and surrounded by exasperated mobs. When Josh Hamilton's car was stopped by an angry surge of people in Binza village, his driver fled into the crowd, and Josh, returning from a dressage class at the Cercle Hippique, climbed out of the back seat and slashed about in the screaming mob with his riding whip, shouting the only word he knew in Lingala, *Keba! Keba!*—which he had often heard his servants use and which meant "watch out!"—until he could get back into his car and make his way up the hill to Djelo Binza. Europeans remained behind the locked gates of their villas, exchanging rumors of violence picked up from each other and off the street from the *radio trottoir*, while their embassies worked out evacuation plans. Sarah attended the embassy meetings on emergency procedures, though she knew full well that she would never leave Jacques and his country.

The riots and looting continued for three days, and on the fourth day, Joe Snead sent up his company's helicopter with someone from the government to get an estimate of the size of the mobs emptying out of the shanty towns along the road to the airport.

And then the rains came. Torrents of rain, a typical rainy season downpour, beginning in midmorning and, unusually, continuing into the afternoon. Better than a firing squad, the rains. The crowds dispersed to the shelter of beer gardens and dank mud-and-wattle huts, and the city waited expectantly for two days, but the riots did not begin again. The price of manioc remained three times what it was before, and the value of the zaïre became so erratic and fragile that each day a half-dozen Lebanese started gathering along the Avenue des Aviateurs with open suitcases of hard currencies and buying and selling local money. By the end of the week everyone was calling the avenue that ran in front of the American Embassy "Wall Street" and went there to shop among the Lebanese in pastel polyester leisure suits with Louis Vuitton luggage filled with stacks of bank notes in red rubber bands for the best rate of exchange for their money.

"The only thing we can do now is to look after our own people," Jacques said. So every time that Johann Verhaegen flew into the interior, Jacques gave him enough money to buy all the yams he could find to bring back to give to the servants and their extended families. Soon a fine layer of red dust powdered the interior of the small Beechcraft, until it smelled of damp earth and yams like the inside of huts in Iyondo. Sam Wofford, in and out of South Africa, brought back quinine and malarial suppressants. With Dieudonné's help, Sarah had become an adept nurse, with a good eye for malaria dosages, even with the servants' children.

After the riots Jacques withdrew into a brooding melancholy that even Sarah could not dispel. He would sit for hours in silence on the terrace, watching the river, and when, nearing sunset, fishermen, black silhouettes against the sky, poled out into the river in their pirogues, he would rise from his chair and stand absolutely still, as if waiting for a message, while the fishermen, in slow, graceful dips and turns, cast their diaphanous nets over the shimmering, sun-struck water.

"Jacques, sometimes I think your mother may be right. You love this country too much. You care too much. Don't hate me for saying that."

"Oh, Sarah," he said, taking her into his arms. "How can I not care for a country where so many I have loved lie buried? My sister, my father, my little Sabine." He kissed her face gently. "And where, on an idle afternoon, walking across an Italian ambassador's garden, I looked up and found the woman I love with all my heart."

He became obsessed with Sarah's safety—though she was not in the least bit afraid—insisting, in a tone that she had never heard before, that she give up driving her car and accept Louis as her bodyguard and driver when she went to the Cultural Center and on errands around town. His hunger for Sarah, for her body, for her warm, fragrant presence, tormented him. At night sometimes, more and more often now, after making love, a bewildered question lurked in the depths of her clear, candid eyes, he saw it there, but he could not stop himself. The merest brush of her hand aroused his wild beating heart, and he reached out, blindly, voraciously, for the sweet excitement of her body.

More and more spare wheels in the government turned up in the waiting room at his office, ex-secretaries of this or that, who wanted to talk of the hard times and *l'effervescence du peuple*, as they put it. Jacques could never tell whether they were seeking information from him or some channel to the president or to Boketsu, or whether they were trying to warn him, as old friends and acquaintances, that the jerry-built dam holding back the people's wrath was about to break.

In the evenings he and Sarah stayed home and saw few people other than Sam Wofford, when he was in town, or Gussie Pearce, in tight-fitting cream jodhpurs, on her way to or from the Cercle Hippique, or Carter Everett, who had lately fallen into a habit of dropping in for a beer and sometimes dinner on his way home from the embassy. They talked of the riots and what faction of malcontents had started them and for what purpose, for no one believed any more that the trouble had truly started over the price of manioc.

One morning at the end of March the older of Jacques' Rhodesian ridgebacks failed to wake up, and a few days later, Chili Dog, the younger ridgeback, began to struggle getting to his feet. He would straighten his front legs, then whimper and moan as he dragged his rear end along the concrete next to the swimming pool until his hind legs would somehow engage and he could get up on all fours.

"Put him down, Jacques," the young Belgian veterinarian said. "That's what you have to do." Gérard Wanzoul, dressed in well-worn cowboy boots and blue jeans and a white tee shirt with a pack of cigarettes rolled up in one sleeve, stood next to the swimming pool, rippling dark azure in the late afternoon breeze off the river. His faded blue jeans were skin tight and had bleached, or rubbed out, in revealing lines over the bulge of his crotch. "The old lady died of old age, but this one has a tumor wrapped around his spine. It'll only get worse. Put him down." Wanzoul flicked his cigarette into a hibiscus bush.

The air was filled with the tangy aroma of freshly cut grass. Célestin, the frail, diminutive yard boy, who had never used a lawnmower and would not learn to use one, crouched close to the ground, and with methodical side steps, swished his sharpened *coupe-coupe* across the grass.

Jacques looked down at Chili Dog, swaying a little on his front legs against the dead weight of his rear end. Jacques had gone with little Suzanne to fetch him as a puppy from an elderly German woman who ran a curio shop on the Route des Poids-Lourds, and Suzanne had named the coppery brown pup Chili Dog, because that was her favorite treat when she went with her nanny to the American Club on Saturday mornings to watch her father play tennis. Jacques bent down and rubbed the dog's head. Chili Dog gave a tentative thump of his tail and slowly eased down onto his stomach.

"Can't be removed, believe me," Wanzoul said. "I don't like to put them down, but for this one, it would be a blessing."

"Well," Jacques said, trailing his hand along the thick ridge of hair along the dog's back, "Do it then."

Wanzoul walked to the drive and lifted a bag from the rear of his station wagon.

"That's fine just the way he is," Wanzoul said, loosening a leather case. "Hold him that way. But, here—" He took Jacques' hand and moved it back from the dog's head. "After the shot hits him, he'll try to bite. It's a reflex. Just keep your hand back."

Wanzoul shook a vial back and forth a few times, filled a large hypodermic needle, dropped to his knees quickly, and inserted the needle. As the needle burrowed into his muscles, Chili Dog twitched a little and yelped faintly, as if his lungs were being squeezed. Jacques stroked his back and murmured reassuringly.

It seemed a long time before Wanzoul slowly withdrew the needle. A hind leg pumped furiously in the air as if trying to reach a flea on the belly before going limp and dropping to the ground, and just as Wanzoul was getting to his feet, Chili Dog jerked his head back toward Jacques' hand and bared his teeth. His neck arching rigidly, the dog looked at Jacques, his eyes filled with the awful bewilderment of betrayal. Straining, Chili Dog held his head up a moment longer, then the menacing mouth disappeared, his jaws closed, and his eyes darkened with sorrow. With an imperceptible sigh Chili Dog slumped down, his brass tags . . . *clink*, and again *clink* . . . rattling against the concrete, as his head settled down to rest.

Wanzoul had taken out a cigarette and was trying to extricate his lighter from the pocket of his tight jeans when a hideous sound broke from Jacques Delpech's chest, and he flung himself prostrate in an attitude of protection over the dying dog's body.

In the kitchen where she was explaining a recipe to Dieudonné, the hoarse, bellowing sound came to Sarah as something inhuman, a *déchirement,* a fierce, husky, inarticulate bark. She and Dieudonné looked up, astonished, at the same moment, and she turned and raced from the kitchen, down the long hallway, and out the French doors of the living room to the swimming pool terrace.

To Sarah the scene in the garden looked like a melodrama of catastrophe and doom. Purple black clouds had suddenly cloaked the skies and a slow, soft rain was falling. Wanzoul, embarrassed, gazed toward the river and stood flicking and shaking his lighter as the unlit cigarette in his mouth soaked up the rain. Célestin, on his knees, his hands drawn up to his mouth in an attitude of prayer, his arms so thin and his elbows so knobby that he looked like a stick man in a child's drawing, whimpered, "*Oh, non, patron, oh, non, oh, non, oh, non, patron, s'il te plaît, patron! s'il te plaît!*" And Jacques lay sobbing, hunched over the dog, his tanned shoulders showing through his rain-soaked shirt.

"Jacques. Jacques," she whispered, pulling at his shoulders. "Come in out of the rain. Jacques. Come away."

He rose to his feet, stumbling awkwardly as he turned away from Chili Dog.

"He sure must have loved that dog," Wanzoul said.

"Yes," Sarah said, guiding Jacques toward the steps of the terrace, though she knew that for Jacques the two dogs had simply been a part of the place, little more than the frangipani and the flame trees and the brilliant swirls of magenta bougainvillea drooping over the walls. The dogs came, drooling and humble, for his absentminded caresses under the breakfast table in the mornings and spent the heat of the day with the servants in the breezeway of the *boyerie* and their nights snoring and snuffling around the swimming pool.

Inside the house Jacques stared out the window as Wanzoul and Dieudonné carried the limp body of the dog across the grass and lowered it into the back of the station wagon, while Célestin, still kneeling in the rain, his fist rammed into his mouth, turned his head fearfully and watched.

35

Jacques had gone beyond his own understanding of himself, and he was frightened, so when Abe Farber invited him and Sarah to join his table at the Israeli Ball, Jacques accepted without a moment's hesitation. In the past couple of years, he had fallen into the careless habit of humoring friends by buying expensive tickets to their balls and galas, then going, or not going, as the mood struck him at the time. Now he was determined to bring back the gaiety in their life together; he would not drag Sarah down into the mourning that enshrouded him. Grieving, mourning, that was what it felt like, gnawing away at him through sleepless nights. Why should his ghosts dim Sarah's gentle, blue-eyed joy in life?

They were delayed by some flap at Sarah's office the day of the ball—an American poet on a lecture tour working his way down the coast from Lomé had overslept and missed his flight and could not get to Kinshasa for another five days.

She came out onto the terrace where he was having a whisky, listening to the sounds of the dark river. She stood a moment, waiting for his attention to turn to her, then twisted and twirled her skirts flirtatiously and took a long sip from his drink.

"Ready?" she said.

"Ready for what?"

"The ball."

"If that's your preference," he said and laughed, taking her arm.

Her skirts tangled voluptuously around his legs as he walked her to the car, and he felt weak with desire for her.

"Where's Louis?" she said.

"Off tonight. He'd be up all night. The Israelis give a real bash."

The ball was held, not at the Israeli Club, but in the large ballroom of the InterContinental. At the wide double doors of the ballroom a dozen or so burly Israeli security guards, squeezed into dinner jackets, paced about, studying the crowds coming in and out, as if searching for a temperamental date who had wandered off to the ladies' room and never returned.

They were six at table: Abe Farber and his wife Lorraine, who had the rosy, round-faced look of a woman who has just delivered a baby, and a willowy, dark officer in army uniform whom Farber introduced as Colonel Lou Pinsky and his date, a stunning mulatto woman named Francine, who worked for Air Zaïre.

Sarah recognized Colonel Pinsky as the Mossad officer who had stood beside her on the platform at Camp Tshatshi during Kowalski's anti-terrorist exercises. She glanced at him and looked quickly away, ignoring his insistent, slightly leering look of complicity when he squeezed her hand.

"Jacques Delpech?" Pinsky said. "I've heard of you."

"Every beer drinker in Kinshasa has heard of Jacques," Farber said. "Jacques and I used to play tennis together. Did Jacques tell you that, Sarah? Won the Cercle Royale de Belgique prize for doubles in '68, didn't we, Jacques? We were just kids. Just innocent kids, eh, Jacques? And my old man beat the hell out of me that night because we went out and got drunk at that Italian girl's house because her parents were in Rome. What was the name of that girl, hmm? Remember that, Jacques?"

Abe Farber had pudgy chipmunk cheeks and talked with his head thrown far back as if he had some sort of peculiar eye problem that made it hard for him to focus on people's faces at any other angle.

"Luciana. Her name was Luciana," Jacques said.

"You sure it wasn't Sophia?"

Loud, recharged, the band came back from a break, and the spacious dance floor filled up with sweating men, huffing and gyrating, and women, stiff and cautious, determined to keep their expensive coiffures intact for a few more hours. The ball committee had flown down a popular group of Israeli musicians called The Gaza Strippers, who performed in nightclubs in Paris. The songs, a jumble of Hebrew, Yiddish, and French, involved strenuous rhythms and a good deal of shouting from the musicians.

"What's your riot story?" Pinsky said, bending low over the table to make himself heard.

"What?" Jacques said.

"Did you get caught up in the riots?"

"No." That was the great thing about being an expatriate, Jacques thought, the skies could be falling, people could be dropping like flies, but what the hell, there was always a good story, an anecdote, something entertaining, amusing. A laugh. Crazy old Africa.

"What do you think? Is the Man losing his grip?" Pinsky said.

"Looks like it." Jacques was determined not to let the Israeli pick him over. He sat watching Sarah, moving as quickly as a drop of mercury, dancing with Abe Farber. Pinsky's Zaïrian girlfriend had left the table for her second or third trip to the ladies' room.

"You don't really believe that, Jacques," Lorraine Farber said. "It will take more than a three-day riot in the rainy season to shake loose Mobutu's hold on this country. Outside of Kinshasa he's as popular as ever. Abe says."

"What about Tshisekedi?" Pinsky said. "Think he has a chance, Jacques?"

"They'll all have a chance if Mobutu goes."

"That's it. It'll be a mob scene. There's no organized opposition," Lorraine said. "And Tshisekedi's no saint. He can't wait to get his hands on the goodies. That's what Abe says."

"Whatever happened to the one mixed up in that coup *monté et manqué* back in 1982, the one who set up an office in Brussels, you know the one."

Pinsky had sounded another false note. Jacques lit a cigarette and looked at him appraisingly. Pinsky was not really searching for the right name to put on the coup *monté et manqué*. And it was not an accident that Pinsky was seated at this particular table.

"Oh, you're talking about Boketsu Bika," Lorraine said. "He's the one you mean." Colonel Pinsky looked annoyed.

"Lorraine, you're a nursing mother. No more champagne. Let's dance," Jacques said.

"I thought you'd never ask," Lorraine said.

At two in the morning, when the crowd had dwindled down to a hundred or so dancers, the horah began. On the second turn, as the women sang and shouted encouragement in a hoarse roar, the men took off their jackets and ties. On the fourth turn, they removed their shirts which the women grabbed and whipped round and round over their heads as they danced. The men moved to the center and crouched down to kick and turn, their naked torsos slippery with sweat.

Jacques was not surprised to see that Colonel Pinsky was one of several men in the circle with a Browning 9-mm automatic shoved into his belt band at the small of his back.

36

Dieudonné came shuffling down the hallway behind them. He had obviously gone to sleep still wearing his white uniform.

"It's after three, Dieudonné," Jacques said. "You should be in bed."

"Bula's been here, *patron*," Dieudonné said, holding back a yawn, his eyes watering.

"Bula?"

"The Mongo with the small head," Dieudonné said, making a small circle with his hands. "I told him where you were, but he said to come tonight to *Citoyen Ministre* Boketsu. Urgent, he said." Urgent enough for Bula to give Dieudonné 200 zaïres to stay awake to deliver the message to Monsieur Delpech as soon as he came home.

"I'll see him tomorrow. *Bonne nuit,* Dieudonné."

"He said come tonight, *patron*."

The only car he met on the road up to Djelo Binza was a small green taxi, coughing and lurching up the hill, the interior jammed with passengers and outside, spread-eagled across the trunk, two young men holding onto each other, their feet braced on the back bumper.

When Jacques pulled up to Bika's gate, he had to flash his lights several times to wake up the guards. They let him drive into the entrance, although the oldest guard kept saying that *patron* had not been at the house all evening. Jacques wandered through the deserted house where only the cheerless blue gray light from overhead fluorescent strips burned in Bika's small study and in the large boxy living room full of overstuffed sofas. Ashtrays scattered along end tables made of garish ceramic chips spilled over with matches and cigarette butts, but the air in the room smelled stale, as if it had been closed up for several days. In the kitchen there were no pots on the stove, none in the sink. A cat jumped down from the top of a refrigerator as it started up with a loud, rasping burr.

He was annoyed with himself as he got back into the car. He shouldn't have bothered. He should have listened to Sarah. The truth was that he missed Bika and wanted to see him. But even during the day Bika played fast and loose with his appointments. Whatever it was, Bika must have decided that it could wait. Suddenly tired, Jacques picked up speed as he turned onto the Matadi road and headed down the hill toward the river.

He had just cleared a grove of mango trees and was approaching the bend in the road next to the Chanimétal plant when a heavy-duty truck ablaze with light rounded the curve and seemed to head straight toward him. He braked, blew the horn, and flashed his lights. The truck came straight on, hurtling closer. He could hear the side panels of the truck rattling on the bumpy road as the truck bore down on him. He was startled by a loud, prolonged noise and realized that it was the sound of his tires squealing against the pavement. He steered sharply to the right, pumping his brakes, fighting to keep from braking too hard and sending the car swerving broadside into the path of the truck. Any second he thought the driver of the truck would wake up and pull to the other side of the road. But he didn't. Jacques jammed his foot on the brakes and braced himself. Suddenly he was surrounded by light and noise and the wide metal bumpers of the truck landed a glancing blow on his left fender that shot the car into the deep rain ditch, and then the steering wheel wrenched out of his hands and the car started rolling over, and over again, squalling and screeching, the mangled metal and shattered glass coming to rest finally against the wall of the Chanimétal plant.

37

"Look, Marceau, it's not a fucking money-back guarantee proposition," Chehab said. "You asked me to do it clean. I did it clean."

Chehab was sitting on a high stool at the blackjack table of the InterContinental casino. The dealer, a young woman in a tuxedo with a jacket nipped tightly around her waist, motioned to Marceau with a deck of cards, but he shook his head.

Drink in hand, Marceau turned around and leaned with his back against the table. "You wonder where that shithead manager gets these goddamn dealers," he said crossly. These days he went from one cock-up to another. A man who liked plans, and Marceau knew that he was goddamn good at plans, he hated cock-ups. Everything had been worked out, the miracle plan that had come to him in a flash on the flight up to Paris, like the touch of a fairy godmother's wand on his shoulder, had been just that: miraculous. With a flourish he had signed Jacques Delpech's name to the new account forms and sent them back to Guichard, and voilà, in a matter of days, one million U.S. dollars pitter-pattering down into the account. A peppery fax to Guichard, and the rest of the loot, another four million plumped up the old nest egg. No cock-ups there. Not with Marceau in control. The problem was having to depend on somebody else.

"I've had fake identity papers made up for you. Passport, driver's license—Belgian, just like you said—the whole thing," Chehab said. A thick, shiny scar cut through and separated into two parts his left eyebrow, placing one side higher than the other so that he had a constant look of extraordinary surprise on his large, round face.

"I don't need them yet," Marceau said. He didn't think he would ever need the identity papers to get at the money. After all, it was his signature on the account. But just in case. He was a goddamn good planner.

"Well, they're ready when you are." Chehab winked at the dealer. "How about a game?"

"No," Marceau said, lighting a cigarette. "We gotta talk about this other . . . thing, this problem."

"Well, I gotta play. That's what I do at night. I don't know what you do at night, but I play blackjack. What do you want to talk about? There's nothing to say. He was wearing a seat belt," Chehab said sourly. "He's American."

"He's not American. He sleeps with an American."

"Same thing," Chehab said. "And we cleaned up after ourselves." He took out a Cuban cigar and began to score it. "That costs money. Cleaning up after ourselves."

Marceau pulled on his cigarette and stared out over the large, high ceilinged room, entirely in darkness except for spots of light brought down low over the gaming tables. Faces were dimmed and obscured, rising into the shadows above illuminated torsos. It was a weeknight, a slow night with a dozen regulars and a handful of prostitutes milling around the tables and running back and forth to the ladies' room.

Marceau figured that he had two possibilities: he could stop where he was and save himself a bundle of money that he could maybe use buying Margot another, smaller annuity. Or he could go ahead and do what he had decided up there on his bedroom terrace that night listening to Stevie Wonder singing his heart out to all those beer-besotted mourners down there at the end of the street. He had decided to do what he had to do and to do it as quickly as possible. If he stopped now, if he didn't go through with it, he would be sitting up all night on some bedroom terrace sometime, some place for the rest of his life. The Swiss bank account, who knows what kind of cock-up Delpech could cause. It was through watching Chehab and his guys that he figured out how easy it could be. Unless there was a goddamn cock-up.

"Well," Marceau said, "Can you get it done right this time?"

"What the hell you mean, get it done right this time?"

"I mean . . ." Marceau hesitated, avoiding Chehab's eyes. "I mean. Get it done. This time."

"It'll cost."

"I'll pay."

"You haven't heard how much yet."

"I'll pay," Marceau said wearily. "Just get it done."

38

"When is Sarah getting back from Dakar?" Carter Everett had broken up the poker game early and had persuaded Jacques Delpech to stay on for another beer by the pool. The two men were easy with each other; they had become friends during Carter's first tour in Kinshasa when Jacques had provided a cover for one of Carter's operatives and had seen each other over the intervening years when Carter came in and out on temporary duty assignments.

"I'm meeting her flight over in Brazzaville on Monday. The Air Afrique hedgehopper. But a few days quicker getting back that way than waiting for a plane into Kinshasa."

Carter put his beer down and lit three bowls of citronella candles on the low table. "When the mosquitoes start getting down to the bone, let me know, and we can go in."

"I'm fine," Jacques said. He kicked off his loafers and rubbed his bare feet against the grainy tiles around the pool. It was a still, humid night, and the walled garden smelled of chlorine and mossy decay and the heavy perfume of angel trumpet flowers.

"Not too sore?"

"Not bad. My right shoulder is still stiff. Especially in the mornings."

"Well, I saw your car over at Tito's garage, and you ought to be stiff all over. Permanently stiff. I still don't know how you got out of that thing alive."

"Sarah and her sermons on seat belts."

"Even so. It's a miracle. What were you doing up there on the Matadi road anyway?"

"Coming back from Boketsu's. He sent one of his men to the house while we were at the Israeli ball."

"Boketsu? I heard that he's been up country."

"I suppose he was. At least, he wasn't at the house when I got up there. No one was there."

"Funny," Carter said.

"Bika's like that. He's never been very dependable where meetings are concerned. I should have known better myself."

"I think maybe Boketsu's still lying low after the riots, staying out of the Man's line of vision."

"The riots didn't look much like Bika's work to me. More like Tshisekedi. He's running the *cité* crowds, not Bika. Bika's support has always been in the interior," Jacques said.

"They're coming at the Man on all sides now, aren't they?"

"Yeah."

"And rightly so. There hasn't been any government to speak of for over a year now. Mobutu's so busy putting out brush fires and saving his ass that nothing gets done. If the army doesn't get a raise and doesn't get paid on time, all hell is going to break loose. Last month's riots are going to look like pretty small beer."

"He ought to hang it up, call it quits," Jacques said. He could hear a phone ringing somewhere in the house behind them.

"But he won't, will he?"

"No. I hear he's going to make a big speech soon promising democratization. Elections. African style, I suppose he means."

Carter laughed. "Where did you hear that?"

"One of his ex-*chefs de cabinet.*"

"The one dying of AIDS?"

"Yes. He's still keyed in."

"Jesus Christ," Carter said, "Mobutu's not dumb. Why can't he read the tea leaves any better? Why doesn't he take the money and run?"

"He's too encumbered. Too many people depend on him and his cow. On his being able to milk that cow when he needs to. He can't take care of them all without the cow. He's never known the first thing about economics, including his own. He wouldn't know an investment if it bit him in the ass. He doesn't understand the concept of making money grow. And in his heart of hearts, I think he still sees himself as that slim young colonel with a vision of nationalism and independence. *Le Guide.* The only one out there brave enough to bring the country out of its colonial sleep. The only real leader this country has produced."

"And he may be right."

"Yes. That's the real tragedy, isn't it?"

"You don't think your friend Boketsu could do the job?"

"Sometimes I do. Sometimes I wake up in the morning and think that Bika can't miss. He's smart as hell, well educated, next in line to head one of the biggest tribes in the country. You Americans like him. And he wouldn't be trying to get into power so that he can clean out the store and gobble up all the candy. Whatever Bika's faults, greed is not one of them. I would swear to that."

"So then why wouldn't you bet on him?"

"I don't know. He's not the same guy who left here in '82. Something's happened. He's rigid. Impatient. To be honest, he's become devious. He could be brutal, I think. He's better where he is now: in the undeclared opposition. He's not a politician like Mobutu. Never has been. Pretty soon Bika would have to start killing off his enemies . . . or doling out money, buying off his opposition right and left, dipping deeper and deeper to hold things together."

"Well, money is the only glue African politicians really understand."

"Sure, but that leaves us back on square one. Exactly where we are right now under Mobutu. Somebody's got to come along with enough vision to find a better glue."

"Everybody pretty much has an eye on Boketsu these days. We aren't the only ones." Carter slapped at a mosquito, and rubbed his hand on his pants, then turned to look at Jacques. "You have any enemies among the Lebs that you know of?"

"The Lebanese? None. They float in and out. I can't tell them apart. Why?"

"Just that two Congolese turned up in an alleyway off Kasavubu the night you had your accident. Shot in the back of the head. Back of head, signature Lebanese." Carter drained his glass of beer. "One of the Congolese was driving the truck that drove you off the road."

For a long while, Jacques said nothing. "I don't get it."

"Well, I'm not sure I do either. But, it might help if you told me one thing." Carter said. At the Playboy Club down the street, a car door slammed, and there was the sound of someone shouting angrily and kicking against a car. "You aren't fronting for Boketsu, are you?"

"What?"

"I mean, are you making any purchases for him? Negotiating. Traveling. Making contacts that he can't make himself? In Angola, for instance."

"Angola?" Jacques said, leaning forward to pick up his beer. "No, no, Carter. Bika had nothing to do with my trip to Angola. I'm not fronting for him or for anyone else. That was business. Just some harmless business. Otherwise, I wouldn't have let Sarah come along."

"Yes. There's Sarah to think about." Carter had taken a good look at the smashed Mercedes. Seat belt or no, Sarah would not have walked away from the crash.

He could not see Carter's face in the dim candlelight, but his voice told him what he wanted to know.

"You have to think of Sarah," Carter said again. "What happened on Matadi road was not an accident. Take my word for it. Look, have you ever thought of leaving? Getting out of Zaïre while the getting's good?"

"No." There was an ambiguous trace of hostility in Jacques' swift reply.

"Too much money tied up here?"

"There's that. But not really. Things have worked out better on that score than I had anticipated. The divorce has forced me to get my shit together."

"Then, get out. The country's already on a slippery slope. It's going to go down fast. And it's going to be messy. Sell up while you still can and clear out. Best advice you'll ever get, Jacques."

"Carter, for God's sake, you people really don't understand, do you?" Jacques slouched forward, his head in his hands, and ran his fingers nervously through his hair.

He raised his head and stared through the darkness toward the pale patch of Carter's face. "Listen, Carter, this is my home. I can't just walk away. Don't you see that? This is where I belong."

When it finally made no sense to pass the night tossing and turning, Jacques got out of bed, picked up his cigarettes, and headed for the back terrace. The security lights in the garden cast a bleak light over the terrace, and it was still too dark and early for the fishermen to be out in their pirogues. With daybreak he would try to locate Bika, in the past an early riser. Where could he possibly be, Jacques wondered. He seemed to have disappeared as suddenly and as mysteriously as he had appeared in the country. Bika had to know why his man Bula had insisted to Dieudonné that his boss wanted to see Jacques urgently in the middle of the night. At the house in Djela Binza it was clear that no one, not even Bula, had been there for days, even weeks. Stale kitchen odors, stale cigarette butts in messy ashtrays, stale beer in half-empty bottles.

Carter had said that the accident was no accident and had linked the driver to the Lebanese. Jacques sat down on the wall of the terrace and lit a cigarette. So the accident was arranged. Arranged to kill him. And it was Bika who put him on the Matadi road at that hour of the night. But what connection could there be between Bika and the Lebanese? As far as Jacques knew, among the expats, Bika was fairly close to Petro-France. Especially to Guy Marceau. Even so, where did the Lebanese come in? And why would anyone in that bunch of riff-raff hustlers want to kill him?

Never, even during periods of unrest in the country, had Jacques felt fear for his safety. Jacques sprang to his feet. *There's*

Sarah to think about, Carter had said in a flat, stern voice. *You have to think of Sarah.*

"Where the hell are you, Bika?" he shouted, his angry voice carrying his fear across the dark, softly murmuring expanse of the river.

39

At night, from across the river, Kinshasa looked like a glamorous modern city on the glossy cover of a chic travel magazine. Tall buildings filled with light cast a glow over the swiftly flowing water. The city looked inviting, full of romantic promises, of luxurious hotels and rich dinners in elegant courtyard restaurants under moonlit skies where native bands played discreetly while waiters topped off champagne glasses with a nimble twist of the wrist.

The dilapidated, rust-corroded ferry, however, listing at anchor at Brazzaville beach, was a serious clue that the city glittering magically across the river did not belong in the world of glossy travel magazines.

"Will we make it?" Sarah said, holding onto Jacques as people swarmed past, their plastic flip-flop sandals sending up sprays of sand as they rushed toward the ferry. Deformed men and boys with eyes or legs or arms twisted or missing pushed themselves along the beach and onto the planks leading to the deck of the ferry. Sarah had always been puzzled by the swarms of handicapped people on the ferries until Dieudonné laughed and told her that these deformed cripples were protected by special *jujus*; so they carried out most of the smuggling, mainly gold and diamonds, between the two countries, for police and customs officers on both sides of the river superstitiously refrained from searching them. This was the last ferry to Kinshasa, and tonight, like any other night, it was filled with cripples and makeshift wheelchairs and homemade contraptions meant to take the place of hands and arms and legs.

"Doesn't look like it. We should be able to get a vedette, even if we have to share one. Or else we can stay over at a hotel."

"I want to go home," Sarah said.

"Good. So do I."

The Congolese captain of the vedette complained that a bad storm was in the making and that he did not want to risk getting caught and having to spend the night on the other side.

"Looks like a fine night to me," Jacques said. It was a sparkling clear night, the skies washed clean, the heavens a black velvet jeweler's tray with splashes of diamonds scattered carelessly by a lavish hand.

"I smell the rain, *patron*. Coming from the south. Oh, I smell the rain, for sure, *patron*."

For a price the captain decided to set aside his misgivings about the bad storm and promised that he would get them to the other side so fast that in future they would never dream of making the crossing with any other captain.

Down below in the snug little cabin Sarah's bags and all the supplies that she had lugged to the meeting in Dakar took up most of the floor space so that Jacques had to spread his long legs from the narrow banquette seat out over the bags. He sprawled awkwardly on the banquette with his head cradled in Sarah's arms. To Sarah, he seemed happier than he had ever been since Iyondo.

"So, tell me, Sarah, what *exactly* did this conference do for three days?"

"I told you. Professors from the States gave papers on the American colonial experience," she said, watching the play of fine lines around his dusty blue eyes as he looked up at her.

"Did it make you think of New England and turkeys and snow?"

"No." She smiled down at him. "It made me think of the widow bird with the long black tail that comes to sit in the papaya tree and the smell of Dieudonné's orchid plants hanging in the trees outside our bedroom window."

"Sarah." He reached up and touched her face. "Do you ever think of Michael?"

"Sometimes. Not often," she said. "What makes you ask that? It's not like you."

"I don't know. New England. The widow bird."

He suddenly looked forlorn. With her fingertip she rubbed the two deep creases between his eyebrows.

"So, tell me, Jacques, what *exactly* did you do while I was far away in Dakar?"

"Not much. Worked. Played poker with Carter's gang on Saturday night. Tried all day yesterday to get in touch with Bika." He frowned again. After a moment, he said, "Bika seems to have disappeared." He was about to tell her what Carter had said about the accident but, without quite understanding why, checked himself. He was determined to find Bika, even if it meant flying out to Mbandaka.

When the vedette swung round to the dock at Kinshasa, the beach was almost deserted, for the decrepit old ferry still labored across the river.

They had not quite finished loading Sarah's things into the trunk of the car when the skies opened up. "My God," Jacques said, slamming down the trunk, "That captain has sure got a nose for rain."

They hurried to get inside the car. "We'll have to wait," Jacques said, "The wipers can't handle it."

Inside, the car smelled of new leather. The light of a lone street lamp wavered through thick rivulets of water streaming down the windshield.

"It's always so peaceful in the rain," Jacques said.

"Yes. And tomorrow morning the garden will be gorged with new flowers. Dakar was full of dust. A thick layer of gray dust on everything. I'm so glad to be home."

The ferry landed, and passengers scurried past, running for the shelter of trees, except for one tall woman who strolled slowly by the car, withdrawn into her own thoughts, on top of her head a dead monkey, looking like a sad but dutiful child, his face turned sideways from the rain, one arm flung backwards, the other tiny hand drooping alongside the woman's ear.

Jacques started the car. "It's slackening. *Eh bien, Madame,*" he said, kissing her damp cheek, "My place or yours?"

"Yours. I want Dieudonné to spoil me with his chamomile tea."

"You must be careful. Malu will be jealous."

"Really? You think so?"

"No. Malu's fine. He's been over at the house since you left. Helping Alphonse with some silver polishing is the way they put it, I think."

Sarah smiled. "I found some vanilla beans in Dakar so that Dieudonné can make you a proper Belgian *flan.*"

"Sarah, please. I am well past the age when I can be bribed by a good *flan.* Well, almost past the age. Anyway, you're not going to make me forget so easily that you have been away for almost a week, cavorting in wild, demonic abandon with Phil Olmstead in exotic, romantic Dakar, the Paris of Africa."

Sarah laughed, a soft, husky laugh. "Oh, big, big news. Phil is wearing a toupee now."

"Sarah, not even Phil would be dumb enough to wear a toupee in the tropics."

"Well, it's very black and shiny. And you don't see his pink scalp anymore."

"He probably spray paints it on every morning."

They had turned into Avenue des Nations-Unies leading toward the river. "I'm so *happy* to be home, Jacques." She leaned against him and playfully ran the tip of her tongue around his ear.

"Naughty girl. Fasten your seat belt." Sarah laughed, but the words suddenly made him feel guilty, as if he had betrayed her in some way. He lifted her hand and brought it to his lips.

Fallen branches and debris that had washed into the street crackled as the car passed over them. The rain had settled into a dense, steady purr.

At the Villa Bondeko the gates were closed, and there was no sign of the sentinels anywhere in the garden. Most of the villa was plunged in darkness except for a small splash of light coming from the back terrace.

"Goddamn. The circuits have blown." Jacques got out of the car and pushed back the gates, then drove the car into the entranceway.

"Maybe the storm knocked out the lights. Maybe a line is down," Sarah said.

"No. I see lights up and down the street."

"You're right. The street lights are okay," Sarah said.

"Stay here. I'll go inside and get an umbrella. No need for you to get soaked. The guards are probably in the back of the house drinking coffee with Dieudonné. Damn. You'd think they'd notice that the rest of the place is dark."

In the foyer he stood for a moment in the darkness and listened for the servants' voices and the sound of Dieudonné's transistor radio in the kitchen. The house seemed empty, shrouded in silence except for the noisy drumming of rain on the outside terraces.

As he groped along the long, wide hallway leading to the back of the house, he stumbled and almost fell across something on the floor. He stooped down and ran his hand over the floor in the darkness until he came to the object, a large ceramic cache-pot, broken in pieces against the marble floor. His hands passed over the dirt and the palm plant scattered over the floor. The storm must have whipped a strong draught through the hallway.

Toward the end of the passageway he could see light from the back terrace shining dully through the French doors of the dining room. He thought he heard a faucet running full force further off in the kitchen. As he moved slowly toward the darkened kitchen and the breezeway leading to the *boyerie*, his foot caught under a lumpy, loose bundle. He lost his balance and pitched forward onto the floor. He had fallen into something wet. His knees slipped as he tried to get up. Cautiously, he raised himself to a crouching position and ran his hand back and forth over the wet floor until his hand found the bundle he had stumbled across. Just as he grabbed a fistful of the stiff cloth of the bundle, a chalky flash of lightning lit up the hallway, and he found himself kneeling in a pool of dark blood next to the decapitated body of Dieudonné. In falling Jacques had turned the body over onto its stomach, while the head, eyes open and serenely blank, stared at the ceiling.

Darkness engulfed him again. He stumbled to his feet and ran down the hallway, arms stretched wide to keep his balance, nearly falling again over the broken plants, shouting, "*Sarah! Sarah! Run! Sarah! Get away!*"

Sarah was already out of the car and running toward the house as he reached the front steps that his feet knew so well. When the shot came, he felt nothing except a jolt, a shock, a kick to his head, and heard nothing except the roar of the rain, inside his head now, and Sarah, her mouth a great round O of fear running toward him, the car door open, the light behind her, her arms straining forward toward him, and he, missing the familiar step, and, finally, falling, gratefully, easefully, lifelessly into her arms.

40

Shortly after noon, Carter Everett met Sarah in the lobby of the Foreign Service Institute. It was a fiercely cold day, the skies a glacial blue with puffs of white clouds scudding along before the wind. Pulling their chins down into their heavy coats, they braced themselves against the gale blowing up from the Potomac and walked briskly down the hill to the Key Bridge.

"The Bistrot Français," Carter said. "We'll go there."

"What?" She raised her head and stared up at him.

"The Bistrot Français. It's just across the bridge in Georgetown. On M Street."

Sarah said nothing. With both hands she held the collar of her coat tightly around her ears. Her blond curls looked darker, Carter thought, chastened by a dour Washington winter.

In the restaurant when she shrugged off her coat, Carter was shaken by her thinness. Not drawn or gaunt, she looked instead almost diaphanous. She wore a black cashmere sweater and a white satin blouse with a broad shawl collar. Her cheeks, the tip of her nose, and her earlobes had been whipped into a rosy glow by the wind. Her beauty caused him so much pain that he felt light-headed.

"Carter?" she said finally, her huge, blue eyes watching him. "Is something the matter?"

"Just a guy who needs a drink. Ah, here comes the miracle man."

The waiter swung his gaze expectantly from Sarah to Carter, then back again to Sarah.

"A white wine," Sarah said.

"A gin martini. Extra dry. Really dry. Tanqueray gin. Don't overdo the vermouth. Make it dry." He folded his hands on the table. "Ah, wait a minute . . . wait a minute. On second thought, just give me a double Tanqueray on the rocks with olives."

"Still taking no chances with your martinis," Sarah said, and Carter thought that she tried to smile.

"Sarah, my dear, there are some things even a brave man does not take chances with."

When their drinks arrived, Sarah raised her glass.

"Congratulations, Carter."

"For what? For managing to lure you out of your cubbyhole for lunch?"

"For your promotion. Chief of Africa Division. Even I know what that means."

Beyond the misted windows of the restaurant the dense, unrestful flow of traffic and pedestrians moved crabbily through Georgetown's narrow streets. Around small tables pale men and earnest young women chatted and ate in a businesslike manner, periodically flicking their watches from their jacket sleeves. A handful of smartly dressed lunching ladies, maybe they had been unable to get reservations at the Jockey Club that day, sat at tables near the street. Carter and Sarah seemed strangely isolated from the noise and bustle of the restaurant and the muffled street sounds, lost in some peculiar kind of shared loneliness.

"So, with your new job you go back often then?" Sarah said finally, when the remnants of lunch had been taken away and they had moved on to coffee. "You go back . . . there."

Carter watched her for a moment, then said, "Yes. There's a lot going on now. None of it good. I have to make the rounds of my parish more often than I had figured. I see some of the old bunch. Your boss Phil Olmstead and Patty aren't suffering too much out on Mauritius. Seems the ambassador is a bridge Grand Master."

At that, Sarah laughed, a short, mirthless chuckle. "Oh, I'm glad, I really am. Good for him." The brightness faded. She gazed down gravely at her hands. "He was awfully sweet, you know. Getting me back here in Washington after what happened . . . After that night."

"I know," Carter said. "And he has a better toupee." But Sarah remained unsmiling. "You would have a hard time recognizing the place. Kinshasa, I mean. Everything's burned, looted, gutted. The GM factory's smashed, so is Goodyear and all the textile mills. There wouldn't be any jobs to go to even if the economy were hitting on all cylinders. The day after the Old Man announced free elections somewhere around the corner, two hundred and forty-seven political parties popped up. Like poisonous mushrooms in a shady grove. And they just keep on popping. Boketsu's heading up the Party of the Future of Zaïre. If he sees any future for Zaïre, he must know something we don't know. Or else he's smoking some pretty strong stuff."

Carter lifted his cup of coffee. Sarah sat quite still, staring down at her hands.

"So? How's the Hausa coming along?" Carter said.

"Oh, not too bad." She lifted her eyes to look at him, but her round blue eyes looked dull and blank. "I keep putting one foot in front of the other. Then somehow I get there. I make some progress. I've become a plodder."

"That doesn't sound like you."

She gazed past him toward the gray, chill street.

"Sarah?" He reached for her hand. "Why don't you give it up?"

"Give up what?"

"The Turd World," Carter said.

Sarah's luminous face twisted slowly into a grin. "Poor old Marceau. Such a funny little man. So intense. I never could figure out what his problem was."

"Well, for starters, Nicole jerked him around so much, he didn't know which end was up. He's still out there. Hitting the bottle. Gambling. In debt to the Lebanese. A year or so ago, Nicole up and left him, making a lot of noise about a pile of money that Marceau had promised would contribute to their married bliss.

Then, Nicole hooked up with a Chevron executive. He's divorced his wife of twenty-eight years and married Nicole. I suspect that Marceau got tripped up in the intricacies of a Swiss bank account. Tricky things, those Swiss accounts, especially if a Petro-France dragon is guarding the golden hoard." Carter tapped her hand. "So, what I mean is, why don't you chuck this assignment to Nigeria?"

"I can't."

"Why not? Of course you can."

"I must. I want to go back to Africa. I can't leave him there. Alone. I have to do what I can. That's where I belong."

"Sarah. For God's sake."

The restaurant, almost emptied out now, had grown quieter. Their waiter smoked a cigarette in the doorway of the kitchen.

"It's not what you think, Carter. I'm not the cotton-headed dreamer you think I am. I don't have many illusions left. How could I?" Absentmindedly, she rubbed the small diamond of her necklace, but did not take her eyes off Carter. "You know, during the riots when it looked as if all hell would break loose at any minute, Jacques came in one day and said, 'Sarah, we have to lower our sights now. The best we can do is to look after our people. Feed them, keep them well.' Jacques was an idealist, full of pipe-dreams about Zaire, most people would say, but he also knew how to get things done on a practical level, too."

"So what does that mean?"

"It means I'm going to Nigeria to teach."

"Teach what? With USIA?"

"No. With AID. I'm going to teach native midwives some basic hygiene. The tribes in the north have an ancient custom of putting goat dung on the umbilical cords of newborns. The infant mortality rates are incredible. Naturally."

"Naturally. Well, it's basic, as you say, and practical."

"And you want to laugh at me but you're too polite," Sarah said.

Carter said nothing. He lowered his eyes and pushed his coffee cup aside.

"It's a practice that has a lot of complicated cultural roots. I'm not naive enough to expect to have blazing success. But I'll try."

She stared out at the slick streets. "Everything used to seem so easy. The strong must help the weak. The rich must help the poor. It seemed so simple."

"Nothing's ever simple," Carter said.

About the Author

For several years in the eighties, Mary Martin Devlin lectured in francophone Africa for the United States Information Agency. During one of those tours she met, and later married, the legendary CIA officer, Larry Devlin, in Kinshasa, Zaire. Because of his many years in Africa, she was welcomed in his circles of friends in all levels of Zairian society. She spent many hours with Mobutu, his family, and his entourage as well as with opposition leaders eager to share their grievances. After leaving Africa, she didn't want to forget what life was like there: the breathtaking beauty of the country along with its squalor and misery, the chronic political maneuvering, the abusive power of corporations like big oil, and, of course, the expatriate life. In all those years, the individuals who touched her the most were the Europeans who had grown up in Zaire, the children of missionaries, for example, or of Belgian colonials. They felt like foreigners in Europe, they believed with all their heart that Africa was their home, and they were devoted to Zaire and optimistic about its future. When she decided to write this novel, she knew that it would revolve around the plight of one of these Europeans.